# Three Extraordinary Years:
# The Coleridges at Stowey

# THREE EXTRAORDINARY YEARS: THE COLERIDGES AT STOWEY

# BETHANY ASKEW

Blue Poppy Publishing 2020

Blue Poppy Publishing 2020
ISBN: 978-1-911438-71-7

For my husband Anthony and all the other volunteers at Coleridge Cottage in Nether Stowey who work so enthusiastically to keep the Coleridge story alive.

# Preface

My interest in Coleridge and Wordsworth goes back many years but for the last six years I have been working as a volunteer room guide at the National Trust Coleridge Cottage in Nether Stowey in Somerset. In my time spent in this little house I have lived and breathed the presence of Sara and Samuel Taylor Coleridge.

In the three years Coleridge lived here, he wrote some of the most beautiful and famous poems in the English language. This was one of the happiest times of his life. When he moved here, he was still very much in love with his wife Sara. His relationship with the Wordsworths, who lived in Somerset for a year, changed all that.

The poetry Coleridge wrote here was influenced not only by the humble cottage he lived in and the beautiful countryside of the Quantock hills, but by his relationships with Sara, Wordsworth and Dorothy. When I show visitors around the cottage, I try to bring their story to life. And this is what I have done in this book. It is not a biography. Events and dates are factually correct, but conversations are obviously made up.

Names are always a problem in this sort of book. Many of the men have the same first names: William, Tom, George, Robert, so to avoid confusion I have referred to them by their surnames throughout. Samuel Taylor Coleridge famously hated his first name. He preferred to be called Coleridge, STC or 'Col'. However, I have called him Samuel because it is what Sara called him and this is an intimate story about him, going back to his childhood. I have called the women by their first names and dropped the 'h' off Sarah because that's what she did (at Coleridge's request).

# Chapter One

*"My own lowly cottage where my babe and my babe's mother dwell in peace"* January 1797

Sara rubbed a space in the misted-up windowpane with the back of her hand. It was snowing again, tiny flakes flurrying around in the icy wind. There was no one around in the street. Surely even Samuel would be hurrying home soon from wherever he was this afternoon. She had stoked up the fire to cook a dish of stew for dinner but the room was still glacial, cold draughts seeping in through the gaps in the windowpanes and the damp rising under the doors and from the bare earth floor below her feet. Sara stopped midway through folding and sorting the laundry to check that Hartley hadn't kicked off his blanket but it was still wrapped tightly around him. She was dead tired. She hadn't stopped all day. Hartley had woken before dawn to be fed and all too soon it was time to start the daily chores.

She sorted the laundry into three piles: one to be put away; one, still damp, to go back up on the airing rack strung across the room; one to be mended, mostly Samuel's stockings, worn through at the heel from all his miles of walking. Thank goodness for her expertise with her needle, the one skill that had stood her in good stead in her adulthood. All the others, the French, the maths, well, none of them were any use to her now.

1

Hartley began to whimper and by the time she'd folded the last petticoat he was bawling loudly.

"I'll take him," Betty said, clattering down the stairs.

"No," Sara said quickly. Betty was a good nurse but Sara liked to see to him herself.

"Here," she said, thrusting the pile of clothes at Betty, "you put these away. He needs feeding," she added more gently. She couldn't afford to alienate Betty, who had been good enough to come down from Bristol with them even though, like Sara, she had only ever known city life.

"I was making up the bed," Betty said. "Master was up so late this morning I didn't get the chance. What with the chickens and pigs to feed…"

"It doesn't matter," Sara reassured her. "Let me see to the baby."

She changed his nappy, putting it to soak with the others in the damp little scullery at the back of the cottage while he wailed incessantly, then settled him at her breast in the chair by the fire, enjoying this moment of quiet, the steady chug-chug of his mouth, the unwavering gaze of his eyes on her.

Hearing the sound of the front door being shoved open, Sara hurriedly covered her breast with a spare napkin. Samuel often brought visitors home, strangers sometimes, but even their good friend Tom Poole, a confirmed bachelor, would blush to see her bare breast. But Samuel was alone. A blast of cold air and a flurry of snow blew in with him. He pushed the door closed again and stamped his feet on the mat, pulling off his heavy, wet coat and hat.

"Freezing out there," he said boisterously. "The pavements are treacherous. The gutter completely iced over. I saw several people slip. I wouldn't go out if I were you."

Sara stopped herself saying she'd been out to the yard while he was still fast asleep this morning to break the ice on the well. She saw his face soften as he saw her with the baby. She knew he loved to see her feeding Hartley.

"Good to be home," he said fondly, bending to kiss her and resting his hand gently on Hartley's head.

"Poole's place is warm enough," he went on. "There's a fire in the book room. Why's it still so cold in here?" He crossed to the window, lifted the sodden green material they'd used to plug the gaps in the windowpanes. "I'll write to Cottle, ask him to send some more of this stuff," he said.

It never ceased to amaze Sara how Joseph Cottle, ostensibly engaged only as Samuel's publisher, should be called upon to supply anything from books to money to material for their house.

"Everything's so damp here. I can endure the cold but not a cold room. You know how it upsets my neuralgia."

Samuel suffered so from his aches and pains brought on, he told her, by the rheumatic fever he'd had as a child.

"I ran away one night," he had recounted dramatically, "after an argument with one of my brothers over some toasted cheese. I spent the night out in the open." He shivered at the thought. "The next morning, I could hardly move. That's what started it."

3

Sometimes he spent days in bed or hunched over in the chair by the fire. He had only just got over the last bout of neuralgia just before they moved here. His face had swollen up and was agonisingly painful. The apothecary had prescribed laudanum and advised him against walking the forty-two miles from Bristol to Stowey, so they had all travelled by cart instead. In the end it had been such a rush: Samuel had forgotten a report he had promised for a newspaper editor, then he went down with a cold. It was hard work being the wife of a writer, especially one as quixotic as Samuel.

"The Cruikshanks live just up the road from Poole," Samuel said, watching her lay the baby over her shoulder to wind him. "I knew Anna before she married John. They have a baby now, about the same age as Hartley I understand. When the weather's better we can walk up and visit them."

Sara smiled. "Oh, that would be lovely," she said. "I'm so lonely here."

"You've got me."

"Yes, but I miss everyone. My friends, Mother, Mary, Edith…"

"It was chaos there, you know it was, Sara. I couldn't hear myself think, let alone write. I need peace and tranquillity."

"And the people here," Sara went on, "they don't like me. I've seen the way they look at me."

"That's only because they don't know you. They'd be the same with any newcomer."

"No, it's more than that," Sara insisted. She knew they thought it was odd that she and Samuel, so obviously cultured people, were living in a worker's cottage. And Samuel already had a reputation as a radical, a supporter of the revolution, a man who had strong political views and, what's more, was not afraid to write and publish them. They wondered what sort of woman would marry a man like him.

"You should've seen the way that Reverend Holland looked at me last Sunday," Sara went on.

"Mrs Poole likes you," Samuel said quickly.

"That's different. She's Tom's mother. She thinks the world of you."

He shrugged, used to compliments, confident in the effect he had on everyone.

"It's all right for you," she went on, "you can go out. I'm stuck here all day."

She laid Hartley down gently in his cradle, tucked him in. When she straightened up Samuel saw tears falling down her face.

"Sara, don't…" he said, as she wiped them away with the back of her hand. It was the second time today he had found her crying. He felt so helpless when she was like this.

"The snow will soon be gone," he said, "then we can go out for a walk on the hills. You'll love it there. The gorse will be out, you can see for miles, you can breathe the fresh air…"

Sara knew she wouldn't. She had been brought up in the city: Bath first and then Bristol. She loved the noise and bustle, the sights and smells of city streets. It had been Samuel's idea to come here.

"I want my family to be brought up in the country," he had said, "close to nature. We can live off the land and I'll be free to write what I want when I want."

There was more to it than that, of course. Samuel had run up debts. Down here in Nether Stowey, more

5

than a day's ride from Bristol, they could escape their creditors. Sara had no choice but to agree. The first house Samuel had considered was a cottage in Adscombe and when that was no longer available Tom Poole had found them this place. He had been a bit worried about it. "It's not the sort of house I'd like for you," he had written, "but there's nothing else available." And Samuel was getting desperate. His latest project, a radical newspaper called *The Watchman*, had failed and he owed money. They had no choice. Their rented rooms in Bristol had been spacious with high ceilings, wooden floors and long windows: quite a contrast. But it wasn't the first time they had lived in a small cottage. Their first few weeks of married life had been spent in a tiny thatched cottage in Clevedon. They had been so happy there; they had talked late into the night, walked in the moonlight, made love in their tiny bed under the eaves, lain in bed late day after day.

Carried away by their own romance, they had taken so little with them that Samuel had to write to Cottle to ask for essentials like a kettle, candlesticks, spoons and glasses. Samuel had loved it there: the white jasmine over the porch, the myrtles in the garden. He had written two poems, the *Eolian Harp* and *Reflections on Having Left a Place of Retirement*. But that was before they had Hartley. In those halcyon honeymoon days they had been two young lovers without a care in the world. Now they had a child to look after, clothe and feed.

It was a precarious profession, writing, but Sara had known that when she married him. Her mother had hoped she might marry someone with wealth, someone who could provide for the family. And there had been just such a man; he had even made an offer. She had been tempted but he just wasn't Samuel. Even Sara's mother had found Samuel fascinating. And two of her sisters, Edith and Mary, had married poets. It was only fair that Sara should be free to marry for love rather than for money. Would she have chosen differently if she could see what she had now? No, she knew she wouldn't. Better to be poor with someone she loved than rich with someone she disliked. Oh, there were times when she wished Samuel to the devil, as he sat hunched over the fire grumbling about his aches and pains. But she missed him when he went out, looked forward to him coming home again. And when he looked at her with love in his eyes, the way he was looking now, she would forgive him anything. And better times would come, she knew they would. If people like Cottle and Poole believed in Samuel's talents, then so did she. His articles were published in newspapers, his poetry praised. It was only a matter of time before they would be financially secure.

Samuel had picked up a book from the pile he kept next to his chair. It was beginning to get dark now and he bent his head and the book towards the window to make the most of the light.

"Shall I light a candle?" Sara asked, though she would have preferred to wait a while. The tallow candles were cheap but nonetheless they needed to eke them out.

"No, no," Samuel said. "I can manage."

With the darkening light came the familiar scurrying of the mice in the cupboards.

"I wish you'd let me trap them," Sara complained as one she saw one dart across the floor.

"You know I don't like to," Samuel responded. "They're God's creatures and it seems so unfair to invite them to eat and then kill them."

"But you don't have to battle to keep them out of our food," Sara replied.

She stirred the stew hanging in a pot over the fire. "This is ready if you'd like to eat."

Samuel set the book to one side and sat at the table while she spooned the stew into bowls. Her husband ate quickly, talking all the time. Food was little more than fuel for him, something to sustain him and give him the energy for the multitude of thoughts that coursed through his mind. Much of what he said was lost on Sara but she liked listening to him anyway. He pushed his long dark hair away from his face impatiently, his grey eyes burning with enthusiasm, and waved his free hand in the air to emphasise his words. This was what had made her fall in love with him, not his looks. He was far from good-looking: she had thought him plain and scruffy when she first met him. But he was so full of life and spirit, so obviously brilliant and gifted, like no other man she had ever known.

"You go on up to bed," Samuel said when she had finished clearing the dishes and scraping them clean in the scullery out the back. "You know I don't sleep well if I come to bed too early. Leave Hartley here with me. I'll bring him up later."

She should be starting the pile of mending but it would wait. She bent to kiss Samuel. He took her hand and squeezed it.

"Sleep well, my love."

At the feel of his hand, the touch of his lips, she was tempted for a moment to suggest he join her in bed. But the thought of rest and the few hours' sleep she would snatch before Hartley woke again was more tempting, so she took the sputtering candle and climbed the narrow staircase.

The bedroom was icy and she undressed quickly, sliding under the cold covers and shivering until the warmth from her body began to warm the bed. The sheets smelled smokily of the fire and the food that had been cooking when they had been drying on the airing rack above. She could hear the sounds of mice scurrying in the rafters overhead, the distant hoot of an owl, the bark of a dog. All these sounds quickly faded away as blissful sleep overcame her.

# Chapter Two

This was the time of day Samuel liked the best. He had the cottage to himself, to think and write. Well, he couldn't do much writing in the dim light from the rushlight candle and the glow from the dying fire, but he could make notes and write down the odd phrases that had come to his mind now he had the time. During the day it was so hard. The cottage was so small. Sara and Betty were always darting around doing something or another, needing the part of the table he was trying to write on or hanging up the washing over his head if he sat reading by the fire. He had never realised how much there was to do in the house. And baby Hartley added to it, always crying and needing to be fed or changed. But this was what he wanted: his family to be brought up in the country, close to nature, not in the city like he told everyone he had been.

Of course, that wasn't strictly true. For the first nine years of his life he had lived in Devon, in Ottery St Mary, where his father was a vicar. Samuel was the youngest. He knew he was his parents' favourite. His brother Frank was so jealous of him. "It's not fair," he would say when their mother let Samuel have cake when he had none. Luckily for Frank their nursemaid Molly preferred him to Samuel and did her best to make it up to him.

Samuel was closest to his sister Nancy who was always on his side. She would cuddle him and sing to him. She was his dearest friend when they were young. In fact, he couldn't remember actually having any other friends. He was different from the other boys, a loner; the older boys teased him. Samuel took to his books, his only allies, which he bought from a shop in Crediton run by his Aunt Susannah. He loved adventure stories, tales like *The Arabian Nights,* and when he put his book down he would leap to his feet to act them out, running up and down the churchyard, pretending to be the characters he had just read about. The church and churchyard, so close to his home, became his sanctuary, the place he could escape to where no one could bother him.

Samuel was small for his age and had a reputation for being a troublemaker and not to be trusted among the older schoolboys, so he was kept in a dame school until he was six. When he finally moved onto King's School he was thrown more into the daily company of his brother Frank who continued to bate him. Frank hated reading and thought Samuel should do the things *he* loved: climbing, fighting, playing and stealing apples. Left alone more and more, Samuel wandered around the lanes and fields, along the River Otter, where he paddled barefoot and sailed his paper boats, and down to the Pixies' Parlour, a sandstone cave below the roots of an ancient oak tree. Here, following tradition, Samuel carved his initials in the soft stone of the walls, alongside those of his older brothers. By then three of them, William, James and Edward, were leaving home to become professional men.

In Samuel's first year at King's School an epidemic swept the school and both he and his brother George became dangerously ill, turning and sweating in their beds on the top floor of the schoolhouse, well away from the other boys. This was when Samuel first started having dreadful nightmares, hellish visions so real and terrifying that he would wake everyone else up with his screams. He began to dread falling asleep and tried to ward them off with the poem, "Four angels round me spread. Two at my feet and two at my head..." He clung to this vision, seeing the angels fighting off the armies of deathly demons who swarmed through his fevered imagination. This was the only time he could remember his brother Frank being kind to him, sneaking upstairs to read Pope's Homer to him. His illness brought him closer to his brother George too, thrown together as they were in their lonely sick room. George was sixteen at the time but seemed so much older and even then Samuel began to think of him as a father figure.

His parents must have been worried about him and George, but it was his sister Nancy whom Samuel remembered visiting him daily, nursing him with tender care and listening patiently to his every complaint.

Once Samuel was well again, he reinstated himself firmly as his mother's favourite. One incident would remain forever etched in Samuel's memory. He was seven years old at the time. Samuel asked his mother to slice some cheese for him for his favourite snack of cheese on toast. When his brother Frank found the sliced cheese on the kitchen table he decided to crumble it up deliberately to upset Samuel. When

Samuel saw it there he lost his temper. He ran at Frank and hit him. Frank fell to the ground, pretending to be far worse than he was and Samuel, thinking he had really hurt him, bent over him, whimpering. Suddenly Frank jumped up laughing and punched Samuel in the face. Samuel was furious. He grabbed a kitchen knife and ran at him.

At this point their mother came in and pulled Samuel away. Samuel knew he was in trouble so he struggled out of her grasp and ran away sobbing, down through the garden, along by the banks of the river. On and on he ran, tears streaming down his cheeks, almost as far as Cadhay Bridge. Here he stopped to ease the painful stitch in his side. He had stopped crying and now he wiped his face with the back of his grubby hand and sniffed until his nose gradually cleared. As dusk fell he sat and watched the cattle munching gently on the grass, listened to the raucous crows making their way back to the tall trees, the smaller birds twittering their evening song. Gradually all these sounds fell silent and despite the cattle in the fields he felt all alone. It was October. It soon grew cold. Damp rose from the fields. It began to rain and soon a strong wind started blowing. Samuel had no warm coat, nothing to shelter him. But he didn't dare go home. And in any case he felt a warm glow of self-satisfaction every time he thought of how worried his mother would be. He needed shelter though from the wind and rain and, seeing a mass of old thorn bush cuttings close to the river edge, he crept under them, said his prayers and fell into a restless sleep.

It was only later that Samuel found out how much trouble he had caused. His mother was beside herself with worry; now that Samuel had a child himself he had some small understanding of what she must have gone through. She sent people out first to search the churchyard where she knew he often played, then sent them around the streets. By nightfall a general alarm was raised; anyone in the village who could leave their houses turned out to search for Samuel. The ponds and the mill race were dragged and the town crier was sent to neighbouring villages. The search went on all night.

Samuel woke at five in the morning, frozen stiff and too weak to move. Hearing voices calling his name he tried to call back but his voice came out as a tiny mewling cry. The men had been out all night. They were tired, hungry, cold and wet through. When Samuel heard them turn back, their voices retreating into the distance, he honestly thought he would be left there to die. One man, however, Sir Stafford Northcote, the local squire, turned back for one more try and this time he came close enough to hear Samuel's faint voice. He lifted him up and carried him in his arms for nearly a quarter of a mile until they met Samuel's father and Sir Stafford's servants. Samuel knew he would never forget the look on his father's face when he saw him. He seemed so calm but the tears were rolling down his face. Samuel's mother was beside herself with joy. Samuel was put to bed and in a day or so he was fully recovered except for the bouts of rheumatism that had attacked him ever since.

Samuel would always look back on the following year, 1780, with fond nostalgia. After that night his father seemed especially close to him. In the evenings he would take him on his lap and talk at length with him. One cold wintry evening they were walking together and his father pointed up to the starlit sky and told him the names of the stars. Samuel listened, entranced, as he explained how the stars were all suns and other worlds rolled around them.

These happy memories stood in stark contrast to what happened the following year, a memory so painful that Samuel's mind darted away from it whenever he thought of it. Just before his ninth birthday his father, the man he had loved so much, who had given him such happiness and chosen him as his special child, died suddenly.

Samuel's world was turned upside down. His mother had no income. The family had to move out of the vicarage and into lodgings in the warden's house nearby. There were fees to pay for both George at Oxford and Luke at medical school and only James, who was in the navy, and John in India, to pay them. Nancy found work as a shop assistant in Exeter. Frank was already in the navy. That only left Samuel who, they decided, would have to go to a boarding school on a charity grant.

It was Samuel's godfather, Samuel Taylor, after whom he was named, who put his name down for Christ's Hospital in London.

Samuel wasn't due to start there until the Michaelmas term of 1782 but his mother sent him straight up to London to spend the next three months with her brother, his Uncle Bowdon, who ran a tobacconists near the Stock Exchange and also worked part-time for an underwriter. Samuel really enjoyed himself there. Uncle Bowdon was proud of him. He took him along to inns and coffee houses, where Samuel talked and drank and argued as though he were every bit an adult. He revelled in the adulation, hearing the other men describe him as a prodigy.

It couldn't last of course and in July he had to put on his school uniform and go to the prep school in Hertford for six weeks. He was happy there with plenty to eat and drink but that, too, was only too brief. In September 1782 he started at the Under Grammar School of Christ's Hospital with its iron bedsteads, its harsh regime and meagre portions of food.

The school was divided into three main divisions. The Writing School prepared boys for commercial apprenticeship at the age of fourteen or so, the Mathematics and Drawing schools sent them into the navy at sixteen, and the Grammar School kept the brightest boys until they were old enough to go on to study for law, the church or the army. The cleverest of these went into a Classical Sixth Form, tutored by James Bowyer, the headmaster. They were known as the Deputy Grecians and from this group three or four boys a year would go to Oxford or Cambridge.

Samuel looked back on his time at Christ's Hospital as one of endless misery, yet it was here he met Charles Lamb, now such a good and faithful friend. And there was the odd happy time: the illegal swimming expeditions down to the New River in the East End and the equally illegal visits to the public lending library for extra-curricular books. He was still a loner though and spent most of his time reading voraciously. The lessons themselves, however, he found tedious and he didn't bother to work hard.

One day, one of the Deputy Grecians saw Samuel engrossed in a book. "What are you reading?" he asked.

Samuel looked up. He knew Thomas Middleton, but only from a distance.

"Virgil," he replied.

"Have you been set it for class?" Middleton asked, surprised.

"No. I just like reading it."

Middleton was so impressed that he told Mr Bowyer, the headmaster, about it. Mr Bowyer asked Samuel's form teacher, Mr Field, about Samuel.

"Coleridge?" Mr Field said, surprised. "He's nothing but a lazy simpleton."

"But he's reading Virgil in his spare time," Mr Bowyer countered.

Samuel was sent for, flogged severely and told that he was clever enough to be a Deputy Grecian, he just needed to apply himself. After that any signs of laziness resulted in punishment and Samuel's schoolwork improved dramatically. So did his popularity. In the company now of Deputy Grecians he made new friends. Thomas Middleton, who had singled him out in the first place, was a few years older than him but became his protector and mentor. Nearer his own age were Robert Allan and Valentine Le Grice and the three often spent time together.

Two of Samuel's brothers were also now living nearby: Luke was training at the London Hospital under Sir William Blizard and George was teaching at Newcombe's Academy in Hackney. Since their father's death Samuel had always looked on George, who was eight years older than him, as a second father. At this time, however, Samuel was inspired by Luke's profession and decided he wanted to be apprenticed to a surgeon. Samuel could see, looking back on it, that it was just a passing fancy as he remembered also wanting to be apprenticed to a local shoemaker, mostly because the man and his wife had been so kind to him but partly because it would have given him an escape from Christ's Hospital.

Samuel wrote his first poem in 1789, inspired by the Fall of the Bastille. The following year, his final one at Christ's Hospital, at the tender age of eighteen he fell in love for the first time. Mary Evans was a milliner and on Saturdays he would escort her home from work with her two sisters, Anne and Eliza, and his two friends Robert Allen and Valentine Le Grice.

It was early in 1791 that he heard of his brother Luke's sudden death in Exeter from a fever, followed only too swiftly of news of his beloved sister's death from consumption. She had been ill for some time but it still hit Samuel hard.

In autumn of that year Samuel went up to Jesus College, Cambridge with a school exhibition prize worth £40, renewable for four years and the promise of a Rustat scholarship of £30, especially reserved for the sons of clergyman who showed outstanding merit. Samuel's family were thrilled, especially George who would have had to support Samuel otherwise.

Samuel was poorly much of the winter with the rheumatism that affected him regularly. This time he put it down to swimming in the New River so late in the year. He spent months in the school sanatorium, dosed up with laudanum and writing poetry.

Samuel hated university when he first arrived. Jesus College was on the outskirts of the city and was a dreary-looking place exposed to the winter wind, his rooms on the ground floor cold and damp. He frittered away much of his allowance trying to make them more cosy and soon found himself in debt; his debts would only increase as time went on. At least he had a friend already there, Thomas Middleton, who was in his final year by then. If it hadn't been for him Samuel would have been lost. Thomas took him under his wing like he had at school, inviting him over to his rooms in the evenings to study.

The Christmas holidays were spent with the Evans family, where he fell once again to walking the three sisters to their milliner's shop in Jermyn Street. He liked both Anne and Mary. Mary was easily the more intelligent but Anne had lovely ankles. Most of all though he liked Mrs Evans, who treated him the way he wished his own mother had.

Back at Cambridge he did the usual student things: went to parties and drank too much, boated on the river, wasted his money on clothes he didn't need. Somehow he still managed to work hard and submitted work for university awards in the Greek Sapphic ode, the Latin ode and the Greek epigrams. Samuel chose the topic of the slave trade for his Greek Sapphic ode, a subject that had recently been debated in parliament, and he was thrilled when his entry won. It was a rare achievement for a first-year student and he wrote proudly to his brother George to tell him. George told everyone he knew and when Samuel went home for the university holidays that summer he was made a great fuss of.

Now that he felt he had experienced something of the world, now that he was able to talk confidently of the slave trade and the French Revolution, Samuel found his relatives dull and provincial: his brother

Edward in Salisbury vain and eccentric, James in Exeter equally vain and cold and only interested in local events. Apart from George, whom he still looked up to as a second father, Frank, out in India, seemed to be the only brother he could be proud of.

His infatuation with Mary Evans grew in his second year at university, where he spent much of his time earnestly discussing politics, drinking hard and running up huge debts. In December he sent in another piece of work for the Sapphic Ode, this time on astronomy, and came second, but his Rustat scholarship was renewed and he was awarded the chapel clerk's place, which brought him £33 a year towards expenses.

Samuel had now made something of a name for himself at university. He saw people pointing him out; they knew he was a good speaker and held strong views on politics and religion. He was set for academic success. When he failed to win the Craven scholarship, however, he began to lose heart. The chance of getting a fellowship was now remote. For some time he had been having religious doubts so he couldn't think of a career in the church. What he wanted was to be free to write poetry, to philosophise, to study metaphysics and involve himself in politics. But how could he tell his brothers this? After all their financial support, they expected him to have a glittering career. Desperately unhappy and confused, he spent money wildly on books, heavy drinking sessions and visits to the whorehouse. When he heard that his brother Frank had died he fell into deep depression, followed by more heavy drinking.

He dreaded going home at the end of that summer term. By then he owed just over £148. He could scarcely admit it to himself, let alone James and George who were supporting him, trusting him to spend the money on his education, not in bars and brothels. So he confessed only to a part of it and after a severe telling off and promises to reform, they paid up.

He was still courting Mary Evans, writing her long affectionate letters, but now he wondered how long he could go on. He had no career prospects to offer her, he still owed money. There was no way he could make her an offer of marriage.

In September 1793, when he should have been back at Cambridge for the start of the new term, Samuel was still in London, alternating between heavy drinking sessions and periods of reform. In November he finally returned to college. Despite his turmoil, or maybe because of it, he found himself writing some wonderful poems at this time. Most of the time though, when he wasn't drunk, he was in the depths of despair. What could he do? He had no future; his debts were out of control. He couldn't tell anyone about them. What would his brothers think, having supported him all these years, expecting the best of him, only to find he had squandered all their money on drink and whores?

He was at his wit's end and in a moment of madness he ran away. He changed his name to Silas Tomkyn Comberbache and enlisted in the 15th Light Dragoons. It was a ridiculous thing to do. He knew nothing about horses and was totally unsuited to army life. It was a period of his life that he looked back on with embarrassment. When his brothers tracked him down they managed to get him discharged as being insane, which really was the only explanation. They paid off all his debts this time and he went back to Cambridge, promising to work hard and enter all the prizes. It would be an end to all the late night parties, he said. He would get up at six and drop all his unsuitable friends, the ones who encouraged him to drink.

But Samuel had seen something now of the outside world. College life seemed dull and boring. He longed for a great cause, something to channel his energies into.

That summer he embarked on a walking tour with one of his friends, Joseph Hucks. On the way they stopped off at Oxford to see his old school friend Robert Allen, who introduced him to Robert Southey. Southey was a tall, rather forbidding-looking man with dark hair and a dark beard. He was quiet and rather shy but once he got to know people he opened up. He and Samuel had a lot in common: he was a writer too, and a poet, and they shared similar political views. They spent long hours discussing religion, politics and metaphysics.

"It's so good to talk to someone with the same ideas as me," Samuel said. "There must be a lot of others like us who would like to do the same. Wouldn't it be good to get them all together? Living together I mean. In a community."

"Sharing the workload," Southey said, warming to the idea, "and using their spare time to study religion and philosophy."

"Men and women — and children obviously." Samuel was thinking of Mary Evans, if she could be persuaded. "We could call it..." He thought for a few minutes. "Pantisocracy," he finished triumphantly.

Southey looked at him blankly. He was studying anatomy, not the classics.

"It's Greek," Samuel explained. "It means equal rule by all."

"Do you think it would work here in England?" Southey asked doubtfully. "What will people make of it?"

"We could emigrate," Samuel declared. "America. I've read about it. We can build our settlement on the banks of the Susquehanna river in Pennsylvania.

"We just need to find people to join us," Southey said.

"And the money. It'll take a bit of financing…"

Southey's brother Tom was an early convert and a friend of Southey's, Robert Lovell, was soon persuaded. Lovell was courting a girl called Mary Fricker, one of five sisters. Mary's younger sister Edith soon caught Southey's eye and the two girls agreed to join them in the Pantisocracy scheme, once they were married. And this was one of the problems of course. The twelve men and women that Samuel and Southey had foreseen living together in a community would need to be married to each other. Samuel was still courting Mary Evans but still had nothing to offer her. He had no idea what she might make of the Pantisocracy scheme.

There was a girl, however, who was all for it. Sarah was the eldest of the Fricker sisters, a dark-haired beauty with the plump full-bosomed figure that Samuel had always admired. She had a reputation for having a quick temper but she was bright, intelligent, vivacious and not averse to risk. In fact all the Fricker family was swept away by the Pantisocracy scheme. Even the widowed Mrs Fricker was prepared to emigrate, taking the younger children with her. Sarah, Mary and Edith were seamstresses, an occupation not unlike Mary Evans' who was a milliner. But Samuel only needed to spend a few moments in Sarah's company to realise that she was vastly better educated. Although the family was now impoverished, a situation they found demeaning, Sarah and her sisters had been to a good school in Bristol. Sarah was particularly gifted in French and maths. She was well read and had been brought up to believe in the Mary Wollstonecraft views of female emancipation. She held strong views on religion and politics and could hold her own in conversation. Here was surely the right wife for Samuel, a woman who would be his equal.

In August Samuel set out on another walking tour, this time with Southey so that they could work out more details about the Pantisocracy plan and drum up support. Southey wanted to walk down to Somerset.

"My family are originally from Wellington," he told Samuel, "and my grandfather was a farmer on the Quantocks. It's beautiful there. You'll love it."

They walked to Bath first to stay the night with Southey's mother. Samuel was delighted to find Sarah Fricker staying with her.

"I invited her here to talk over the American affair," Mrs Southey explained. It was only nine days since Samuel had first met Sarah. He saw how her face lit up and her eyes shone when he walked in.

They left early the next morning, Southey insisting on bringing his dog with him.

"Are you sure your dog will manage the distance?" Samuel asked uncertainly, looking down at the aged animal plodding along beside them.

"Rover? Yes, of course he will. And he's a good companion, you'll see. Come on Rover! We'll go down to Wells first, I think," Southey suggested, "then on to Cheddar."

"I thought we were going to see George Burnett first?" Samuel asked.

"Tomorrow probably," Southey said. "Depending on how long it takes us."

Burnett was one of Southey's friends from Balliol College and a recent convert to the Pantisocracy project. He had proposed to the youngest Fricker sister Martha in order to secure his place but she had refused him, feeling, quite rightly, that she was only being made use of.

Ten miles from Bath they reached the village of Chilcompton.

"It's beautiful here," Samuel said. "What a lovely stream."

Words for a poem drifted into his mind, inspired by the quiet village with its few scattered cottages, children playing with paper boats in the stream...

The road onwards dropped over the Mendip Hills and down into Wells, the cathedral walls and towers glowing in the early evening sunshine.

"We don't have much time to look around," Southey said, "not if we're to make Cheddar tonight."

"How far is it?"

"I have no idea. We'll ask someone."

But everyone they met had a different answer: some said two and a half miles, some seven. In fact it turned out to be nearly nine miles and they walked on through gathering gloom and finally darkness until they reached the town at ten o'clock.

"We'd better find somewhere to stay," Southey decided.

The inns were all closing for the night, candles being extinguished at all windows. The innkeepers gave them dubious looks when they knocked for admittance.

"Do we look that bad?" Southey asked, looking down at himself.

"No worse than anyone else who's walked twenty-odd miles," Samuel replied.

But it was the same answer everywhere: "Full up tonight."

"What are we going to do?" Samuel asked. The thought of sleeping on the street, on a cold damp pavement where they might be robbed...

"Let's try one more," Southey said wearily.

The innkeeper looked at them ruefully.

"You can sleep in the garret if you like," he offered.

"Well, I don't trust 'em," they heard his wife mutter. She was still grumbling as she made up their beds and as she left the room they heard the bolt being drawn across the door.

"She's locked us in," Southey said incredulously.

"Maybe she thinks we were going to rob the place," Samuel laughed.

They had a bad night: the tiny truckle beds were hard, the room damp and musty, the dog whined in his sleep and Samuel had his usual nightmares. "I'm lost..." he whimpered mournfully.

"For Lord's sake, Samuel. You're in an attic with me. Settle down and go to sleep," Southey said.

The next day dawned clear and sunny again and it was still early when they reached the gorge.

"Astonishing!" Samuel breathed, as he gazed in wonder at the huge limestone cliffs, the tiny sheep grazing perilously on the edge, the dizzying view looking up. Nothing could have prepared them for the sight.

They arrived at Huntspill later that day and found the house where George Burnett lived, a little way away from the turnpike and with a large sundial above the front door.

"He doesn't seem very pleased to see us," Samuel whispered to Southey when George's father had shuffled off to find George himself.

"He was hoping George would be ordained when he left Balliol," Southey whispered back. "Now George is telling him he wants to give it all up and come to America with us."

Burnett was indeed still keen on Pantisocracy. He spoke about nothing else the whole time they were there. "We're on our way to see Henry Poole next," Samuel told him.

"I don't think I know him," Burnett said.

"He's a fellow student of mine at Jesus College in Cambridge," Samuel explained. "We're hoping he'll join us. He's just the right sort. And if he isn't interested himself he comes from a large wealthy family. His father might back us. Or an uncle or something…"

Henry Poole was living at his grandfather's home at Shurton Court, recently converted from a large farmhouse to a modern fashionable mansion. To get there they had to cross the river by ferry at Combwich Reach.

Henry Poole listened patiently while they expounded their scheme. "Well, it's not something I'd like to do," he said. "And I can't imagine my father or my grandfather being interested. I know someone who might be though. My cousin Tom."

"What does he do?" Samuel asked. *"A doctor maybe, or a clergyman. Someone influential,"* he thought.

"He's a tanner," Henry replied. "Not by choice," he added quickly, seeing Samuel's face. "He wanted to go to university but his father apprenticed him to his tannery business. So he's educated himself. He's well read, he collects books. He's interested in politics and he's not afraid to speak out. A few years ago he was elected by a group of tanners to go up to London to meet the prime minister about the poor state of the tanning trade."

"Really?" Samuel was impressed.

"He came back full of French revolutionary politics and other democratic views. Shocked the hell out of his father and the other Stowey cousins. Apparently..." Henry dropped his voice even though they were alone, "all the letters he sends are opened by the government and they've dubbed him the most dangerous person in the county of Somerset."

Samuel hid a smile. It was hard to imagine a country tanner in a Somerset village could be considered dangerous.

"He lives in Stowey," Henry said. "It's not far. I'll take you over there."

They approached the village through Lime Street, the poorest in the village. One of the cottages served as the poorhouse to the village, the rest were the homes of the workers of the village: the weavers and candlemakers, quarrymen, saddlers and wheelwrights. The insides of the cottages were so dark that people worked outside in the street as much as possible and the air around them rang with the sound of weavers' looms clacking and people talking as they sat sewing their gloves and saddles.

As the three young men walked by, everyone looked at them suspiciously and Samuel couldn't imagine anyone here having the remotest interest in their Pantisocratic ideals.

"My uncle lives this way," Henry said, turning right at the end of Lime Street into Castle Street. Here the houses were more substantial, made of brick, stone and stucco and clearly lived in by wealthier tradesmen and professionals. They stopped outside an elegant-looking house built in the local red Quantock stone.

Henry hesitated before he knocked. "My uncle is inclined to be a bit…" He searched for a word. "Well, he has a lot of pain from his gout," he went on. "It makes him a little impatient at times."

Remembering the welcome they had received from George Burnett's father earlier, Samuel felt a feeling of dread settle in his stomach.

Fortunately Henry's uncle was not at home and his aunt received them, exclaiming delightedly at the unexpected sight of her nephew and bustling around organising refreshments to be served.

"My other son Richard is home at the moment too," she told them. "He's a doctor in Sherborne," she added proudly.

Samuel could see how that would rankle: Tom Poole, the older brother, having to take over the family tannery while his younger brother went to university to study medicine.

His first sight of Tom only confirmed his doubts that he would be of any help to them: he was a broad man, strongly built like the Somerset farmers they saw in the fields, with a round ruddy complexion and a crushing handshake. His voice had the local Somerset bur, a variation on the Devon accent Samuel was used to hearing at home. He must have been about six or seven years older than them but he was a working man — he had been working since he was seventeen — and he seemed infinitely more mature.

Ten minutes in his company though was enough to change Samuel's mind about him. Here was an educated man, a man who took an interest not only in the politics of his county but the politics of the whole country. Finding him an easy man to confide in, Samuel told him about the mistakes he had made recently and his resolve to be sober and rational. They talked about religion and politics.

"I'm a Unitarian," Samuel said, "and a democrat to the utmost extent of the word. Let me explain to you my Pantisocracy scheme. Twelve like-minded couples will emigrate to America on the banks of the Susquehanna river…"

"America?" Tom Poole interjected. "Why, I have been thinking of emigrating there myself."

As Samuel spoke, gathering confidence as he went along, he could see Henry's cousin listening and nodding sympathetically. It was doubly disappointing then when he finally spoke in a calm measured voice.

"It is a very laudable scheme," he said, "with much to praise. But I cannot give it my support. It doesn't mean we can't be friends though does it? We have so much in common."

Samuel felt the same. In the short period of time he had spent with Tom Poole he knew he had found a good friend. And more than that he had seen the admiration in Tom's eyes as he spoke. Here was a man he could look to for support, if not in Pantisocracy, then maybe in other projects.

"Would you like to walk over to Marshmills after lunch?" Tom asked Henry. "It would be a shame to go back without seeing your other cousins."

"I'd love to," Henry said. "It's only a few miles," he explained to Samuel and Southey. "Our uncle has a fine house there. More Pooles for you to meet!" He laughed, "Though Tom is only interested in one of them."

Tom blushed.

"Can't say I blame you!" Henry gave Tom's arm a little shove. "You wait 'til you meet the lovely Miss Penelope Poole. You'll see what I mean."

"You'll come with us, won't you Richard?" Tom asked, turning to his quieter younger brother. "You haven't seen them since you've been home, have you?"

Tom and Richard were very close to their cousins at Marshmills, as Tom explained to Samuel on the way there.

"There's Charlotte, Penelope and John," Tom said. "John and I have been friends since we were children. I was so jealous of him, going to Tiverton Grammar School and then up to Oxford, but he's helped me such a lot, reading Latin with me in his holidays and advising me which books to collect. You'll like him, I know you will."

Charlotte and Penelope were there to greet them. Charlotte had sharp, knowing eyes. Penelope was every bit as lovely as Henry had said, with beautiful dark eyes and thick dark hair. "I think John's in the parlour," Charlotte said. "Go on through."

John Poole was sitting reading and Samuel had the impression they were spoiling the afternoon he had planned for himself.

"*Life of Johnson*," Samuel remarked, picking up the book John had reluctantly put down. "Are you enjoying it?"

"It's excellent," John said. "I borrowed it from my friend Mr Lewis this morning. He's our curate. So what have you been up to, Tom?" he went on. "More mischief-making politics?"

Tom instantly realised the mistake he had made bringing these young men here. John was a staunch Tory with firm conventional Church of England beliefs and his new friends' Unitarian and democratic views went against everything he stood for. As the conversation turned rapidly to politics it became more and more heated.

"I read in the *Western Flying Post* this morning that Robespierre has been executed," John said.

"Oh no! How awful; I would rather have heard of the death of my own father," Southey said.

"That's a dreadful thing to say!" John said, outraged.

They were still arguing loudly when the rector of nearby Aisholt called in later on.

"I don't think anyone here will forget your visit in a hurry!" Tom Poole laughed.

On their way back to Bristol, Samuel and Southey stopped off again at Mrs Southey's house in Bath, and again found Sarah Fricker there to greet them.

"Will you write to me, Miss Fricker?" Samuel asked her when he left.

"Of course," Sarah smiled at him.

Back in Bristol in late August, Samuel, Southey and Lovell decided to raise money by writing a play about Robespierre's death, based on the newspaper reports. Samuel dashed off the first act, writing all one night to get it finished, Southey wrote the second nearly as quickly, but Lovell struggled with the pace set by the others.

"What about a publisher?" Southey asked.

"Oh, Cottle will do it," Samuel said confidently. "When I met him last year he said he would publish anything I wrote."

But Cottle refused, so Samuel said he would publish it himself when he went back to Cambridge.

It was a wrench to leave Bristol in early September, to say goodbye to the people who believed in him and his scheme: the Frickers, Lovell, Burnett and Southey.

"In a year's time we will be in America," he told them, "on the banks of the Susquehanna, living our new life."

He spent a fortnight in London talking to anyone and everyone about Pantisocracy. He also researched how to buy land in Pennsylvania, sending back details to Southey and Lovell. By the time he got to Cambridge everyone was talking about Pantisocracy — not just the students but the tutors and dons — and Samuel had long heated discussions with some of them.

He had found a publisher for their play *The Fall of Robespierre* and it was circulated in Cambridge, London and Bath, bringing in the funds that they badly needed.

It was around now, however, that Samuel sensed Southey was having doubts. He bombarded Samuel with letters: how would the children be educated, he asked, what status would the servants have, what religious beliefs should be taught and how could women, who would have to bear children and look after them, be free from domestic chores.

Samuel did his best to mollify him. "Let the married women do only what is absolutely convenient and customary for pregnant women or nurses," he wrote back. "Let the husbands do all the rest."

Samuel's brothers George and James were also set against Samuel emigrating. His escapade in the dragoons had been bad enough but this time they thought he really had lost his mind. They threatened to cut off his allowance. They said they would take him away from Cambridge and send him to study law at the Temple.

Another letter arrived, this one unsigned, but he knew the writing. Mary Evans wrote saying she had heard of his "absurd and extravagant" scheme and wondering, like his brothers, if he was going mad. In fact her words were so similar to his brother George's that Samuel wondered if he had put her up to it. "There is eagerness in your nature," she wrote, "which is ever hurrying you into the sad extreme… I often reflect on the happy hours we spent together and regret the loss of your society. I cannot easily forget those whom I once loved…"

Guilt washed over Samuel when he read the letter. He had loved Mary but dropped her almost instantly when Sarah Fricker seemed to fit so easily into his plan for the future. Had he made a mistake? Which one did he really love? Mary, his first love, who had shared so many happy times with him, but who disapproved of what he was doing? Or Sarah, whom he scarcely knew, but who looked at him with such admiration shining in her eyes when he talked about Pantisocracy, who was prepared to go with him to America and start a new life?

With Southey and George both berating him for his disloyalty he buried himself in his work — not college work, but poetry, sonnets and another play called *The Robbers*.

By November he had pulled himself together enough to go up to London to see George and try to convince him that Pantisocracy was a reasonable plan.

Realising he also needed to straighten things out with Mary, he wrote to her describing his feelings for her and asking what she felt for him and whether she was actually engaged to someone else, as he had heard she was. While he waited impatiently for her reply he threw himself into publicity seeking, dashing off more sonnets which were published in the *Morning Chronicle*. His plays were performed by actresses like Mrs Siddons and at last he was beginning to be known as a writer.

Pantisocracy was always on his mind though. He continued to work through the details and difficulties in long letters to Southey. In his letters back, Southey often reminded him of his duty towards Sarah, whom he had rather abandoned while he was waiting to hear back from Mary.

They planned to emigrate in March the following year, April at the very latest. They had reckoned on an outlay of £2,000 but by Christmas that year they still had none of it. With no practical experience of farming between them, Southey and Lovell suggested maybe they should spend some time on a farm in Wales beforehand to learn the necessary agricultural skills. As far as Samuel could see this was all procrastination. Southey was constantly coming up with objections and criticisms, and wasting time arguing them, whereas Samuel just wanted to push ahead as quickly as possible.

And yet his career as a writer was taking off. His sonnets were being published and the editor of the *Morning Chronicle* wanted him to consider a career in journalism. He hadn't given up altogether on the idea of returning to Cambridge, then he was offered a post as a family tutor to the Earl of Buchan. Added to this his brother George was still pushing him towards a career in law.

He didn't know what to do. Pantisocracy was still his first choice but there was no money to finance the trip to America.

It was late December when he received the letter from Mary Evans telling him she was engaged to someone else. This left him free to marry Sarah of course, but now he wasn't sure that he really loved her.

He couldn't deny his physical attraction to her, but was this love? Was it enough to base a marriage on? And yet he didn't need Southey to remind him that he had a duty towards Sarah. He had led her on. It would be unfair to drop her now.

By the new year of 1795 he still hadn't made up his mind what to do, either about Sarah or about his future. He had lately become friendly again with an old schoolfriend, Charles Lamb. Lamb was devoted to his sister Mary in the way that Samuel had been to his sister Nancy and they sat for hours together in the Salutation and Cat public house, talking about their sisters, discussing philosophy, religion and of course Pantisocracy.

When Samuel received a letter from Southey insisting he come down to Bath to discuss things properly with him and Lovell, he honestly meant to go, but somehow he couldn't bring himself to and finally Southey arrived in London to berate him in person.

"You're getting nowhere up here," he told him. "You have to make a decision; if you really believe in Pantisocracy this is your chance to prove it."

"But I don't want to go to Wales," Samuel said. "Why don't you come up here? We could both find work. I could teach. You could work on a newspaper. We can raise enough money..."

"I've promised Edith we will marry," Southey cut in. "I can't just come up here. I owe it to her to stay in Bristol. And what about Sarah? If you won't come to Wales you must come down to Bristol, marry Sarah, find work and then we can raise the funds to go."

And so his decision was made for him. He came down to Bristol, moving into lodgings with Southey in

College Street. Bristol was a busy, hustling, bustling city, much of its wealth founded on the slave trade, which Samuel firmly opposed. There was plenty of opportunity for Samuel to establish himself here. His university career abandoned, he decided to earn his living as a writer. He sent his poems to Joseph Cottle for publication, he borrowed books from the Bristol Library on travel, philosophy and theology in order to write articles about them. He also gave a series of three moral and political lectures in rooms above the Corn Market with entrance tickets at a shilling each. He found he had a natural talent for speaking but his subject matter didn't go down well with everyone. It was dangerous to show revolutionary sympathies at this time and he quickly earned a reputation as a Jacobin and a radical, even receiving death-threats. The lectures paid so well, however,  that he planned a further series once the heat had settled down.

Once he set eyes on Sarah again, Samuel had realised that what he felt for her wasn't just physical attraction. He had forgotten her intelligence, her independent spirit, her sympathy for him and most importantly her belief in him. He truly loved her and she loved him. Ironically, Sarah's family were now advising her not to marry Samuel. In his absence, she had had two proposals of marriage, one from a wealthy man who could support her and her widowed mother and brother and sister.

By late March Samuel was beginning to think the Pantisocracy plan would come together. Southey had persuaded him that the farm in Wales was the only way forward. He too had begun lecturing and he reckoned that if they could count on a definite £150 a year from the lecturing and their writing they could marry the Fricker sisters, move to Wales and learn how to run a farm until they had saved enough money to emigrate to America, which was still their ultimate goal.

Samuel's lectures were now financially supported by some of Bristol's leading citizens: Joseph Cottle and his brother; John Prior Estlin, an influential Unitarian, and the Morgan family. Samuel was flattered when they commissioned a portrait of him by Peter Vandyke.

Samuel found he spoke best when he prepared least. He borrowed books from Bristol Library the day before a lecture and he spoke from the heart, waiting dramatically until his audience was ready and then allowing his thoughts to roam freely, whilst keeping basically to his theme. Pantisocracy was still his main topic of course but religion and philosophy featured highly and on the 16th June he delivered a boisterous talk on the slave trade. This was a contentious subject of course, since it was the source of much of Bristol's wealth. Samuel was becoming notorious for his radical views: anti-war, anti-Pitt, anti-slave trade.

Despite the success of the lectures, money was still tight and they often had to borrow from Cottle to pay the rent. Living in these cramped quarters in such close proximity, Samuel found himself constantly at loggerheads with Southey. Southey had been brought up by a maiden aunt. He was meticulously neat and well-organised, always perfectly dressed and well-organised in his work.

"You're always in such a muddle!" Southey told Samuel exasperatedly.

"But it all gets done in the end," Samuel said, blithely.

"Not always. You promised you'd do my historical lecture and never turned up!"

"I forgot."

"And you could smarten yourself up a bit. Put on clean stockings. Comb your hair…"

"Those things don't matter, my friend: it's what's up here that's important." Samuel tapped the side of his head.

But he and Southey were drifting apart. He could feel it. Southey was only interested in himself and Edith, in making enough money for them to live on. He seemed to have forgotten the principles of Pantisocracy, that they were all in it together. They began to argue. It was a painful time. Just as Samuel had come to terms with the Wales scheme, Southey and Lovell seemed to have gone off the idea. Samuel turned to George Burnett for support but he was just as uncertain. Everyone was against Samuel. The only one who stood up for him was Sarah. She was his staunchest ally, taking his side against Edith and Southey. He didn't know what he would have done without her and suddenly he realised how much he loved her.

Things came to a head with a violent argument over money. Southey had been offered an annuity of £160 a year. As far as Samuel was concerned the principles of Pantisocracy meant that that money belonged to the whole group. Southey, however, felt that his private money was his own, to be used for himself and Edith.

"So you're saying we each manage our finances individually?" Samuel said. "Even when we're living communally in Wales? That goes against everything we've been talking about."

"Just because we're living together, striving towards a common goal, it doesn't mean we have to pool our financial resources."

With these sorts of fundamental differences still not resolved, the Welsh project seemed to be slipping away.

"Just tell me once and for all," Samuel asked, "are you or are you not joining me in Pantisocracy?"

"I'm not," Southey declared. "Maybe one day. Say, in fourteen years or so. When Edith and I are married and settled."

"It'll never happen then," Samuel said. "You may as well go now. We've got nothing in common. I relied on you but you've let me down."

So Southey went, back to his mother's house in Bath to save enough money to marry Edith.

Samuel was lost without him. He had relied on him for so much. What could he do now? He turned to Sarah, his only friend. "We'll get married as soon as possible," he told her. "We'll find somewhere to live. By the sea maybe. I can write the poems I've promised for Cottle."

It was just as well really. Sarah and Edith, with their belief in female emancipation, had thought nothing of going about Bristol unchaperoned. But their reputation had suffered. People began to say that they were immodest and there were rumours that Pantisocracy meant the couples didn't need to be married.

When the two girls went to Wales with Southey and Coleridge and stayed overnight at an inn unchaperoned they found when they came back that they were considered to be 'ruined'.

"Can you not smile at the envy and absurdity of the many?" Southey asked. But society judged women harshly.

Samuel's wedding to Sarah was booked for October. In the meantime, Samuel went around visiting old friends and making new ones, influential people who could help him in his writing career. One day he was invited to the house of John Pinney, a rich West Indies sugar merchant. The Pinneys were a liberal family, even though their fortune was founded on the slave trade.

"My slaves never go hungry," John Pinney asserted. "They own their own goats, pigs and poultry. In fact, they have better living standards than the free poor on the island."

It was an argument always used by slavers. But Coleridge couldn't afford to be fussy about a potential patron.

"Ah, there's someone here you might like to meet," his host told him when he arrived. "William Wordsworth, the poet. I expect you've heard of him?"

Samuel looked across the room. Wordsworth was a tall, gaunt man, dressed in strange old-fashioned country clothes. He looked uncomfortable and oddly out of place in this city setting but when they finally managed to speak, Samuel was struck by how much they seemed to have in common: both struggling writers, both radicals, both looking for a way to lead the life they wanted.

Samuel went down to see Tom Poole again in Nether Stowey. Poole listened sympathetically as Samuel recounted the failure of the Pantisocracy scheme. "Something else will come up," he assured him. "You're destined for better things."

As Samuel wandered along the shoreline near Bridgwater his thoughts turned again to Sarah, his one true love, he knew now, the woman who loved him and believed in him and who would help shape his life.

The words for a poem came into his mind, a poem to Sarah, *Lines Written at Shurton Bars*, celebrating their love.

"O ever present to my view!

My wafted spirit is with you,

 And soothes your boding fears."

He made a reference to Wordsworth in the poem, borrowing his phrase 'green radiance'.

Samuel married Sarah on 4th October 1795 at St Mary Redcliffe in Bristol. No one from Samuel's family came and it was nearly a year before they met Sarah.

"I think you should change your name," Samuel told Sarah after the wedding.

"What? I just have, haven't I?" she laughed. "Mrs Coleridge."

"Mrs Coleridge," Samuel repeated, savouring the sound of the name in his voice. "No," he went on, "your Christian name. The spelling of it: S-A-R-A," he spelled out. "Without the 'h'. It's more refined."

He knew that would appeal to her. Despite their evident poverty nowadays, Sarah had never forgotten her privileged upbringing: she sealed her letters with a stamp saying *'Toujours gai'* and peppered her sentences with French expressions.

"Whatever you say, husband." She smiled now, winding her arm through his, pressing herself to his side. He felt the round softness of her breast against his arm, felt himself becoming aroused. He recognised in Sara the same sensual longings that he had. He knew instinctively she would be a good and responsive lover. And she was. In their tiny cottage in Clevedon he found a whole new meaning to the sexual encounter. Where before he had simply been satisfying his needs with whores, now he found a warm responsive woman, as eager for him as he was for her. It was such a happy time. In their eagerness and innocence, they had forgotten so many of the essentials and Samuel sent a shopping list to the ever-reliable Cottle:

"A riddle slice; a candle box; two ventilators; two glasses for the wash-hand stand; one tin dustpan; one small tin tea kettle; one pair of candlesticks; one carpet brush; one flour dredge; three tin extinguishers; two mats; a pair of slippers; a cheese toaster; two large tin spoons; a bible; a keg of porter; coffee; raisins; currants; catsup; nutmegs; allspice; cinnamon; rice; ginger and mace."

"Are you sure he won't mind getting all this?" Sara laughed when she saw it.

"Oh, that's just the essentials!" Samuel said. "There are *desiderata* as well: 'Set of better china, tubs and a pail, urine pots, beds, blanket, a pair of sheets of the finer order, two pairs for the servant, a set of curtains and pewter and earthenware.'"

Cottle obliged, of course, with the essentials anyway. Many of the other items remained even now on his *desiderata* list.

They hung an Eolian harp in their window: a simple frame with a few strings which played notes when the breeze blew through it.

The tiny cottage with its roses and jasmine climbing around the windows, the warmth of the late Indian summer, the long walks they took along the by the sea: Samuel knew then it would be one of the happiest times of his life and he felt the poetic urge rush upon him. Here he found his voice, as words and phrases flooded into his mind, his love for her and their happiness together reflected in the poems The *Eolian Harp* and *Reflections on having left a Place of Retirement.* She was his muse, his inspiration, the woman he loved best of all humankind.

In their romantic happiness, even Sara found a poetic voice. When she lost her silver thimble and Samuel wrote to Cottle asking him to send a replacement, he sent four to choose from. In return she wrote:

"You much perplex'd me by the various set:
They were indeed an elegant quartet
My mind went to and fro, and waver'd long
At length I've chosen (Samuel thinks me wrong)
That, around whose azure rim
Silver figures seem to swim,
Like fleece-white clouds, that on the sky blue,
Waked by no breeze, the self-same shapes retain;
Of ocean-nymphs, with limbs of snowy hue
Slow-floating o'er the calm cerulean plain
Just such a one, *mon cher ami*
(The finger-shield of industry)
Th'inventive Gods, I deem to Pallas gave…"

"It is remarkable elegant," Samuel said, "and would do honour to any volume of poems."

45

He was still determined to live by his Pantisocratic ideals and had one faithful follower in George Burnett, who came with them to the cottage in Clevedon. It wasn't fair that the woman should do all the chores so he and Burnett got up at six o'clock every morning to clean the kitchen, light the fires for Sara and put the kettle on ready for her to do breakfast at eight. They helped her with the dinner and did the dishes afterwards.

It was all so idyllic, too good to last. Clevedon was too much of a backwater for Samuel to stay there for long; he had to go back to Bristol to see about publishing his poems. Sara stayed on with George Burnett, Samuel's only supporter in the Pantisocracy scheme now. He had always intended going back to the cottage and he kept the rent going until the following March but winter set in, the cottage was glacial and remote. Sara came back to Bristol. The only place they could live was with her mother and Samuel found himself responsible for her and her family, as well as the ever-faithful George Burnett, who still supported Samuel and Pantisocracy and had nowhere else to go.

Before they had married, Sara had talked of being an equal to her husband. She had shared his views of female emancipation. Samuel had hoped she would help him with all the new ideas he had now he was back in the city. He published a pamphlet reprinting his first two political lectures, on the English Jacobins and the war against France, and he delivered lectures on the bills that Pitt planned to bring in banning what he saw as provocative meetings and lectures. These all went down so well that Samuel had a brilliant idea: he would set up a newspaper specifically for Unitarians and radicals like himself.

"I shall call it *The Watchman*," he told Sara. "I've worked out I shall need a thousand subscriptions to it to make it work. I reckon I can get that in a month. I'll dedicate two-thirds of it to parliamentary reports, political issues and foreign news and the rest to book reviews, philosophical commentary and poetry."

"That's a lot to do on your own," Sara said.

"But I'll have *you* to help me, my dear love, and Burnett of course. We'll send it an advance notice, "That all may know the Truth, and that the Truth might set us free."

"How are you going to get all those subscriptions?" Sara asked. "A thousand seems like a huge amount."

"I'll have to spread the word," Samuel said. "The Midlands and the north: that's where people will read us the most. The skilled workers in the factories, the book club readers, the people who suffer the most from Pitt's war measures and taxes."

"Will we make enough money from it?"

"If we don't we can go up to London. I can get a job on a newspaper. Or I could teach. We could set up a private school here in Bristol. Or maybe I should go back to Cambridge…"

He had envisaged Sara helping him collect the subscriptions, working with him on the articles. Wives should be the free and equal companions of their husbands, he believed. But, now that they were married, Sara seemed to enjoy domesticity. She had adored their little cottage in Clevedon and now that she was back in Bristol, she was happy at home with her mother and sisters, whom she had missed dreadfully when they were apart.

With four hundred of the subscriptions he needed, he was ready to take Sara with him on a tour of the Midlands and the north to secure the rest when she told him she was expecting a baby. He was overjoyed of course. He wanted children. But suddenly he was beset with responsibilities. He was already expected to support Sara's mother and brother. Then there was George Burnett, essential to him in the new project. And Sara and the new baby of course. It was imperative he should make this work.

So he went alone, trying everything from the individual approach of knocking on doors, which was largely unsuccessful, to preaching in Unitarian chapels, where he drew huge crowds and a lot of support.

He came back full of enthusiasm and with promises of subscriptions. After the excitement and freedom of the tour, life in cramped rooms in Bristol with Sara's mother and brother was an anti-climax. He had come home early because Sara had been ill and they thought she had lost the child. In April they moved to their own rooms in Kingsdown in Bristol, where Samuel ploughed on editing, correcting, packing and despatching copies of *The Watchman* from Cottle's shop and supervising the publication of his collection of poems.

To begin with the newspaper looked like it would be a huge success. In the first few issues he published his own articles on modern patriotism and the slave trade and issue five included an article by his friend Tom Poole in Nether Stowey and sonnets by Robert

Lovell. His book of *Poems on Various Subjects* also attracted some good reviews.

By the end of the month, however, *The Watchman* was in financial difficulties. The political climate had changed, readership dropped, Samuel found it hard to find people to write articles and to keep to his own deadlines. In May he was forced to admit it was a failure, the final ignominy being when he found the maid using old copies of it to light the fire.

It was a bad time. He had huge debts for the printer's bill. The death of his friend Robert Lovell on 3rd May 1796 hit him hard. Lovell was family, since his wife was Sara's sister. He had suffered dreadfully during his long illness. He had been a good friend and one of the original believers in Pantisocracy; it was the end of an era. For the last year or so that Samuel had been involved in politics, lecturing and writing, all his ideas had begun with Pantisocracy. He had to face up to the fact that it was over. Time for a fresh start.

"Come down to Stowey," Tom Poole urged him. "It will do you and Sara good to get away. And you can tell me your plans."

Poole had always believed in him. They sat in the garden at the back of Tom's house in Castle Street, drinking cider while Samuel recited his poetry.

"I have two schemes," Samuel told him, "the first impractical. The second not likely to succeed."

"Yes…?" Poole said encouragingly.

"Sara and I could go to Germany. I could study and translate Schiller. At the University of Jena."

"And how would you finance it?"

"I could teach. I could start a school for a dozen or so men. I have a curriculum all planned. Part One: man

49

as animal, including the complete knowledge of anatomy, chemistry, mechanics and optics. Part Two: man as an intellectual being, including the ancient metaphysics, the systems of Locke and Hartley and of the Scotch philosophers and the new Kantian system. Part Three: man as a religious being including an historic summary of all religions."

Poole nodded vaguely. "And the second scheme?"

"I could stay in Bristol and become a parson. I wouldn't drop the plan for the school. I could do both. I must do something. And soon. Money is tight at the moment, with the baby on the way..."

Back in Bristol at the end of May, Samuel found himself thinking nostalgically of those few weeks in Stowey: Poole's fine house in Castle Street with the gutter running with burbling water outside the front door, the comfort of Poole's fine house with its high ceilings and oak floors, the cool book-lined study, the beautiful garden with shady lime trees and Poole's mother bringing out the jug of cider.

Poole was proving a good friend. He wrote around to various people, admirers of Samuel, people who knew he had talent, and together they promised to contribute enough for £40 to be paid to him every year. And George Dyer, Samuel's old poet friend from London, offered to pay off all the outstanding printer's bills on *The Watchman*. It was good to know people believed in him. Now he must prove he was worth it. Samuel filled his notebooks with new plans: he would write essays on Bowles and Godwin, more on Pantisocracy, on marriage, an opera maybe, a tragedy and an epic poem on The Origin of Evil. He also had ideas for shorter poems: a 'wild poem on maniac', six hymns to the sun and the moon, and the elements, 'Egomist', a metaphysical rhapsody and 'escapes from misery'.

He started writing to William Wordsworth about poetry. Wordsworth had sent him the manuscript of his poem *Salisbury Plain* from where he was now living in Dorset with his sister Dorothy in Racedown Lodge, a house owned the Pinney family. It turned out they weren't paying any rent. John and Azariah Pinney were great admirers of Wordsworth. They knew he had no money and, unknown to their father, allowed him to live there rent-free.

In the summer Samuel had some offers of work. Impressed by his work on *The Watchman*, Perry of the *Morning Chronicle* in London offered him a position as an associate editor. He was also asked to help set up private schools in the Midlands in two separate proposals, one from a Dr Crompton and the second from a Mrs Evans, and in Liverpool William Roscoe, the friend and patron of Mary Wollstonecraft, offered him a position as a lay preacher.

Samuel was flattered by all these proposals. It showed that his reputation as a journalist, lecturer and preacher had spread countrywide. But he had never been very good at making up his mind and he dithered about what to do. On the face of it the editorial position in London was the most appealing, even though he wasn't that keen on returning to London. Luckily the decision was made for him when he applied for it but was turned down.

In July he went down to Ottery St Mary to visit his family for the first time since his marriage. His mother greeted him with delight and his brothers were pleased to see him, especially George who had always supported him. When Samuel returned he took Sara up to Derby so that he could investigate the possibility of setting up a school with Mrs Evans. They spent several weeks there and the whole idea seemed quite feasible but unfortunately the trustees did not sanction Samuel's appointment. Mrs Evans was so disappointed and had been so taken with both Samuel and Sara that she gave Samuel a gift of £95 parcelled up with some beautiful baby clothes for Sara.

There was still the possibility of joining the Unitarian ministry and Samuel went to Birmingham to preach while Sara returned to Bristol. While he was there yet another job offer came up: the Lloyd family asked Samuel if he could be private tutor to Charles Lloyd. The Lloyds were a wealthy Quaker banking family. Charles was twenty-one but mentally unstable and suffering from epilepsy and the Lloyds suggested that Charles should live with Samuel and Sara so that Samuel could give him the personal attention he needed. Samuel liked this idea. It was well paid, it wouldn't take up all his time, he could live wherever he wanted and he would still have time to write and study.

He had just finalised the details with Mr Lloyd when news arrived from Bristol that Sara had had the baby. With still two weeks to go, she had had nothing ready and delivered the baby herself, the nurse only arriving in time to deal with the afterbirth.

Samuel could scarcely believe himself to be a father. A baby boy. The news was shattering. The sudden responsibility for another being seemed overwhelming.

He hurried back to Bristol, taking Charles Lloyd with him. His first sight of the baby surprised him. He had expected to feel a rush of happiness and love but he felt nothing. A couple of hours later, however, he went back in to find Sara feeding him. He saw the utter love in her eyes, the total concentration on the tiny creature in her arms and suddenly he felt an outpouring of emotion. He went over, bent down, kissed the top of the tiny head.

He wrote three sonnets, each one exploring his feelings.

The baby was christened David Hartley, after the philosopher, but they always called him Hartley.

Suddenly, and surprisingly, having Hartley crystallised Samuel's vision for the future. He didn't want his son, or any other children he and Sara might have, to be brought up in Derby or in Birmingham. He wanted a country life for his children, a simple, back-to-nature existence, where they would be free to roam the hills and valleys. He wrote to Tom Poole, asking if he could come and stay with him in Stowey and bring Charles Lloyd with him. Tom's father had died and it was only Poole and his mother living in the big house in Castle Street. "We don't want to be any trouble," Samuel wrote. "We can share a bed like we do here in Bristol. We're quite used to it."

Mrs Poole welcomed them when they arrived.

"We've invited John Cruikshank over," she said. "He lives just up the road from us here. We would have asked his wife as well but she is shortly expecting her confinement."

"I believe I know her," Samuel said. "She was Anna Buckle before she married wasn't she? And lived in Enmore?"

"Yes, that's right."

53

"And now she's to have a child. Why, that's marvellous. My wife has just had a baby you know."

"Yes, Tom told me." Mrs Poole smiled fondly at his fatherly pride.

"And what does Mr Cruikshank do?" Samuel went on.

"He's agent to the Earl of Egmont, who owns a lot of the property around here."

"I'm thinking of coming to live down here," Samuel said to Cruikshank later as they sat drinking beer in the parlour. "Would you be able to find me somewhere?"

"There's a cottage in Adscombe I might be able to get for you," Cruikshank replied. "I can ask Lord Egmont for you. We can walk over there sometime and take a look if you like."

They took the road Samuel had taken with Tom, Henry Poole and Southey the previous summer, but this time walked on through the hamlet of Marshmills and on to Adscombe, just a collection of four cottages and the farmhouse itself.

"Enchanting," Samuel said.

"It would be one of those cottages." Cruikshank gestured to the small group. "But it comes with about six acres of land..."

Samuel saw it clearly. He would be near Poole in the Quantocks, his children would be brought up in the heart of the countryside, they could live off the land and he would be free to write and commune with nature. He had the income from tutoring Charles. It was a perfect plan.

And that was what brought them to Stowey. However, it didn't quite work out as he had planned.

First of all, Charles Lloyd had a series of epileptic fits and had to be sent back to Birmingham to recover, then the cottage at Adscombe was unavailable to rent. By the beginning of November Samuel was getting desperate.

"Has Cruikshank forgotten about me?" he asked Poole. "Or has Lord Thingamabob — I forget the animal's name — refused me?"

"I think they're just trying to make the cottage more habitable for you," Poole wrote back.

"Maybe we might rent some rooms at your uncle's house at Shurton Court in the meantime?" Samuel responded.

Two days later Poole replied. Cruikshank was so taken up with his wife's approaching confinement ("She's very delicate, you know," Poole wrote) that he had done nothing more about it.

"We *must* be out of here by Christmas," Samuel wrote. "Can't you find me somewhere else?"

The only other house to rent was a tiny, dilapidated cottage in Lime Street, known as Gilbard's, which Samuel and Southey would have passed unnoticed when they first came into Nether Stowey that summer. Right on the outskirts of the village, it was a two-up, two-down worker's cottage with an outhouse, a courtyard with a well, and a large garden.

When Poole described it to him, Samuel wasn't put off. He and Sara had lived in a small cottage before in Clevedon. He was sure they could make it habitable. And the garden backed on to Tom Poole's garden. When the summer came they would sit outside in the way they had sat in Tom's garden last year. Samuel was sure this was the place for him. He had had enough of cities and towns. From now on he would make do with a simple life. "I shall have six companions," he wrote to Charles Lloyd's father, "my Sara, my babe, my own shaping and disquisitive mind, my books, my beloved friend Thomas Poole and, lastly, Nature, looking at me with a thousand looks of beauty, and speaking to me in a thousand melodies of love."

Here, Samuel thought, he could live out the principles of Pantisocracy. The cottage had a big garden. They could live off the land. He hadn't completely given up the idea of writing as a career but it wasn't a profession he could live on. If they could be self-sufficient, if he could live a simpler life, he would have time for spiritual self-examination and philosophy.

He hadn't considered how hard it would be in the tiny cottage with Sara and the baby and the nanny around all day every day. Tom Poole was very good to him, allowing him to use his book room when things became too frantic. But now, at this quiet time of day, with Sara in bed and Hartley sleeping quietly by his side, now was the only time for reflection, introspection, reading and writing.

The fire was dying, however, and it was growing cold. Samuel raked over the last of the embers, scooped up the ashes and scattered them on top to keep it going overnight. He lifted Hartley carefully from his cradle. The baby whimpered slightly and Samuel stiffened, waiting for him to start crying and Sara to appear sleepily at the top of the stairs, but Hartley found his fist and sucked on it and Samuel felt the little body relax in his arms again. He climbed the stairs carefully, laid Hartley down in the crib by the bed.

Sara was asleep. He slid carefully in next to her and her warm body rolled towards him. "Samuel…" she murmured. "I love you…"

"I love you too, Sally," he whispered. Sally, Sally Pally, one of his silly nicknames for her, the baby talk of love. He knew she was tired, he didn't want to wake her, but her soft body moulded itself against his. He could feel her naked leg, feel her warm, round arm. "Samuel…" she said again.

It was too much. He turned to her, took her in his arms. His mouth found hers. She was awake now, her arms tightened around him, she pulled him on top of her.

It was quick; she was eager, she was wonderful. His Sara, the woman he loved. She knew how to make him happy. All her sad moods, her tears, her quick temper, they didn't matter as long as he had this.

Samuel fell asleep immediately, his damp face buried in Sara's shoulder. She pushed his dead weight from on top of her, pulled the tangle of bedclothes from around her and fell asleep. It was still dark, still icy cold, when she heard the first sounds of Hartley stirring, the gentle hiccupping sound that soon turned into a full-scale wail.

# Chapter Three

Sara scarcely had a free moment to think about anything other than her daily routine: what they would eat next, whether she needed to buy anything, the next lot of washing to sort out, the next lot of mending to tackle. Her day was full of mundane tasks from the moment Hartley woke her in the small hours of the morning until the moment she laid her head on the pillow at night. She wouldn't have it any other way of course. She loved being a housewife, being busy, looking after a husband and a baby. Yet, just occasionally, when she was scrubbing the muddy vegetables in the scullery or hanging the washing over the airing rack above Samuel's head, she would wonder how she had ended up in this tiny cramped cottage in deepest Somerset.

Sara had enjoyed a genteel upbringing. Her family was middle class. Her father was a wine and spirit merchant, her mother the daughter of a merchant venturer family who owned a large iron foundry. Sara's mother brought her own money into the marriage and wanted the best for her daughters so when it came to education she chose the renowned Hannah More School in Bristol.

It was a large family and Sara was the oldest. She had four younger sisters and a brother and four other children had died when they were babies. Their childhood was divided between a smart house in Bath and a villa in Westbury near Bristol. Sara and her sisters were brought up in liberal, Unitarian surroundings. They were encouraged to think of themselves as equal to men.

In 1786, when Sara was sixteen, her world turned upside down when her father was declared bankrupt. Almost overnight they lost everything: their beautiful houses, all the furniture, everything except the clothes they had on. It was the most shaming time of Sara's life. They had nowhere to live, nowhere to go. The family was separated as friends offered temporary accommodation: Sara and her father stayed with one friend outside Bristol, her mother and the youngest children went to another friend and Mary and Edith, only fourteen and twelve, yet another. Worse was to come when, just a few months later, Sara's father died, leaving her mother with six children and no house or money.

Sara's mother rented lodgings on Redcliffe Hill in Bristol and set up a small private school and, later on, a dress shop. Neither of these made much money so Sara, Mary and Edith did the only thing they had been taught at school that turned out to be any help to them: they became seamstresses. It was an occupation with a dubious reputation, often used as a euphemism for prostitutes.

The three girls now found themselves working for people who had been their friends and social equals, including Margaret Southey, Robert's mother. In fact Sara had known Robert Southey since they were small children. They had always been close and when he went up to Oxford he wrote to her. She was one of the few people he could talk to about his radical ideas.

By then Mary had given up sewing and begun working in the theatre as an actress, where she seemed to have some talent. It was here that she met Robert Lovell. He was the son of a wealthy Bristol Quaker and his family disapproved of his relationship with Mary: she had no money, she was an actress and she wasn't a Quaker. Lovell went to Balliol College, Oxford but he didn't want the career his patents had in mind for him. He had democratic sympathies and he wanted to be a poet. When Sara and Mary introduced him to Southey they became great friends.

Sara's sister Edith often sewed for Southey's Aunt Tyler. Southey had been brought up by his aunt and in the university holidays he went to visit her, so he began to see a lot of Edith. Edith was very shy and nervous and not easy to get to know, but Southey himself was reserved and appreciated her quietness.

In 1794 Mary married Robert Lovell. His parents threw him out of the house and stopped his allowance and he and Mary rented rooms in College Street. It was in August that year that Samuel walked into their sitting room and into Sara's life. She wasn't much taken with him at first; he was far from good-looking, his clothes were in a dreadful state and his long dark hair needed a good cut. She was struck, though, by how learned he was and how eloquent. He had expressive grey eyes. As he talked on and on in his easy melodic voice about Pantisocracy, Sara found herself being won over. So much of what he said seemed to make sense: men and women as equals, sharing the daily tasks, living, working and studying together.

After years in the company of Southey and then Lovell, the Fricker girls were all well versed in the democratic principles behind the scheme. The practicalities lay in finding a group of like-minded men and women willing to put it into action, to emigrate to America, to live the dream. Lovell had Mary, it was clear that Southey would soon have Edith, it seemed destined that Samuel should have Sara. Sara's mother liked Samuel, as she also liked Southey and Lovell. Edith was nervous of emigrating to America without her mother but Mrs Fricker was so won over by the idea of Pantisocracy that she said she would go as well. Sara knew that her mother would have liked her to marry someone with wealth who could support the family. And there was such a man. In fact, in that long period of time when Samuel went up to London and she didn't hear from him, she had two proposals of marriage. She wasn't keen on either suitor but she left the more advantageous one open, just in case. She knew, of course, why Samuel took so long proposing to her. It had all seemed to happen so quickly and she fitted neatly into a slot ready for the Pantisocracy scheme. She wasn't surprised that Samuel suddenly had cold feet. She was sure of his feelings for her though. She could see it in his eyes. She hung onto her belief in him long after others had told her it wouldn't happen. She and Samuel, they belonged together, as though they were bound by an invisible cord. She knew it instinctively.

When he returned she was ecstatically happy. Life couldn't get much better. Here they were, her and Mary and Edith, all either married or engaged to three exciting young man, on the verge of an enterprise that could change society. The only problem was that they had no money. Mary was already expecting a baby. But Coleridge and Southey came up with various money-making plans and they all remained optimistic, their goal still firmly in sight.

When Samuel quarrelled with Southey it caused a rift between Sara and Edith. She had always been close to her sisters and it hurt her dreadfully but she had to put Samuel first: he was her fiancé.

They were deeply in love, their marriage day the happiest of her life. Samuel wrote her some beautiful poetry: *The Kiss* and *Ode to Sara, Lines Written at Shurton Bars*.

At first their time at Clevedon was idyllic, despite the privations of the tiny cottage. It was Sara's first taste of physical love, though she knew it wasn't Samuel's. She had had no idea how happy two people could be together. It was bliss.

But winter set in and the cottage became difficult to heat, Samuel had to go back to Bristol regularly to supervise the work he was doing and, despite the company of the ever-faithful George Burnett, Sara became lonely and unhappy. She was used to being in a big, busy family. She was used to working. The neighbours looked at her suspiciously whenever she went out. In November they moved back to Bristol to live with her mother and her younger sisters and brother. Although she would have liked a home of her own, Sara didn't mind too much. She was used to the noise and the chaos and she had missed her mother and her family. But Samuel hated it. He couldn't find anywhere quiet to work and he didn't like having to share Sara with everyone else.

They began to argue. "I thought you'd want to spend all your time with *me*," Samuel grumbled.

"There are things to do in the house, Samuel."

"Can't you let your mother do them? You could help me with *The Watchman*."

"I thought George Burnett was helping you. That's why he lives with us isn't it? That's why you support him." She didn't know why she was being so horrible to poor old George; she quite liked him. He had been good company when she was on her own in Clevedon. But she was angry with everyone and he was a draw on their resources.

"He *is,* of course he is." Samuel sprung to his defence. "You don't understand, Sara. He's always stuck by me. Not like Southey…"

"Oh, don't start that again," Sara snapped. "He was only thinking of Edith. And now she isn't speaking to me."

"That's not *my* fault."

"Of course it is! You know it is!"

When she found out she was pregnant she was so excited but the excitement soon palled when she felt sick all the time and couldn't keep anything down. Then she and her mother both went down with a fever. She was so ill that she thought she would lose the baby. Samuel was so kind to her then, rushing back from his trip to the north to look after her, that when he suggested they leave her mother's house to find lodgings of their own, she agreed, even though she found that George Burnett was coming with them.

She began to feel better and soon realised she hadn't lost the baby. But she was still feeling sick all the time and as she grew bigger, she began to despair of Samuel's chaotic approach to work.

"It's such a mess in here!" she yelled, picking up sheets of paper and throwing them around the room. "No wonder you never get anything finished. You'll never make any money at this rate!"

"Sara, don't!" Samuel remonstrated, picking up the pieces of paper and trying to put them in order again. "That's my next article."

She wasn't surprised when the magazine failed. She was just worried about how they would manage, especially once they had Hartley. Samuel, as ever, was optimistic. "I can teach," he told her, "or become a parson and still have time to write articles and lectures."

Grand schemes again, none of which came to anything, except for tutoring poor old Charles Lloyd and that didn't work out, although to be fair that wasn't Samuel's fault. Without the charity of friends she didn't know how they would have managed.

"It's an annuity, Sara," Samuel kept correcting her, "because they believe in me."

It was always so important to Samuel that people believed in him. That was how they ended up in Stowey. Because Tom Poole had replaced Robert Southey in Samuel's life. He was his new best friend, the man who believed in him, who supported him financially as well as morally, who found him a bolthole, somewhere he could live the simple life that he had decided he needed.

Samuel described the house he had found in Somerset in glowing terms. "It's in Adscombe. It's a little combe, secluded and quiet, scarcely anyone lives there."

"But I'll be so alone, like I was in Clevedon. All day on my own…"

"It's not far from Tom Poole's cousins at Marshmills. You can visit them. You'll be friends."

She told her mother all about it. "It's just like Samuel's original scheme for Pantisocracy," she said, trying to raise her own enthusiasm for it. "We can live off the land. The children will be brought up in the fresh air…"

"Well, maybe we could come too," her mother said, "George and I." She gestured to Sara's brother sitting by the fire. "If we could find him an apprenticeship."

"That would be lovely," Sara said. Her mother could help her in the house and garden. Samuel had been saying they could manage without a servant, just taking Betty who was mostly a nanny but would turn her hand to anything. "We can send out the washing," he said, "only eat meat on Sundays and do without strong liquor."

Sara wondered if he would give up laudanum too. It was so expensive and Samuel took it at every opportunity, doubling the dose for his rheumatism and neuralgia and relying on it to get him through the stressful periods, especially when they argued. She had watched him pour the drops into his glass, scarcely counting how many went in.

"Didn't the doctor say twenty-four drops every four hours?" she asked.

"It helps steady my nerves," Samuel said.

It was true that he was often anxious and depressed but Sara wasn't sure that the laudanum helped at all.

He had always suffered from dreadful nightmares — she watched him pray every night for a trouble-free sleep but he still woke screaming in fear — but now he suffered from what he called 'day-mares' as well. In addition, he complained of such dreadful joint and muscle pain that he sometimes ran around the house naked to try to relieve it.

Sara wondered how Samuel would take the news that her mother wanted to join them. He used to get on with her but lately he had begun to actively dislike her.

"She's so middle-class and conventional," he said to Sara, "and has such strong religious views."

"You don't have to take any notice of that," Sara said loyally. "She'd be company for me. And she'd bring her own furniture with her."

Samuel brightened. They had little of their own. It would help cut down on expenses.

Sara comforted herself that Samuel might get on better with her mother in new surroundings. Since she'd had Hartley he had made it up with Edith and Southey. They had promised to visit them in Somerset. This would be a new beginning.

It didn't work out like that of course. Like all Samuel's schemes there were changes, one of which included her mother. First of all they couldn't find an apprenticeship for George. Everyone they tried needed a huge premium which they didn't have. Then Sara's mother announced that she had changed her mind about living in the country.

By then the house at Adscombe had fallen through and the only place available was this dilapidated cottage in Lime Street, nothing like the lovely cottage with its six acres of land that Samuel had described.

Even this nearly came to nothing when Tom Poole wrote saying that the cottage simply wouldn't do, that it couldn't be made habitable, it was an unsuitable home for Sara and the baby. Samuel was distraught.

"He thinks we should live in Iron Acton instead."

"Well, it's not far from Bristol," Sara pointed out. "It would be closer to your friends."

"But miles away from Poole," Samuel lamented. "He's my only true friend now, the one I thought I could rely on."

As Samuel raved on, Sara wondered if it was Samuel's reputation that was causing Tom Poole such doubts. What would his friends and fellow villagers think of him bringing such a notorious young radical to the village?

Samuel sat up nearly all that night writing a long, impassioned letter to Poole.

"I haven't quite finished it," he told Sara the following morning, taking up his pen again. "I shall get it off directly."

"What have you said?" Sara asked.

"I've told him that the land around Iron Acton is intolerably flat, I need the hills of Somerset. The only friends I have in Bristol are Cottle and Estlin and they can come and visit us in Stowey, that the cottage will do, we will make it do. I've said that we can live on sixteen shillings a week, which I can earn from writing reviews."

Once it was all settled Samuel began to draw up a timetable for them both:

Six o'clock. Light the fires. Clean out the kitchen. Put on the Tea Kettle. Clean the insides of the boiling pot. Shoes etc. Samuel and Betty.

Eight o'clock. Tea things etc. put out and after clean up. Sara

One o'clock. Spit the meat. Samuel and Betty

Two o'clock. Vegetables etc. Sara

Three o'clock. Dinner.

Half past three 10 minutes for cleaning dishes.

"I'll do all the gardening of course," he told Sara, "and you can look after the baby and do the sewing."

It all sounded perfect and, despite her reservations, Sara found herself looking forward to it. Her heart sank however when she first saw the cottage. She had thought it would be something like the cottage at Clevedon with its roses and honeysuckle around the windows, but this was just a basic worker's cottage with an open gutter flowing outside the front door. The gutter overflowed in wet weather and poured all across the road, causing a dreadful stench. The cottage was right at the end of the village on the turnpike road so a constant flow of traffic made its way past their front door, turning the muddy road into a quagmire.

The front door opened into the main parlour where Sara had to do all the cooking over an open fire. There was no oven and she had to take pies and meat to the bakers to be cooked. The chimney in this room smoked dreadfully. Samuel had talked of having it Rumfordised, whatever that was, but he never got around to doing it, his own remedy being to go out when the room become too smoky because it "inflamed his eyes".

The plan to send washing out had never materialised and Sara and Betty were constantly scrubbing the skirts and petticoats that became streaked with mud in the wet weather. There was a small scullery at the back where Sara could soak Hartley's nappies and the other dirty washing, scrub the muddy vegetables from the garden and wash eggs. They also had a best parlour on the right, a room they scarcely used at first since they knew no one to invite. The back door gave onto a courtyard with a well and a large garden beyond.

Sara didn't know how they would have coped at all at first without Tom Poole to help and advise them. He did whatever he could to make the cottage more bearable and brought over parcels of food. Sara was so lonely without her mother and her sisters and friends nearby to visit. Life was so different here from in the big city. Samuel's timetable for chores was never put into action; everything was left to her. In some ways she didn't mind. She had always wanted her own house to run. Here, she felt in control. Yet it was hard not to resent the freedom Samuel had. He didn't get up until seven, later sometimes when he'd had a bad night, by which time Sara had been up for hours. He might then do a couple of hours' gardening, but that had been impossible recently with the bad weather and the ground so hard, so he sat and read by the fire while she and Betty scurried around him. Sometimes she glanced over his shoulder to see what he was reading but it was mostly philosophy and unintelligible to her. He used the few hours of daylight to write letters and articles for magazines and poetry and at two o'clock he fed the pigs and poultry. After they had eaten he read or wrote again. It was often getting dark by then and he had to use the tallow or rush candles which were all they could afford. Increasingly he went over to Tom Poole's house where Poole had said he could use his comfortable book room. Samuel had joined the Stowey Book Society but Poole's collection of books was more extensive and included the sort of books he missed since he couldn't get to the City Library in Bristol.

It wasn't the life Sara had foreseen for herself. She missed her family and friends in Bristol. She missed the comfort of the big city houses.

"Do you remember Mrs Evans' house in Derbyshire?" she asked Samuel one evening.

For a moment Samuel thought she meant Mrs Evans, the mother of his first sweetheart, and he blushed guiltily. Then he realised what she'd said.

"Mrs Evans in Derbyshire?" he repeated. "Of course. It was lovely. And she was so welcoming. Such a shame nothing came of her school. It would have been ideal."

The comfortable house, the motherly woman to look out for her and introduce her to like-minded people: Sara wouldn't have minded moving all the way up there to have all those things.

Sometimes she found herself thinking how it would have been if she had accepted that wealthy man. She could have had a house like Mrs Evans'. Two in fact, one in the country and one in the city, with beautiful furniture, fine clothes, servants, a carriage, parties. He would have supported her family, given her brother George an education. But what were all these without love? She loved Samuel, she was proud of him, she believed in him. One day he would give her all the things she wanted. She just had to be patient.

# Chapter Four

The cold winter gave way to a mild spring. In late February Charles Lloyd came back to live with them. They couldn't refuse him, they needed the income, but he disrupted the routine they had begun to establish. Betty, their loyal nanny from Bristol, had left, too disgusted by the conditions she had to work in, so Sara had had to employ a local nanny. The girl was about twelve, slow witted and dull eyed. She had learned nothing at school but she was strong and willing and was used to working in cramped cottages. Sara prided herself on her own ability to work hard and the chores didn't seem so bad with someone equally hard-working to share them with. She prided herself on her optimism too. She never stayed downhearted for long. It was an attribute that Samuel, with his propensity for doom and gloom, liked about her as well. So she hummed to herself as she hung the washing up on the airing racks, thinking it wouldn't be long before she could peg it outside, and she greeted Samuel with a smile when he came back from Tom Poole's house.

Charles arrived like a whirlwind, turning the house upside down. Sara put him in the spare bedroom but during the day he used the best parlour, the one set aside for receiving guests, as an office. Here he worked on the poetry he had brought with him, written by him and Charles Lamb, that Samuel had generously offered to have printed as an appendix to his own new edition of poetry.

It was unfortunate timing: Samuel had just received a valuable commission to write a verse tragedy for Sheridan which would be put on at Drury Lane Theatre.

"I shall set it in Spain at the time of the Inquisition," he told Sara. "I'm calling it *Osorio*. It will be romantic, wild and somewhat terrible."

He needed time and peace and quiet to concentrate on it but Charles was demanding and Samuel *was* being paid to mentor him. Disorganised at the best of times, Samuel now had difficulty finding time for his own writing, in particular the reviews he wrote which brought in a regular income.

Everyone thought Charles was fully recovered but unfortunately he began to have epileptic fits again. By the middle of March he was having them nearly every day. The fits were bad enough but they were followed by a strange sort of delirium that lasted several hours. Samuel sat up for hours with him at night, trying to soothe him and physically restraining him when he thrashed about. The household was turned upside down by the sleepless nights and the chaos. Samuel's work on the play faltered. His reviews weren't delivered on time. Money stopped coming in.

It was a huge relief when Charles went back to the Midlands and was admitted to a sanatorium. Life could go back to normal even if they had lost the £80 a year they were relying on as part of their income.

No longer trapped in the house by the endless rain and bad weather, Sara began to go out more. She and Samuel called on the Cruikshanks, who lived up the road from Poole in Castle Street. Anna had a baby girl, also called Anna, roughly the same age as Hartley, and they soon became close friends.

"You must come to her baptism," Anna said as she jiggled the baby in her arms, "on 3rd February. Both of you. Mr Roskilly is conducting the service. I can introduce you to his wife. She has a baby about Hartley's age too, Mary Elizabeth, such a sweet little thing…"

The garden of the cottage in Lime Street backed on to Tom Poole's and Poole had a gate made so they could get into his garden and his house or, through his orchard, across a meadow into John Cruikshank's garden. Samuel used the gate to escape into Poole's book room to read and write in peace and quiet but Sara often carried Hartley up to Anna Cruikshank's for a chat or into Mrs Poole's welcoming parlour, its large high-ceilinged room so much more like the houses she was used to in Bristol.

Mrs Poole always made her feel so welcome and she rarely left without a bag of vegetables or a jar of preserve. "Just to keep you going until you're more settled," she would say if Sara tried to demur.

She and Samuel were invited to parties and musical evenings. Samuel was very popular with the pretty young women, whom he charmed with his clever wit, even though they didn't fully understand some of his puns. They tried to teach him to dance, something he had never done before, but he wasn't very good.

Samuel had always made friends easily and soon the curate William Roskilly and Anna Cruikshank's husband John were regular visitors to the cottage. William Roskilly was a Cornishman who kept a boarding school, charging £20 per annum including washing and Latin.

After the Cruikshank baby's christening, Samuel wrote a tribute to her mother Anna, whom he had known as Anna Buckle before she married John Cruikshank.

One morning in 1797 Cruikshank told Samuel about a dream he'd had.

"I saw a spectre ship," he said. "Like a ghost, all white and shimmering, manned by ghostly figures."

Samuel thought it over after he had gone, wrote it down carefully in one of his notebooks. It was the sort of thing he could use in a poem in the future.

With all these new friendships Samuel didn't forget his old friends. He couldn't afford to, of course: many, like his publisher Joseph Cottle, supported him financially. Cottle was a regular visitor to Nether Stowey. He stayed at the cottage and liked to visit Tom Poole to discuss politics and current affairs with him and Samuel. Sometimes Tommy Ward would be lurking in the shadows, contributing little but hanging on every word he heard. Tommy was Poole's apprentice. He was sixteen when Tom Poole's younger brother Richard brought him to Nether Stowey from his home in Sherborne. Originally he had wanted to be a doctor, but once he met Tom Poole he decided instead to be a tanner. He was living in Poole's house while he was learning and soon became like a member of the family. He was a bright-faced, enthusiastic, intelligent lad and Sara and Samuel were both very fond of him. Ward, for his part, hero-worshipped Samuel and took great pleasure in performing tasks and errands for him.

When Samuel wanted to be alone to read or write he would go up to Poole's book room, which he could get to either through the house itself or, more usually, by going up an outside flight of worn steps. This was his haven, a beautiful room with a barrel ceiling made of elm rafters and a floor made of old elm boards.

By the end of March 1797 Samuel had to admit that his verse play was in a dreadful state. "I don't know where I'm going with it," he told Sara, leafing distractedly through sheets of paper. "Maybe I should take a break from it for a while. I'll go up to Bristol. Go to the library, see some friends…"

He had been so depressed recently. The gothic books he had had to review in order to make some money were so vapid.

"I'm fed up with dungeons, old castles and solitary houses by the sea," he grumbled to Sara. "And my play is a mess. I don't know what to do. Every way I choose to earn bread and cheese seems to fail."

Sara waved him off cheerfully. She knew she would miss him but it would do him good to get away and she could get on with the house much better without him constantly moping around and getting in her way.

Samuel's walk to Bristol took him past fields and orchards and through the villages of Cannington and Wembdon, then on to Bridgwater where he would stop for a rest before tackling the thirty-five miles to Bristol. In Bridgwater he usually took refreshment either at the Old Angel Inn or, on the rare occasions he was taking the coach, at the George Inn in George Lane. As he neared the town, he fell in with other walkers and horses and carts also on their way to the town and by the time he reached the narrow thoroughfare of Fore Street he had to weave through a tight, noisy throng of pedestrians, horses and carts.

Fore Street was full of shops of all sorts of trade: stay-makers, hatters, mercers, wig-makers, maltsters, chandlers, tallow-makers, trunk-makers and china-and-earthenware dealers. It was also full of inns including the Bridgwater Arms, the Ship and Castle and the King's Head. Then there was the Castle Inn with its stables and the town gaol. Ahead of him the tall spire of St Mary's Church rose into the sky above the half-timbered houses of the marketplace. Behind here were the newly built corn and provision markets. On market days it was noisy with the bargaining going on in the open air outside the Crown Inn in High Street, where Samuel was now heading.

High Street was also lined with shops and yet more inns: the Golden Ball, the Greyhound, the Lamb, the Bull and Butcher, the Mansion House, the unusually named Noah's Ark and the Woolpack. On one side stood the old Guildhall and the Assize Hall where assizes were held in rotation with Wells and Taunton. Further down, High Street was divided in two by a narrow line of shops called the Island. Here there was a butcher's shop called The Shambles, which was always busy with customers going in and out.

The Old Angel was in a small street at the back of the Crown Inn in High Street and this was where Samuel would find books, letters and parcels left to be collected either by himself or Milton, the Stowey carrier, or a messenger from Tom Poole.

Once rested and refreshed, he walked over the stone bridge with its three arches and massive piers that crossed the River Parrett; the water, already muddy from the local red-brown earth that lined the banks, made worse when it passed by the quay.

*"Never was a river so aptly named,"* Samuel thought. *"As filthy as if all the parrots in the House of Commons had been washing their consciences in it."*

The river below the bridge was crowded with ships: local ones bringing various goods from Bristol, slate from Cornwall, fleeces from Ireland and coals from Wales and international ones trading with Spain, Portugal, the West Indies, Virginia and Newfoundland. Standing on the bridge, Samuel saw the tidal bore glide silently up from the estuary, washing over the sides of the coal barges as they carried coal up the river towards the River Tone and Taunton. The woollen cloth industry that had sustained the town for some time had begun to decline and many people now relied on the shipping industry to provide work with jobs in the shipyards such as rope-making, sail-making and boat-building as well as the chandleries and general merchants, whose shops lined the quayside. Here, too, were more inns: the Dolphin, the Anchor, the Fountain, the King's Arms, the Ship in Launch, and the

Salmon, named after the fish which, despite the muddy water, still swam as far up as the bridge.

And so Samuel walked on, through Eastover and out through East Gate and on to the busy turnpike road from Bridgwater to Bath and London, always crowded with carts, goods wagons, men on horseback and, on market day, livestock being driven in the opposite direction, to the famous Bridgwater market.

The first thing he did in Bristol was to go to the City Library where he cheered himself up by borrowing two volumes of Brucker's *Critical History of Philosophy*.

He stayed with Joseph Cottle in his rooms above his bookshop on the corner of Wine Street and High Street. Cottle was only two years older than Samuel. They had met through Robert Lovell when the Pantisocracy scheme was at its height; Cottle had loved Samuel's work and offered him five times the amount of money he had been offered in London for the copyright of his poems. Later, when Samuel had told him he didn't know how he could afford to get married, Cottle had promised him a guinea and a half for every hundred lines of poetry he could write, on top of the work he was already contracted for. And he had supported and published Samuel's radical newspaper *The Watchman*. More of a friend than a business associate, Cottle, like Poole, was always there to listen to Samuel.

"My play is such a mess," Samuel told him. "I just can't move it on."

"It'll be better when you get back to it," Cottle reassured him. "The break from it will do you good. You'll see it with different eyes."

Samuel took a circuitous route home, walking across the Somerset Levels to visit George Burnett in Huntspill. They were still good friends and Burnett sometimes walked over to Stowey to visit him and stay a day or two. When he got there he found Burnett ill with jaundice. "I wish my pockets were as yellow as George's phiz!" he wrote later, thinking of the yellow guineas that never seemed to line his pockets.

On the way back to Stowey he came across a garrulous old woman.

"You've been to see George Burnett?" she asked. "Such a nice young man. But he's fallen in with a bad lot, a vile Jacobin villain called Coleridge."

"Dear me!" Samuel said politely.

"Dreadful it is. I don't know what's going to happen to him."

"I hadn't the heart to undeceive her," Samuel told Sara when he got home.

\*\*\*

Samuel's Pantisocratic radicalism was still firmly based on religion. Where Thomas Paine and William Godwin spoke of the rights of man, Samuel was more concerned with Christ's teaching about wealth, property, temporal power and the brotherhood of man. Unitarianism was the one branch of the Christian faith that attracted Samuel. Its tolerant and loosely defined system of belief seemed best suited to link his views on philosophy and religion and the feeling of the absolute unity of God and his creation. Keen to continue the preaching he had done in the Unitarian chapels in Bristol and Bath, he asked one of his supporters, John Prior Estlin, the influential Unitarian minister in Bristol, to write letters of introduction to the Unitarian chapels in Taunton and Bridgwater. Soon he was being asked to preach regularly.

"Maybe I should take it up properly after all," he mused to Sara, "as a profession. It's not badly paid…"

"It would be a regular income," she agreed readily, as she passed him the white waistcoat and blue coat he always wore for preaching. "This is getting a bit tatty," she added, shaking it out.

"Poole said I could have one of his old ones," Samuel said. "This will do for the time being. It'll look even worse by the time I've walked over there. And no one will look at me. They're only interested in what I have to say."

Sara wondered what the congregation must make of the dishevelled, dusty figure with the long unkempt hair, in comparison with the usual sober black-clad minsters. But Samuel's sermons were becoming popular, he was a good speaker, truly inspirational with his fiery rhetoric. He could earn a good living this way. She pictured a neat little house to go with the ministry, in a town like Taunton or Bridgwater with more going on than in this dreary backwater. But she knew Samuel's heart was still set on his writing. Maybe this play would prove a great success. It was only fair to give it a good chance first.

One afternoon in early April there was a knock at the door. Sara had just finished feeding Hartley and was putting him down in his cot and she heard Samuel exclaim delightedly as he opened the door. "Wordsworth! How lovely to see you." Then, as she joined them, "Sara, this is my friend William Wordsworth, a great poet."

The man standing in the open doorway was tall and thin with dark hair and dark eyes. He was dressed in strange old-fashioned clothes, covered with dust from the road.

"Come into the garden," Samuel was saying. "The babe's just settled and we don't want to wake him. Sara will bring refreshments."

Samuel led him out, talking constantly as always so that Sara could only hear the odd mumble of assent from Wordsworth. She arranged a jug of cider and some bread and cheese on a tray. They were the only things she could find at such short notice but if Wordsworth was anything like Samuel and all his writing and philosophical friends, they didn't mind what they ate as long as it kept them sustained for their next bout of creative work.

As she stepped out into the courtyard, blinking in the sudden blast of sunshine, Samuel hurried towards her to take the tray. She saw the appreciation in his eyes as he looked at her and she smiled up at him. It was good to know he was still proud of her despite all the niggles and disagreements they had.

"Your health!" He saluted them all, once the drinks were poured.

"This is a beautiful part of England, Mrs Coleridge," Wordsworth said. It was the first time she had heard his voice and she could see it was a real effort for him. A shy man, perhaps, or maybe just one who only spoke when necessary, not like her dear Samuel who spoke incessantly. Wordsworth's voice had an odd drawn out accent, quite different from the West Country accents she was used to, but not dissimilar to the accent she had heard in Derbyshire.

"We like it," she said politely, although it was actually Samuel who liked it, loved it deeply in fact, in a way she could never, would never, understand.

Samuel was already talking again. "There are some beautiful walks. You must stay awhile, Wordsworth. I can't wait to show them to you."

"My sister Dorothy will be expecting me back," Wordsworth said quickly. "She is on her own at Racedown with little Basil Montagu, my friend's son. His mother died a few days after he was born."

"Oh, how dreadful," Sara said. "The poor little mite. How old is he?"

"Nearly five. His father lives in London. He found it hard to look after him and Dorothy loves children…"

Sara realised they must be being paid to look after him, the same sort of arrangement she and Samuel had had for Charles Lloyd.

"We are bringing him up on the principles of Rousseau," Wordsworth was saying. "Our prime intention is that he should be happy. When he first came to us he used to cry almost all the time."

"Of course," Sara said. "He must have missed his father. And he didn't know either of you."

Wordsworth didn't seem to have heard her. "So whenever he cried we told him the noise was unpleasant to us," he went on, "and we put him in a room on his own where we couldn't hear him. We called it 'The Apartment of Tears'. It worked wonderfully. Now whenever he starts to cry he says to us, 'I think I am going to cry,' and he goes into the room of his own accord."

Sara listened in amazement as Wordsworth went on to describe how, if the little boy was late getting up, the maid was forbidden to dress him or get him breakfast and he had to go back to bed until the afternoon. "That soon cured him," William said triumphantly. "Now he does what he's told when he's told and he has learnt to keep his emotions under control."

"And it's a big house?" Sara asked.

"Racedown Lodge? Oh, yes. Not very attractive though. One of old Pinney's country houses. A merchant's house, if you know what I mean. Montagu tutors the Pinney boys. They're not charging us any rent. And it's fully furnished."

Sara thought enviously of the big house, the large airy rooms (the tiny cottage had gone from glacial in the winter to stifling in the summer), the fine furniture, beautiful curtains…

"It's three storeys high," Wordsworth was saying. "We have two parlours with big sash windows, the library is wonderfully stocked, there are views down the valley to the river and across the Vale of Taunton Deane. There are both fruit and vegetable gardens as well as a formal garden and we can walk over to Lyme Regis and to the market at Crewkerne. And shorter strolls with Basil, of course, into the woodland. We teach him about nature in his natural surroundings rather than spending hours in the school room. The principles of Rousseau, as I said."

"Wordsworth was in France during the Revolution," Samuel said proudly.

This was the sort of subject that Sara would have found fascinating at one time; she recalled the hours she had spent listening to Samuel and Southey talking about politics. Now though, her mind drifted instead to the chores she had to do: the bed to make up for Wordsworth, who would obviously stay the night, the washing to bring in off the line and put away, the animals to be fed. She couldn't expect Samuel to do anything now they had a visitor. She stood up and straightened her skirt.

"Oh, do you have to go?" Samuel asked.

"Things to do," she answered lightly.

"Can't you let Nanny do them?"

"She needs to be watched," Sara said, "supervised. She can't think for herself."

Nanny must have some other name but her job was children's nurse and everyone always called her Nanny so they did the same. Although she had looked after other people's children quite satisfactorily Sara didn't trust her on her own with Hartley. She was better with the menial tasks like bringing in the washing, making the bed, scrubbing the vegetables.

As Sara checked on Hartley, still sleeping peacefully in his cot, she wondered about the sort of woman who said she loved children but left a four-year-old to sob his heart out on his own uncomforted.

"Are you sure Dorothy is his sister?" she asked Samuel in bed that night.

"Shh," Samuel admonished her, aware of Wordsworth in the next bedroom. "Of course she is," he added indignantly.

"He seems inordinately fond of her. He never stops talking about her."

"I loved my sister too," Samuel said wistfully. "In just the same way. It's a sacred bond Sara. Think of how Lamb still loves Mary."

"Poor mad Mary," Sara said.

Mary Lamb had attacked and killed her mother in a fit of insanity the year before and was now locked up in an asylum.

Despite the extra work it entailed for Sara she saw that Wordsworth's stay did Samuel good. She smiled to herself as she heard them grumbling together about how easy it was for Southey to produce verse when they laboured and sweated to do the same. Wordsworth was writing a verse play too, *The Borderers,* and they wondered if they could get them produced together in London.

Knowing that they would have a lot in common, Samuel took Wordsworth to meet Tom Poole and the three of them went out walking together, discussing politics, poetry and books as they walked.

One day Poole took them to Walford's Gibbet, between Stowey and Holford, and told them the story of John Walford. Walford was a local charcoal burner, who had spent his life alone in a woodland shelter made of poles and turf.

"He was a man remarkable for his good temper and generosity," Poole said. "But he also had ardent feelings and strong passions. He was in love with a woman from Over Stowey called Ann Rice but the girl's mother disapproved of him and put a stop to the marriage. Deeply disappointed, he drifted into drunkenness and when a local half-mad girl visited him in his shelter he took her in and she bore him two illegitimate children. Forced into marriage with her, but filled with loathing and self-disgust, he murdered her one night as they walked in the darkness to the Castle of Comfort Inn. My father was involved in Walford's arrest," Poole went on. "He was sentenced to be hanged in chains. I was at his execution. There was an enormous crowd. When he saw Ann Rice at the back he asked if she could be brought to him. She looked almost lifeless. They talked for nearly ten minutes and, as the officers pulled her away, Walford snatched her hand and kissed it, tears rolling down his cheeks. That was the first time he had shown remorse. When he spoke to the crowd he admitted his guilt but said he had done it without any fore-intention and that he hoped God would forgive him."

This was just the sort of story that Wordsworth liked to use for his poetry and he asked Poole to write it down for him.

Spurred on by his long talks with Wordsworth and by listening to him reading from his manuscript *Salisbury Plain,* Samuel went back to work with a vengeance once Wordsworth had gone, completing 1500 words of his verse play *Osorio.*

"Poole loves it," he told Sara enthusiastically. "He says it has passion, a well conducted plot, stage effect and the spirit of poetic language without the technicalities."

In a burst of enthusiastic hard work he also finally finished his volume of *Poems* and delivered it to Cottle in Bristol. After this he set off for a long walk through the Vale of Taunton Deane. His ultimate goal was to visit Wordsworth in Racedown but first of all he had to go to Bridgwater to preach in the Unitarian Chapel in Dampiet Street.

When he had finished there, he set off to walk the forty-odd miles to Crewkerne, achieving it in a day and a half and arriving at Racedown in the early evening of 5th June.

It was a beautiful summer's evening, the sun still high in the sky, the heat rising from the hard-baked mud of the lane. Samuel stopped and leaned on a gate to gaze over the valley below him, taking in the yellow fields of corn, the rolling hills, the tall green trees. Below him, across the field, he saw a distinctive square brick house — the 'merchant's house' Wordsworth had described — and a woman's figure bent over, working in the garden. He saw her look up and, rather than walking all the way around to the front door, he vaulted the gate and hurried down through the field of corn to meet her.

He didn't know exactly what he had expected but Dorothy Wordsworth was not a pretty woman. She was small and slight with olive skin, dark hair and eyes and a slightly hooked nose. But the dark eyes were bright with intelligence, her movements quick and lively. She was like a dancing sprite, alive with animation. She was sensitive, interested in everything and everyone around her. She clearly adored William. She followed his every move, anxious to pre-determine what he needed. A few minutes in her company and Samuel had forgotten her appearance and saw only her personality.

Wordsworth was delighted to see him again.

"You must stay," he said, "as long as you like. I will read you my play."

"I've finished the first draft of mine too. It still needs work but you can tell me what you think."

Dinner over, the chores done, the two men read their work out loud to each other, while Dorothy sat and listened.

"It's excellent," Wordsworth told Samuel.

"But nothing compared with yours," Samuel said. "Such profound touches of the human heart, such as I find in Schiller and Shakespeare, but with you there are no inequalities."

Samuel had only intended staying a few days but he ended up staying two weeks. The three of them found they had so much in common. Leaving little Basil with Peggy, the maid who, like their own Nanny, did everything from cleaning and cooking to looking after the child, they walked for miles, William wearing the double-soled boots he had had made in London especially for the purpose. "I ordered six pairs," he told Samuel. "The strongest soles and upper leather."

They talked the whole time, sitting down wherever they could find a good spot to eat the bread and cheese they had brought with them.

They were about three miles from Lyme Regis when Dorothy suddenly stopped in the middle of the path and held up her hand.

"Listen!" she exclaimed. "You can hear the first murmurings of the waves. I remember distinctly the first time I saw the sea."

"You were only five," William said wistfully. "Our parents took us to Whitehaven. You cried when you first heard the sound of the waves and saw the scene spread out below you."

Samuel was struck by the difference between Dorothy and Sara. Sara had none of Dorothy's sensibility. She was practical, down to earth. She was a good mother, he reminded himself, and he missed her when he was away from her, especially in bed at night when he thought of her longingly in their cosy bed in their humble cottage bedroom. But Dorothy, like Wordsworth, was a kindred spirit to Samuel. He couldn't imagine being friends with one without being friends with the other. They were inseparable. She strode alongside them, oblivious to the stony paths, the steep hillsides and the wind that whipped her hair from the confines of her bonnet. Sara didn't see the point of walking unless it was to get to someone's house. The idea of walking just for the pleasure of observing nature and the surrounding countryside was completely alien to her.

Dorothy stayed up late at night with them, discussing everything from poetry to politics to philosophy. She was amazingly observant. "See how the sea sparkles in the sunlight," she would say, or, "the way that leaf dances in the breeze." Wordsworth often jotted down the things she said and she assiduously copied out his poems, suggesting corrections and amendments. She did the same with Samuel too, criticising his work in a way he had never known a woman to do before.

"She's exquisite," he told Wordsworth.

"I don't know what I would do without her," Wordsworth agreed. "She has dedicated herself to me in a way no one else has. Given up everything to be with me, risked her future and her reputation in her belief that I will be a great poet."

"I believe it too," said Samuel. "You must come and live in Stowey," he went on. "There's nothing to keep you here, is there? Then we can see each other like this every day. I'll ask Lamb as well. And Thelwall." He could see it: a new Pantisocratic circle of his friends living in the Quantocks with him, along with Thelwall, a notorious radical whom he had never met but with whom he had corresponded for years. "Southey too," he said in a burst of enthusiasm. "He would love the Quantocks. And Sara would like to have Edith near her again."

It was true, there was nothing to keep Wordsworth and Dorothy at Racedown.

"We had hoped our brothers John and Christopher would be able to visit us here," Dorothy said, "but John is away at sea and Christopher is studying hard at Cambridge to become a fellow of his college and enter the church and cannot take the time off. My friend Mary Hutchinson came to stay, all the way from Sockburn by coach. What a journey for her: York, London and then Crewkerne. She stayed six months. It was so lovely to have her here. She transcribed William's work and made fair copies. But really we are very isolated here. And cut off from news; we cannot afford a London newspaper. Everything is so expensive…"

"The war has raised the price of everything," Samuel remarked. "We eat very little meat and live off the produce from our garden."

Dorothy was nodding. "Tea is our only luxury," she said. "We get it sent from Bristol. And we dry the tea leaves and re-use them until they are almost tasteless."

The house at Racedown might be rent-free but their plans to have more paying pupils had come to nothing. They had received no money from little Basil's father for his upkeep and education and they were still owed a large portion of a legacy they were due to receive. If Wordsworth were to make money from his writing he needed to be somewhere that inspired him, in the company of like-minded people.

"I'll go back with Samuel," he told Dorothy. "See what I make of the idea of living there and come back for you if I think it's feasible."

"I can't wait to tell Sara," Samuel said. "She'll be so pleased. You'll be great friends, Dorothy. And we have the sweetest little baby. You'll be bringing little Basil I suppose?"

"I don't know," Dorothy said. "Maybe his father would prefer to take him back to London."

Samuel and Wordsworth walked the whole way back to Nether Stowey, talking as they went. The moment they arrived at the little cottage, Samuel burst through the door.

"Sara! Sara!" he called, but there came no answer. He turned to Nanny, who looked at him, bewilderment clouding her already dull eyes.

"Where is she?" he asked.

"Out the back, Master," she said, "bringing in the washing."

Leaving Wordsworth trailing in his wake, Samuel hurried into the courtyard. "Sara! Sara! Look who I've brought back with me!" He grabbed her by the waist and hugged her. "Wordsworth has decided to come and live here," he gasped, putting her down breathlessly. "And Dorothy. We'll go and see Poole, he will find him somewhere to live. And Lamb is coming too. And Thelwall. Just think, Sara, it's what I've always wanted. All of them living here; our own Pantisocratic circle."

And he was away as usual, extolling the beauties of the countryside, the principles they would all live under, the conversation they would have, the writing they would do. Sara's mind, meanwhile, flew to the practicalities: the bed to make up for Wordsworth, who would surely stay a few days while he looked for a property, the food she would need, the meals to plan and prepare. She knew Samuel. He would rashly invite people without a thought. Much as she enjoyed company, Sara knew that she would be doing all the hard work.

"And where will they all live?" Her voice came out sharper than she'd intended.

"Poole..." he began.

"He had enough trouble finding somewhere for us to live, Samuel." She dropped her voice, away from Wordsworth standing uncertainly to one side. "How is he going to find somewhere for all these other people?"

She hadn't meant to start arguing the minute he came home. She had missed him. But she needn't have worried. When Samuel was in one of these moods nothing could dent his enthusiasm. "It'll be fine Sara!" he laughed. "Don't worry so!" He pulled her close to him and kissed her on the cheek. "They can always stay here while they look for somewhere. We'll manage. Just think of the fun we'll all have. I can't wait to show Lamb and Mary the Quantocks."

Four days later Samuel was on his way back to Racedown in a trap borrowed from Tom Poole to collect Dorothy, the books and the luggage.

"What a journey!" he grumbled when they returned. "The roads are so bumpy. And I'm a good driver..."

Sara couldn't wait to meet Dorothy. Samuel and Wordsworth had talked so much about her. It would be good to have female company, someone to talk to while the men chatted politics and poetry. Her first sight of the diminutive woman alighting from the cart caught her unawares. She was expecting someone more like herself or her sisters, she realised, someone rounded, feminine, womanly. But the figure standing next to Wordsworth was small and slight, more like a young girl. Her face was hidden from view by the bonnet. Then she turned to look up at the cottage. Her profile showed a hooked nose, a pointed chin. Her eyes were arresting, deep brown and sparkling with energy and interest, but she was no beauty, Sara noted smugly. The thought of her alone with Samuel gave her no qualms.

"Oh, but this is charming!" she heard Dorothy say, taking her brother's arm. "We shall be happy here William, I know we shall."

She saw Dorothy examining her with the same interest but more discreetly.

"Thank you for having us here," she said.

"I don't know how we're going to manage," Sara said. "There isn't much room."

"Oh, it will be fine," Dorothy said airily. "William and I aren't fussy where we sleep or what we eat."

At least the fine weather meant that they could spend most of their time outside. They ate on a trestle table in the garden, happy to survive on the bread and cheese and cider that Sara rustled up for them.

Dorothy offered to help but the cottage was so small that it was easier for Sara to manage on her own. Dorothy seemed happy with the arrangement, her every waking moment dedicated to making sure Wordsworth was happy. She treated him like a lover, her eyes constantly turning to him, whether he was speaking or not. In the odd moments they were apart she peppered her conversation with his name: "William thinks... William feels... William says..." They were all in all to each other, scarcely needing anyone else's company, often disappearing for walks alone together or sitting in the garden talking quietly together.

One morning Sara was just lifting a skillet of boiling milk from the fireplace when Samuel darted past her to pick up a book from the chair by the fire. "Careful!" she called but it was too late. Samuel had jogged her arm and the milk poured all over his foot.

"Nanny! Nanny!" she called as she helped him to a chair. Removing his shoe and stocking she found that the foot was badly burnt. She bandaged it but he was still hobbling around on a stick three days later when Charles Lamb arrived. With so little room in the cottage it was lucky that his sister Mary couldn't come. She had been released from the asylum under Lamb's care and power of attorney but he had left her to be looked after by a nurse in London, worried that the excitement of coming down to Somerset and all the people around her would upset her delicate mental state.

Samuel had been looking forward to showing Lamb all his favourite places on the Quantocks. A picnic had been planned. They were all going, including Sara who had prepared the food. Samuel's foot, however, was still too painful. "You go!" he told everyone generously. "I don't want to spoil your fun."

The cottage was deathly quiet when they left. Samuel felt suddenly bereft and lonely. He would have loved to have gone with them. He sat in his chair for a while but it was warm in the parlour with the fire banked up with ash to keep it going for their return. He looked out of the window. It was a beautiful day. Clear blue sky, just a few wispy clouds. He reached for his walking stick and hauled himself up. Hobbling on his bad foot he made his way up the garden to the gate that led to Poole's garden. Here, under the cool shade of a lime tree he sat down to write.

"Well, they are gone, and here must I remain,
This lime-tree bower my prison!"

The finished poem ran to seventy-six lines. He called it *This Lime Tree Bower My Prison* and dedicated it to, "My gentle-hearted Charles ... my Sara and my Friends."

"I'm not keen on the gentle-hearted epithet," Lamb said. "Drunken-dog maybe or ragged head, odd-eyed, stuttering... Something that properly belongs."

Samuel was pleased with the poem. He could see it was similar to some of his others, especially *Low Was Our Pretty Cot,* which he thought was his best.

As Wordsworth had foreseen, Dorothy loved the Quantocks and surrounding area. "There is everything here," she wrote excitedly to her friend Mary Hutchinson. "Sea, woods, wild as ever fancy painted, brooks, clear and pebbly as in Cumberland, villages so romantic...Walks extend for miles over the hill-tops; the great beauty of which is their wild simplicity..."

Out on a walk one day on their own, Wordsworth and Dorothy found what seemed like a secret waterfall in a steep combe surrounded by tall trees.

"It's beautiful here," Dorothy said. "Wouldn't it be lovely if we could find a little cottage nearby to live in?"

They came back a few days later to explore further and found a driveway, overhung by ancient oak trees and large holly bushes, that led not to a humble cottage but to a large country mansion.

"That's Alfoxton Park," Tom Poole told them when they described it to him. "It belongs to the St Albyn family. It's empty."

"Maybe we could rent it?" Dorothy asked.

Poole looked doubtful. "I can look into it for you. But are you sure you wouldn't mind being so far from Stowey? Mrs Coleridge likes to be near people so she's not lonely."

"It's only four miles," Dorothy laughed. "I can walk that easily!"

The next thing they knew Poole was drawing up a lease for the rental, having it witnessed and offering to stand as guarantor, the same as he had for Samuel and Sara.

"Twenty-three pounds a year, including taxes!" Wordsworth repeated. "I can hardly believe it. For nine bedrooms and three parlours, all furnished. And a park and woods. With seventy head of deer."

It was a beautiful house, elegant and simple, two storeys high with large gabled attic windows. A short flight of steps led up to the front door. The front of the house gave on to landscaped gardens with a glimpse of the Quantocks beyond, the back onto woods and meadows, the thin grey strip of the Bristol

Channel in the distance, the pale blue coastline of South Wales rising beyond.

Wordsworth and Dorothy excitedly explored the surrounding area, from the woods of Holford Glen, cool and dark with ferns and mosses, to the beaches of East Quantoxhead. One of their favourite walks was up a narrow combe, where the stream was little more than a trickle, the trees gradually thinning out until, with a final scramble on hands and knees, they were out at the top with a sweeping view of moorland, villages and churches nestling in the valleys, and the coastline beyond.

It was perfect. Here they had the rural lifestyle they wanted without being cut off from society as they were at Racedown. Bristol was easily accessible and Samuel was nearby with his constant stream of interesting and stimulating visitors.

One warm July evening there was a knock at the Coleridge's cottage door.

"Whoever can that be?" Sara asked. "Oh, go and answer it will you, Nanny? I've got my hands full here." With the heavy basket of washing balanced on one hip, she pushed the back door open and went out into the courtyard to hang it on the line.

The sound of voices drifted out to her: a man's deep voice and Nanny's high slow-to-comprehend-voice.

"I've told him the master's not here…" Nanny said as she came out, followed by a small dark-haired man. He was on the stout side and looked hot from walking on a warm day but he had a good-looking face, a kind face, warm, dark eyes, looking at her rather uncertainly.

"I beg your pardon, Mrs Coleridge." He bowed slightly, then reached in his pocket for his handkerchief to wipe his brow. "My name is John Thelwall. Your husband invited me."

Sara hurriedly dropped the long petticoat she had been about to peg on the line.

"Mr Thelwall." She bobbed a curtsey, suddenly acutely aware of her dishevelled hair, her sweaty face and damp red arms. "My husband's not here," she said, flustered. "You're lucky to find *me* here actually. We were over at Alfoxton with the Wordsworths but I had to come back early to superintend the washing. Nanny is so hopeless without me."

"Oh, please don't let me disturb you," the man said, smiling. "If you'll just give me directions to Alfoxton I'll be on my way."

"It'll be dark by the time you're half-way there," Sara laughed. "Let me give you refreshments and make you up a bed. You can go tomorrow morning instead. As early as you like. I'll come with you to show you the way."

"Nanny," Sara said, sharply. The girl was in a dream as usual and she jumped. "Here, get on with this," Sara gestured to the basket of washing at her feet, "while I find something for our guest. Why don't you go on up to the garden, Mr Thelwall? It's so warm inside."

"Please don't hurry on my part. I had refreshments not long ago. I'm happy to wait until you've finished what you're doing."

Sara hesitated. The clothes in the copper pan over the fire needed agitating. Nanny really wasn't strong enough to do it properly. Left alone she would give them a few half-hearted stirs and take them out still covered in stains. "As long as you don't mind," she said, relieved.

To her surprise, Thelwall followed her back inside. Sara was acutely aware of the tiny, cramped parlour, stiflingly hot from the fire under the big pan, steam filling the room despite the open doors and windows. But Thelwall chose the chair furthest from the fire and leaned back in it, mopping his sweaty brow every so often and watching her intently.

"It's hard work for you here, Mrs Coleridge," he said as she stirred the clothes with the big wooden bat.

She shrugged nonchalantly, but she was pleased. No one else ever seemed to notice what she did, least of all the Wordsworths. Dorothy was a slapdash sort of housekeeper, rushing through her chores to spend as much time as possible with the men. And she didn't have a ten-month-old baby to look after. Sara would have to go on breastfeeding Hartley for as long as possible, something most women of her class would abhor. But they couldn't possibly afford a wet nurse. She didn't have the freedom that Dorothy had.

"Your reputation goes before you, Citizen Thelwall," she said, smiling over at him. When she first knew Samuel, Thelwall was one of the men they talked about the most; he had been tried twice on charges of sedition and high treason.

"I've given all that up now," Thelwall told her. "I went on for a while, even after my trials, but it became far too dangerous. I was followed everywhere by government spies. Magistrates paid trouble-makers to disrupt my lectures and cause riots. I was threatened with physical violence. No, I've done my bit and now I've retired from politics."

"Nonetheless my husband will be delighted to meet you at last. You will have a lot to talk about with Mr Wordsworth and Mr Poole."

The household was woken early the next morning by Hartley's wails. "I do apologise," Sara said as Thelwall made his way down the narrow winding staircase.

"Please, don't," he smiled. "I have babes of my own."

"We can go over to Alfoxton as soon as you like," Sara said. "It looks like it will be another warm day. It will be cooler to walk in the morning."

She was aware of his eyes on her as she moved around the kitchen, lifting the kettle from the fire, pouring the water onto the tea leaves.

"You have a very comely figure, Mrs Coleridge," he said.

She smiled and blushed. She was unused to compliments nowadays. Samuel no longer thought he needed to tell her how she looked and the Wordsworths scarcely seemed to notice her. She had hoped she and Dorothy could be friends but Dorothy was too caught up with Wordsworth to need female company. It was surprising how subservient she was. Sara had been brought up to believe she was a man's equal, not his inferior, yet Dorothy would drop anything she was doing immediately if Wordsworth wanted to do something different.

Sara and Thelwall walked companionably along the cool, leafy lanes, taking it in turns to carry Hartley. Alfoxton House was in silence when they arrived.

"They don't have a servant," Sara explained. "There's an old woman in the cottage next door who comes in occasionally to scour the range and help with the laundry but otherwise they manage alone."

"Hello!" she called, her voice echoing in the spacious hallway.

There was a clattering sound overhead and Wordsworth appeared at the top of the stairs.

"See, I've brought a friend!" Sara called, laughing at the confusion on his face to find her there so early with Hartley on her hip and a stranger by her side. "This is Citizen Thelwall," she said, "come to talk with you and Samuel."

"Mr Thelwall, at last! We have heard so much about you. A pleasure…"

Wordsworth, in his rumpled, open necked shirt without a stock, unshaven and his hair sticking up from sleep, made a flourishing bow, removing his imaginary hat from his head.

Samuel came down next, woken by the commotion. "Sara!" he said in surprise, "My beautiful boy!" He kissed them both.

"And who is this?"

"John Thelwall, at your service."

"Thelwall, at last. We are honoured. I feel I know you already."

Sara and Thelwall had eaten already but they breakfasted again with the Wordsworths, in the dark wood panelled dining room at a vast table that could seat twelve, Dorothy bringing in bowls of porridge.

"We live on porridge," she confessed. "William doesn't care what he eats as long as it keeps him alive to write. And I have so much trouble with my teeth."

She passed a bowl of sugar around almost reluctantly. Along with tea it was their biggest expense.

"You must stay here," Wordsworth urged Thelwall as they ate. "We have plenty of room."

"We are a most philosophical party," Thelwall wrote to his wife Stella, "Coleridge and his wife Sara, Wordsworth and his sister. An enthusiastic group, a literary and political triumvirate."

Uncertain whether their new city-bred friend, with his interest in politics, would appreciate the beauties of nature, they took him nonetheless on their favourite walks.

"But this is beautiful!" he exclaimed, standing at the foot of the Alfoxton waterfall.

"It's the most beautiful part of the most beautiful glen of Alfoxton," Wordsworth said.

"A place to reconcile one to all the jarrings and conflicts of the wide world," Samuel agreed.

"Nay," said Thelwall, "to make one forget them altogether."

"You must bring Stella and the children," Samuel urged. "We'll find a house for you. We can all be together."

"In this enchanting retreat," Thelwall said longingly. "The Academus of Stowey."

Sara was keen to have Thelwall and Stella as neighbours too. She liked Thelwall. He always had time for her. He would join her while she did her chores, talk to her about Hartley and about Stella and the children. She was pretty sure she was pregnant again; it would be lovely to have the company of another young family nearby.

Then, one morning, she woke early with an agonising pain low down in her stomach.

"Samuel, Samuel!" She nudged him. "I'm losing the baby."

He was out of bed in a shot, standing in his nightshirt next to her.

"Sara, Sara, my dear, surely you're mistaken."

But she could feel the sticky wetness between her legs. She reached down, showed Samuel her fingers, the red streaks of blood.

"I'll get Nanny," he said.

It was only a day but one of the worst days of Sara's life. Samuel, who had been distraught when she thought she had miscarried Hartley, now felt a touch of impatience as she lay in bed clutching her abdomen. His whole routine was disrupted. Nanny ran around uselessly, rushing up every time Sara groaned and taking Hartley up to be laid at Sara's breast every few hours when he cried.

He was relieved the next day when he woke to hear her busying herself in the kitchen as usual.

"It's such an early stage," he said blithely, kissing her. "You'll soon be back to normal. And you can come out with everyone again. No one else needs to know."

She didn't say what would be obvious to anyone else but him: that it was going out with everyone, and having them back here to cook meals for at all times of the day, that had caused the miscarriage. Instead she nodded silently as she blinked back the tears and got on with her chores.

# Chapter Five

"The village is alive with gossip," Poole told Samuel. "Word has got around that Thelwall is here. And now that Wordsworth has Alfoxton, my cousin Charlotte is convinced we are setting up a Jacobin colony here. A group of radicals plotting a revolution."

"Oh dear!" Samuel laughed. "Why would they think that?"

"You're so naïve, Samuel. Villages like this view all strangers with suspicion. And Wordsworth speaks with a north country accent. The servants say he reads French books and talks all the time about French politics. As far as people around here are concerned that makes him a Frenchman."

"How on earth do they get to know all this?" Samuel asked.

"Servant gossip," Poole admitted sheepishly. "You know Thomas Jones, who lives at the farmhouse?"

"Yes," Samuel nodded.

"Well, he had a visit from his old friend Charles Mogg who used to work for the St Albyn family at Alfoxton. Naturally, Mogg wanted to know all about the new tenants and Jones said they were French."

"Because he reads French books," Samuel laughed.

"Yes, and he said that the woman living with him does the chores, like washing and mending, on a

Sunday when godly folk rest, like it tells them to in the Bible."

They were both laughing now.

"Wait," Poole said, "it gets worse. Mogg likes nothing better than a juicy scandal. So he paid a visit to the St Albyn's former huntsman, Christopher Trickie, who lives at the ancient Dog Pound. Do you know it?"

Samuel nodded again. "And...?" he asked.

"Well, he and his wife were even more forthcoming. They said the French people had taken the plan of their house and all the other houses in the area; that they had asked Trickie whether the stream was navigable to the sea and, when he told them that it wasn't, they followed its course down to the sea anyway. Mogg then went around asking other people who lived nearby and they all said that the French people at Alfoxton were suspicious and up to no good. They didn't keep a servant but lots of people came and went at all hours and they were frequently seen walking at night."

"So that's it!" Samuel laughed again. "Wordsworth and Dorothy are French. They're plotting a French invasion!"

"Shh," Poole warned, looking around him. They were in his garden. No one could possibly hear them. But talk of invasion was dangerous. Only the year before, a landing had been attempted in Ireland but failed. And in February this year three French frigates and a lugger had appeared off the North Devon coast near Ilfracombe. They made no attempt to land but they did scuttle several English merchant ships and tried to destroy shipping in the harbour before they sailed. Several days later the ships were spotted again

105

off the Pembrokeshire coast. This time they landed a small force of about 1,200 Frenchmen, under the command of an American veteran William Tate. Two days later they surrendered to the local militia and Captain Tate's orders were seized. From these they discovered that the invasion of Wales was a fallback position: their original mission had been to mount a surprise attack on Bristol, the second city in England for riches and commerce.

"You remember that dinner party we had just after Thelwall arrived?" Poole asked now.

"Yes, of course," Samuel said.

The party had taken place on 23rd July, a beautiful summer's evening. It was Wordsworth's idea, a sort of joint housewarming and welcoming of Thelwall. Poole and Samuel had gone over before the others to hear Wordsworth read his tragedy *The Borderers* outside in the garden. Samuel remembered the shade of the cool green trees, the sound of the wind rustling in the branches, the leaves dappling the faces of the people sitting underneath, Wordsworth reading his play in his slow steady northern voice.

"We were lucky your mother gave them that fore-quarter of lamb," Samuel said to Poole. Fourteen people had sat down to dinner at the vast dining table in the large panelled dining room, welcome respite from the searing heat, friends from Poole's inner circle joining Poole and Samuel, Sara, Wordsworth and Dorothy. Thelwall was guest of honour of course, wearing the white hat that marked him out as a supporter of the French Revolution. He had had the crown reinforced to protect his head from rioters throwing stones at him.

"Thelwall became quite heated, you remember?" Poole went on. "Standing up and spouting forth and hitting the table…"

"Yes," Samuel laughed. "He loves nothing better than a good audience."

"Well, Thomas Jones, from the farmhouse, had been asked to wait at table as Wordsworth has no servant. Apparently," Poole began laughing again, "he told Mogg that he had been so frightened by the speech, so passionate was it, that he didn't like to go anywhere near the Wordsworths or Alfoxton after that."

"Such rubbish!" Samuel said.

"He also said that Wordsworth had been back to Racedown and brought back a 'very chatty woman servant.'"

"That's Peggy Marsh," said Samuel. "She brought little Basil back with her. And the rest of Wordsworth's things."

"Well, Peggy told him that her master was a philosopher."

"Nothing wrong with that is there? Although Wordsworth is a poet really."

"Maybe Jones thinks a philosopher means a revolutionary."

It was only later that they found out the rumours had escalated. On his way home, Mogg called in on another former servant at Alfoxton. This lady was so concerned about what he told her that she reported it all to her new employer, Dr Daniel Lysons, who passed it on to the Duke of Portland, the minister in charge of the Home Office. Dr Lyson wrote two letters, one on

8th August and one on 11th August. The latter said that not only were the new tenants French, but that:

"The man of the house has no wife with him, but only a woman who passes for his sister. The man has camp stools, which he and his visitors carry with them when they go about the country upon their nocturnal or diurnal expeditions and also have a portfolio in which they enter their observations, which they have been heard to say were almost finished. They have been heard to say they should be rewarded for them and were very attentive to the river near them...these people may possibly be under agents to some principal at Bristol."

Even before the second letter had been received, James Walsh, an experienced government agent, had been sent down to Alfoxton to investigate the story. He was sent first to Hungerford to interview Mogg, whom he found to be, "... by no means the most intelligent man in the world."

The Home Office, however, were still alarmed, particularly by the reports about Wordsworth's interest in the course of the river, and they instructed Walsh to:

"Proceed to Alfoxton or its neighbourhood yourself, taking care on your arrival so to conduct yourself as to give no cause of suspicion to the inhabitants of the mansion house there. You will narrowly watch their proceedings...you will of course ascertain if you can the names of the persons and will add their descriptions and above all you will be careful not to give them any cause of alarm, that if necessary they may be found on the spot."

The vast sum of £10 was sent to Walsh to enable him to pursue his enquiries. On 15th August he booked in at the Globe Inn in Nether Stowey and had only just arrived when he overheard someone ask the landlord if he'd seen anything of those "rascals from Alfoxton" and if Thelwall had left yet.

"Are you referring to the famous John Thelwall?" Walsh asked the man.

"Yes."

Now Walsh knew that he was on the right track. He had been following Thelwall for the last five years, reporting his activities to the Home Office, and had arrested him twice.

"I think this will turn out no French affair," Walsh wrote to the permanent under-secretary, "but a mischievous gang of disaffected Englishmen."

The men he spoke to at The Globe agreed. "They're not French," they said. "But they are people that will do as much harm as all the French can do."

Walsh wasted no time in going to Alfoxton Farmhouse to question Jones, who repeated everything he had told Mogg, and Walsh concluded that they were violent democrats.

There was a rumour that Samuel had a printing press in his house. Walsh went back to The Globe with a local magistrate and interrogated the landlord.

"Is Coleridge handing out seditious papers and handbills?" he asked him, "and haranguing people? Does he walk about on the beach with maps and charts?"

"No, nothing like that," the landlord replied, bemused. "Why folks do say, your honour, as how he is a poet and that he is going to put Quantock and all about here in print."

The reason Samuel had been so interested in the course of the river was because he had been planning a poem to be called *The Brook*. Nearly every day he went out with his pencil and notebook in hand, studying where the river went, from its source in the hills at a spring called Lady's Fountain, through Holford Combe and Holford Glen and out into the sea at Kilve. The brook in his poem would flow from the unpopulated hills down to civilisation, first to be channelled into the sheepfold then into remote cottage gardens, on into hamlets, villages, market towns, factories and finally into the sea. He never actually wrote the poem but he used the imagery in later works and kept the odd phrases he was pleased with: his description of the distant cry of seagulls, water dripping one Sunday from the miller's wheel, the snow blown, curling, from a wood, "like pillars of cottage smoke," and a wild Quantock pony racing in the wind.

When he found out years later that he had been thought a spy, he said that if he had written the poem he would have dedicated it to the Home Office, "to our then Committee of Public Safety as containing the charts and maps, with which I was to have supplied the French Government in aid of their plans of invasion."

Samuel might have treated it as a joke, dismissing it as the 'Spy Nosy' affair, because Walsh had apparently misunderstood Wordsworth talking about Spinoza, but at the time it was taken seriously and it was Poole who now found himself under investigation by the Home Office. He was the one who had brought first Samuel, then Wordsworth and, by association, the notorious Thelwall to Nether Stowey.

Walsh's suspicions fell on the Poor Man Benefit Club that Poole had set up for the unemployed. In his report Walsh described Poole as, "a most violent member of the corresponding society. I am told that there are 150 poor men belonging to this club and that Mr Poole has the entire command of all of them."

Having completed his mission, however, and ascertained that the government had nothing to fear from the residents of Alfoxton, Walsh departed.

But the rumours persisted and Mrs St Albyn came to hear about her tenant and the company he kept. The Wordsworths were told that their lease would not be renewed in June next year. They had only been there two months and already they would have to think of somewhere else to live.

Poole was devastated. "If anyone's responsible for William's tenancy, it is me," he said. "I will write to Mrs St Albyn and tell her myself what sort of man he is."

"I believe him to be in every respect a gentleman," he wrote. "Mr Wordsworth is a man fond of retirement — fond of reading and writing." He added that their late vicar, a canon of Windsor, had been a close friend of Wordsworth's Uncle Cookson and that it was unfortunate that the, "most unfortunate falsehoods" had been told about the company Wordsworth kept. Thelwall's visit had been unexpected, he said, and no one at Stowey or Alfoxton had ever spoken to him before. He didn't say that Samuel had been writing to him for ages.

"Be assured," he concluded, "and I speak from my own knowledge, that Mr Wordsworth, of all men alive, is the last who will give anyone cause to complain of his opinions, his conduct, or his disturbing the peace of anyone. Let me beg you, madam, to hearken to no calumnies, no party spirit, nor to join with any in disturbing one who only wishes to live in tranquillity. I will pledge myself in every respect that you will have no cause to complain of Mr Wordsworth. You have known me from my youth and know my family — I should not risk my credit in saying what I could not answer for."

But it was no good. Mrs St Albyn's mind was made up.

Thelwall was the second casualty. He had left Stowey at the end of July to follow his original plan of looking for somewhere quiet to live in Wales. His heart, however, was in Somerset and throughout August he badgered Samuel to find him a permanent home in the Quantock area.

"I'll write to John Chubb," Samuel told Sara.

"Who's he?"

"A magistrate in Bridgwater. An important merchant. I shall ask him to find Thelwall a cottage anywhere in a five- or six-mile radius of Stowey. Truth and liberty make it our duty, I shall say, to find him a home, despite odium and inconvenience."

Behind his back, Sara raised her eyes heavenward, wondering what John Chubb would make of this passionate letter.

"Our community is the place for political discussion and re-education for radicals like Thelwall," Samuel went on, warming to his subject. "Here with us he will find the society of men equal to himself in talents. Superior, probably, in acquired knowledge." Sara knew he was talking about himself and Wordsworth. "We can teach him tolerance, discipline him into patience. And with the influence he has shown he has on the lower class, when revolution does come, that day of darkness and tempest, we will be ready."

But word had got around. John Chubb heard Mrs St Albyn's opinion. He didn't want to be responsible for bringing a radical into the area to join other radicals in some sort of community.

"Very great odium T Poole incurred by bringing *me* here," Samuel wrote sadly to Thelwall. "My peaceable manners and known attachment to Christianity had almost worn it away ... when Wordsworth came and he likewise by T Poole's agency settled here ... You cannot conceive the tumult, calumnies and apparatus of threatened persecutions which this event has occasioned round about us. If you too should come, I am afraid that riots — and dangerous riots — might be the consequence...When the monstrosity of the thing is gone off and the people shall have begun to consider you as a man whose mouth won't eat them, and whose pocket is better adapted for a bundle of sonnets than the transportation of a French army, then you may take a house..."

# Chapter Six

Sara was pregnant again. The look on Samuel's face when she told him was enough to restore any confidence she may have felt about his feelings towards her.

"Why, Sara, that's wonderful!" he said. "A little brother for Hartley."

"It may be a girl, Samuel," she laughed.

"I shall love her like I love her mother," he said. "Though not quite so passionately." He pulled her towards him.

"Careful, Samuel," she said as he led her to the bed. "The baby…"

She didn't want to lose this one. The fine summer lingered on but she stayed at home more. There was always plenty to do anyway since Samuel eschewed his chores in favour of going out every day. Either he walked over to Alfoxton or the Wordsworths came to him. Sara joined them sometimes, if there was someone to carry Hartley for her. She enjoyed going for meals or a picnic lunch but she didn't get the same enjoyment out of walking as they did. And sometimes they walked huge distances, over to Lynton and Lynmouth on the coast, far too far to take Hartley. All their friends and visitors were expected to go with them, to experience the delight Samuel and the Wordsworths felt with the sweep of the hills, the steep

114

cliffs dropping into the sea, the crashing waves below them. But even on the shorter walks on the Quantocks, Samuel was so intent on planning his poems, he didn't pay any attention to Sara and she felt she was in the way.

She missed Citizen Thelwall. That first day by the washing tub hadn't been the only time he spoke to her. He often stayed behind to talk while she was doing the chores. There was a gallantry about him. He made her feel attractive and listened to what she had to say as though she were an intelligent woman. She had the impression that the Wordsworths thought she wasn't very bright, just because she didn't know much about poetry.

Charles Lloyd turned up again in the middle of September. He was keen to hear the last acts of Wordsworth's play *The Borderers*. Unfortunately William was ill when he arrived.

"Why don't you stay for a few days?" Dorothy urged. "Your company will do him good and he can read it to you when he's better. And we're expecting two of the Wedgwood brothers to come soon. William met John in Bristol. He's bringing his youngest brother Tom with him. Tom's just moved to Bristol to have some treatment at Dr Beddoes' Pneumatic Institution."

"I've heard of it," Lloyd said. "Dr Beddoes is studying the medical effects of new gases."

"Yes," Dorothy nodded. "Samuel is very interested in all these scientific experiments. We talk a lot about them."

The Wedgwood brothers, John, Josiah and Tom, sons of the potter Josiah Wedgwood, had all been brought up to take a keen interest in science and the arts and to use their money and influence to further worthy causes. They had houses all over the country, including Cote House at Westbury near Bristol.

Tom Wedgwood came with a proposition for Wordsworth. "I'd like to do something for the furtherance of mankind," he announced.

William nodded. "Very respectable," he said.

"I'm a wealthy man," Tom went on. "I would like to devote a portion of my wealth to the education of a genius."

"Yes…" Wordsworth nodded again.

"I'm a follower of Godwin. Like him I believe that there is no such thing as innate ability and that bad education is responsible for depravity. The child should not be allowed to have its own way or it will develop tyrannical tendencies. I propose that the child should be protected from contact with bad example or sensory overload by not being allowed outside or to leave its bedroom."

William said nothing.

"The bedroom walls should be painted grey and there should only be a couple of brightly coloured objects with hard edges to irritate its palms. The child must be supervised at all times by someone who understands the experiment, so that it connects its pleasures with rational objects and acquires a habit of earnest thought. It needs a bit more planning but I shall get together with Godwin, Dr Beddoes, Holcroft and Tooke to refine the details but I thought *you* would be perfect to supervise the child."

William thought for a while. He and Dorothy were strict with little Basil; he had been taught to control his feelings. But this experiment was going too far.

"I agree that it's important to bring up a child to have an equable temper," he said finally. "But to shut a child up indoors and deny it access to nature? No, I could not do it."

Tom didn't let it go. Day after day he returned to his argument, citing Godwin's principles, the support he had, the chance it was to make a difference in the world. But Wordsworth remained unmoved and five days later Tom left, disappointed and displeased.

Samuel spent the whole of September making preparations for his poem *The Brook* and working on his play *Osorio*. He really needed time on his own to gather his thoughts and work undisturbed. He decided to go on a walking tour around the North Somerset and Devon coast that he loved so much. He would take the manuscript of *Osorio* and work on it in the evenings in the inns or farmhouses he stayed at. He set off on the 9th of October and was gone for five days, returning exhausted but triumphant.

"It's finished," he announced to Sara. "Complete and neatly transcribed. You have no idea the difficulty it caused me."

"At least it's done now," Sara said, kissing him, "and will be a great success I'm sure."

"I went for a long walk one day," Samuel said, "along the coast path between Porlock Bay and Lynton..."

Sara wasn't really listening. She was daydreaming about the play being performed in Drury Lane, people queuing to watch it, a standing ovation at the end, the money that would come in....

"I must go over to Alfoxton," Samuel said, noticing her lack of interest. "Wordsworth and Dorothy will want to hear the play."

His reception there was much more gratifying. Wordsworth and Dorothy were delighted to hear he had finally finished work on *Osorio* and thought it was excellent.

"Something odd happened while I was away," he told them, resuming the story he had tried to tell Sara. "I went for a long walk to clear my head, along the coast path between Porlock Bay and Lynton. The path climbs steeply, zigzagging through woodland from Porlock Weir to Culbone. I saw deer, foxes and badgers and as I climbed I could hear the distant sound of waves crashing on the shore below, the cry of seagulls. I reached the church. It's the smallest in England, you know."

Dorothy laughed. "You've told us many times!" she said.

"And I was on my way back," Samuel went on, "when I was seized with dreadful bowel pains."

"Oh dear," Dorothy said sympathetically. She knew Samuel was prone to upset stomachs. He ate so sporadically, grabbing whatever came to hand when he was hungry. They were all the same: as long as they had something to sustain them for the next bout of writing.

"So I stopped off at Ash Farm above Culbone Church," he went on. "I often stop there. They give me refreshment and sometimes I stay for the night. Either there or Broomstreet Farm. Anyway, I took a couple of grains of opium to settle my bowels," he went on, "and fell into a sort of half-waking sleep, brought on I suppose by the opium. You remember I've been reading Purchas' *Pilgrimage*?"

"No, but it doesn't matter," Wordsworth said. Samuel was always carrying some great tome he had brought home from Tom Poole's book room or borrowed from the City Library in Bristol. They waited for the rest of the story.

"Well, while I was half-asleep I had a dream. Visions rose before me and I composed a poem based on the description of Kubla Khan's house of pleasure. In Xanadu did Kubla Khan a stately pleasure-dome decree," he chanted.

"Go on," said Dorothy, entranced.

"Well, that's just it," Samuel said. "I must have been asleep about three hours and it was a long poem, some two hundred to three hundred lines. When I woke up I started writing it down. But I hadn't got very far when there was a knock at the door."

"Oh no, how annoying. But you went back to it?"

Samuel shook his head. "It was a man on business from Porlock," he said. "He stayed about an hour. When I took up my pen again I had forgotten most of what I was going to write."

"Oh dear," Dorothy said. "Never mind. It will come back to you. And at least you've finished *Osorio.*"

But it didn't come back to him. He tried again and again but never got further than the first three verses. Incomplete as it was, it wasn't worth mentioning to his friends. Except for Dorothy and William, of course, who persuaded him to recite it one evening. They were so taken with it that he took to performing it at small gatherings of people, reading it out in the sing-song chant that it required. "It can never be published," he would say, "until I can finish it."

He went back to it so many times that, later in life, he couldn't remember exactly when he had written it. But the fragment, as he called it, was strongly evocative of that first autumn in Somerset: the steep cliffs running down to the sea, the deep dark woods, even the caves he had visited at Cheddar Gorge with Southey the year before. Much of the imagery in *Osorio* had the same origin, the description of the wooded countryside in Granada, its setting, describing almost exactly the woods at Culbone:

"The hanging woods, that touch'd by autumn seem'd

As they were blossoming hues of fire and gold
The hanging woods, most lovely in decay,
The many clues, the sea, the rock, the sands,
Lay in the silent moonshine, and the owl,
(Strange! very strange!) the scritch owl only waked
Sole voice, sole eye of all that beauty."

Samuel acknowledged the influence of Purchas' *Pilgrimage* on *Kubla Khan*, the first few sentences particularly:

"In Xamadu did Cublai Can build a stately Pallace, encompassing sixteen miles of plaine ground with a wall, wherein are fertile Meadows, pleasant Springs, delightful Streames, and all sorts of beasts of chase and game, and in the midst thereof a sumptuous house of pleasure…"

The passage went on to describe some sort of harvest festival or fertility sacrifice, involving the sacred milk of a herd of snow-white horses, "… the milk whereof none may taste, except he be of the blood of Cingis Can ... According to the directions of his Astrologers or Magicians, he on the eighth and twentieth day of August aforesaid, spendeth and poureth forth with his owne hands the milk of theses Mares in the air and on the earth to give drink to the spirits and idols which they worship, that they may preserve the men, women, beasts, corne, and other things growing on the earth."

To this, Samuel added his own slant: the demon lover, the River Alph, the caves of ice, the Abyssinian maid, the ancestral voices 'prophesying war'.

He wrote it as a ballad, his first attempt at the ballad style that he found so fascinating. Now that he and Wordsworth had finished their tragedies, *Osorio* and *The Borderers,* they needed a new project to work on. They began to discuss the revival of the ballad form. They had already been trying out a couple of other narrative ideas. One was a re-write of a story Wordsworth brought with him from Racedown, *The Three Graves*. Samuel added another two sections to the story but never finished it. It was a story of sexual jealousy in a domestic setting. "I just can't get it right," he told Wordsworth. "I can't identify with it."

In early November, Samuel took Wordsworth and Dorothy on the walk to Porlock that he had taken when he wrote *Kubla Khan,* up the steep woodland track leading from Porlock Weir to Culbone and on to Broomstreet Farm and Yenworthy. It was getting dark by the time they reached Lynmouth, where they stayed the night. The next morning they walked to the Valley of Rocks.

"This is magnificent!" Wordsworth exclaimed. "Quite unlike anything I've ever seen before. The great piles of rocks, the desolate valley. We must use this setting for something…"

"A biblical story maybe," Samuel suggested. "That would work well."

"The Wanderings of Cain…" Wordsworth said.

"We can write it together," Samuel said enthusiastically. "You can do part one, I'll do the second and whichever is finished first can do the third."

With its themes of spiritual guilt and lonely exile this was the sort of subject Samuel related to; he finished his section at full speed and took it triumphantly to Wordsworth. The look on Wordsworth's face was priceless. The piece of paper in front of him was almost blank. They both laughed. "Maybe it wasn't such a good idea!" Wordsworth said. He was writing very little compared with Samuel, who, with the landscape of the Quantocks and Exmoor, and the company of Wordsworth and Dorothy, found himself inspired.

At the end of the year he wrote another fragment in the same musical style as *Kubla Khan*, the setting in Exmoor, the memory from his childhood:

"Encintured with a twine of leaves
That leafy twine his only dress!
A lovely boy was picking fruits,
By moonlight, in a wilderness,
The moon was bright, the air was free,
And fruits and flowers together grew
On many a shrub and many a tree…
Alone, by night, a little child,
In place so silent and so wild—
Has he no friend, no loving mother near?"

# Chapter Seven

"She is a woman indeed! In mind, I mean, and heart ... her manners are simple, ardent, impressive..." Samuel wrote to Cottle. His feelings for Dorothy had grown since he first met her. Every time he saw her he found more to appreciate in her.

"In every motion her most innocent soul
Outbeams so brightly, that who saw would say,
Guilt was a thing impossible in her..."

Three lines from a poem he had begun to write, *Destiny of Nations,* that seemed to sum her up perfectly.

"Her information various, her eye watchful in minutest observation of nature and her taste a perfect electrometer; it bends, protrudes and draws in, at subtlest beauties and most recondite faults," he wrote to Cottle.

Hardly a day went by without him seeing the Wordsworths. Either he would walk up to Alfoxton or they would come to him. They spent hours on the Quantock hills, revelling in the beauties of nature and talking about poetry, philosophy, religion. They agreed about so many things and even those they disagreed about were argued over amicably. Back at Alfoxton they read together companionably and talked about poetry. Dorothy wrote out Samuel's work and helped him correct it for publication  as she did for her brother; Wordsworth and Samuel criticised each other's work.

"We're like a factory," Wordsworth said. "We should call ourselves 'The Concern'."

It was surprising really that they should get on so well. Wordsworth and Samuel were so different: Wordsworth taciturn, deliberate, prosaic, Samuel animated, excitable, bursting with ideas and energy. It was Dorothy who bound them together like glue, with her unerring ability to know just what they were thinking and feeling.

Samuel was spellbound by them. Dorothy and Wordsworth were equally smitten. Sara noticed. How could she not? At first she assumed the novelty would wear off. Samuel was always like this with new friends: enthusiastic, overwhelmed, as though he were in love. But it usually wore off, like it had with Southey, with Burnett, even with Poole and Cottle, and settled into a more normal friendship.

When the Wordsworths first arrived, back in those high-spirited, high-summer months, she had been more included. She would never forget those long hot days. The four of them would set off together, the two men carrying the picnic food. Dorothy would often run ahead through waist-high fern, thrashing a path with a stick. Sara, trailing in their wake, carrying Hartley, pulled her skirts tightly to her, worried about them tearing on brambles, scared of the insects and snakes that lurked up there.

If they were invited to Alfoxton for dinner Sara would change her day dress, take off her cap then brush, re-pin and pile up her long brown hair. They walked up the cool, dappled drive to the big house, with Samuel carrying Hartley, and walked back again in the dark. It was a golden time, everyone happy with everyone else.

But as September came with its cool misty mornings, mornings she spent bent double with nausea from the coming baby, Samuel went out more and she stayed at home. The hills were less attractive when it was cold and clammy, the walks Samuel wanted to go on far too far with Hartley to carry.

Sara was brought up in the city. She could see the beauty of the hillsides, the bright yellow gorse, the stream and waterfall at Holford, but she couldn't spend hours rhapsodising over it like Samuel, Wordsworth and Dorothy did. She didn't really understand their poetry. Not understanding it meant she couldn't appreciate it. And she was too honest to pretend she did.

It was hard not to feel resentful as Samuel spent day after day with the Wordsworths.

"The chimneys are so bad today," he would say. "I can't write here. I'll go over to Alfoxton. Don't wait up for me. I'll probably stay the night."

Sometimes they would walk back with him the next day and expect Sara to provide breakfast or lunch while their damp clothes dried by the fireside. Then they'd be off again on some other jaunt, leaving her on her own.

She reminded herself it was work. This is what Samuel did to provide for her and the family. And Samuel *was* working, writing — at what he called 'full-finger speed' — poems and articles that Dorothy would painstakingly transcribe for him.

But as winter began to set in Sara found herself back where she was almost a year ago, tied to the cold damp cottage on her own. She did have her own friends now, of course, Anna Cruikshank in particular, but she couldn't go there every day or spend all her time visiting other people's houses. And it wasn't as if she wanted Samuel to stay at home all the time. It was the way they excluded her from their charmed circle that hurt her.

Samuel made no secret of his admiration for Dorothy. "She's so good to Wordsworth isn't she?" he said.

"Subservient, you mean," Sara said sharply. "Fawning, admiring, sycophantic, besotted…"

"Sara, you know that's not what I meant."

"But it's true. He only has to suggest a thing and she drops everything to do it."

"I wouldn't mind you doing that occasionally."

"Well, you married the wrong woman then. I was brought up to believe myself equal to a man, not inferior. Anyway, it's different. I've got a baby."

"Dorothy has little Basil."

"He's five years old. He doesn't need breastfeeding. And she leaves him with Peggy Marsh the whole time."

"You could leave Hartley with Nanny."

"You know how hopeless she is without me to tell her what to do," Sara said. "And she can't feed him."

"Anyway," Samuel went on, still determined to make his point. "Dorothy doesn't think herself inferior. She just believes in Wordsworth, totally and absolutely. And in me…"

"I believe in you, too."

To his ears her voice lacked conviction. If she believed in him so wholeheartedly why couldn't she talk to him like Dorothy did? Listen to his work, help him correct it, criticise it and offer improvements? Understand it? Understand him.

"You know how I despise women who are too independent," he went on. "It erodes sensibility and sympathy."

"I'm hardly independent, am I?" Sara snapped, gesturing to her swelling stomach, the baby crawling on the floor.

At least she had Hartley, the one thing that attached her to Samuel, the one thing Dorothy and Wordsworth couldn't join in with. She loved to see Samuel with their son.

"Look, Sara, he's gripping my hand so hard. He knows me, look at him smile. Come to Papa, my sweet boy!" He would scoop Hartley up and hold him high above his head, making him squeal with delight. He was interested in every stage of his development, making notes in his notebook on a page entitled 'Infancy and Infants'.

But these moments were few and far between as she felt the growing distance between her and Samuel.

One day Samuel, Wordsworth and Dorothy burst through the cottage door, laughing and talking all at the same time.

"What a downpour!" Dorothy was saying. "I blame *you,* Mr Coleridge. *You* were the one who said it wasn't going to rain! *Look* at me!" She gestured to her gown, wet through with the rain and spattered with mud almost up to her waist.

"Sara!" she cried, catching sight of her, "Look what your husband has done to us! We're wet through and frozen to the marrow!"

The three of them crowded around the fire, still laughing and chattering, the men divesting themselves of coats and hats that they passed to Sara almost as if she weren't there.

"How am I *ever* going to get dry?" Dorothy laughed, holding her skirts out in her arms and whirling around and around like a dancing doll. "I know!" She picked up her skirts and dashed for the stairs. A moment later she was back, dressed in one of Sara's best gowns, one she wore when they were invited out to musical evenings or dinner with the Cruikshanks. The dress was way too big in the bust and waist for her skinny frame and hung off her hips and she gathered it to her, taking a deep curtsy.

"*Oui, c'est moi!*" she trilled, mimicking Sara's voice, her habit of using French words, exaggerating the accent, "*Madame Colerrridge...*"

The men roared with laughter, "Oh, Dorothy, don't!" Samuel said. He glanced at Sara. He could see the effect it was having on her. But Dorothy was irresistible, prancing around the room, holding her skirts high as though she was trying to avoid any dirt.

Sara's face burned. Hurt settled deep in her chest like a physical pain and tears sprang to her eyes.

"Oh, come on Sara!" Samuel burst out, putting his hand on her arm. "It's only a bit of fun!" She tore her arm away, glared at him. Dorothy caught his eye, looked heavenward. "I think the rain has stopped," she said in a level voice. "Shall we go, William, before it starts up again?"

"I'll come with you," Samuel said quickly, picking up his still-wet coat and hat. He tried to kiss Sara, put his hand on her arm, but she turned away. She didn't care what the Wordsworths might think.

When they had gone she let the tears come, hot wet drops that soon turned into huge heaving sobs. Nanny, all-hearing, all-watching, too young, too inexperienced, too lowly to comfort the mistress she cared for, could only cast sympathetic glances at her from the fireside.

Upstairs on the floor, Sara found Dorothy's dress in a wet crumpled heap. She thought sadly of her best dress, dragged through the mud of the lanes. Dorothy wouldn't think to clean it before she returned it. But she wasn't Dorothy. She picked the dress up, straightened it , took it downstairs and put it to soak with the rest of the dirty clothes.

Every instinct told her not to say anything to Samuel when he returned. It would only prolong the argument, increase the distance. She should greet him with a smile, behave like the sort of subservient woman he wanted. But she couldn't. The hurt was still too deep.

"At one time you'd have taken my side!" she burst out.

"At one time you'd have seen the funny side of it!" he countered. "What is *wrong* with you Sara?' Why can't you like my friends?"

"*Your* friends! *Your* friends! That's just it isn't it, Samuel? They can't be *our* friends. They're just *your* friends!"

"Well, you don't make them feel welcome, do you? With your freezing looks, your grim disapproval of everything we do!"

"They've *changed* you Samuel. Can't you see it? Poole can. And all your other friends. You've left us all. You only want them!"

"Poole?" Samuel said. "Poole doesn't think that. And I still see my other friends. Cruikshank walked up to Alfoxton with me only yesterday."

"But it's not the same, Samuel, you know it isn't."

The friendship with the Cruikshanks had shifted. She still had Anna but they no longer saw each other as a foursome. It was the same with the Roskillys. This was what she wanted. Friends together, as a couple, like other people had. Not Samuel's friends and her friends separately.

But it was true about Poole. He had spoken to her about the Wordsworths.

"They allow him too much free rein," he said. "He's too excitable. He needs to be encouraged to exercise common sense and restraint. They're so selfish and egotistical. I'm afraid they will damage his work."

Maybe Poole was jealous too. Because there was no doubt Samuel was working harder than ever. She was only worried about the effect it was having on their marriage. There was no one she could tell. Not even Anna, who might have been happy to be her confidante. It would be disloyal. It was her own private hurt, to be nursed secretly. She felt it keenly. She wasn't his best friend anymore, his Sally-Pally, the person he came to with his worries, concerns, ideas, thoughts.

What had happened to the man she married? Where had he gone? Samuel had become a stranger to her. A selfish, self-centred man had taken the place of the kind, loving man she had known. She had been so proud of him once; he was so different from anyone she had ever known before with his exciting plans and ideas for the future. Plans that had always included her. But not now. She remembered those halcyon days at Clevedon, the love they had felt for each other, expressed in the poems he had written for her. If something troubled her it also troubled him. Now all the little kindnesses had gone. If she asked him to do something he snapped at her and said she was nagging. He didn't care if she was upset or worried; he didn't even notice.

Oh, there were times when she felt he was still hers, in bed at night when he reached for her, turning her on her side so as not to harm the baby. Clutching him to her, the summer-sweet outdoors scent of the crumpled sheets around her, Sara would remind herself that this was the one thing Dorothy Wordsworth couldn't share with him. She would remind herself how plain Dorothy was, how gaunt and skinny, with her bad teeth and tanned skin like a gypsy's.

But Samuel didn't seem to see that. He couldn't explain it himself; he'd never had a relationship like it before, devoid of romantic or sexual attraction yet inextricably bound. How could Sara understand when he didn't understand it himself? He felt alive in a way he

131

had never felt before, a heightened sense to everything around him. When he was with her and Wordsworth it was as though they were one person, not three; three people but one soul. It was a constantly changing dynamic, conversations that drifted from one to the other, sometimes Wordsworth and Dorothy, sometimes Samuel and Wordsworth, sometimes Dorothy and Samuel, yet all three one being, a synergy that was so special no one could join it, no one break it.

Dorothy had a way of knowing instinctively how both of them felt: she would be silent sometimes, talkative others, perfectly in tune with their moods. In her, he saw an intellect he had never known before in a woman and a readiness to experience everything in life. She liked to sit and look at the countryside around her, allow herself to be completely still and silent, melt into a trance-like state. On one walk together she taught him how to do the same.

"Look at the distant hills," she said. "Let them hover before your eyes, dissolve and melt into one."

Samuel sat next to her, allowed his vision to blur.

"Now lie back," she commanded him, "on your back on the grass." She gave him a little nudge and he lay back, closed his eyes.

"No, open your eyes. Look at the sky, the clouds, the birds above you. Feel the grass below you. How it scratches your back. Ground yourself in it, then let yourself free. You're one of the birds up there, wheeling in the sky. You can look down on us lying here…"

It was the most intimate he had ever been with a woman without making love to her. There was nothing physical in it. It was on a higher plane, a meeting of minds, a connection like he had never known before.

# Chapter Eight

"You're good for William," Dorothy said. "He's writing so much more."

"It's the same for me," Samuel said. "You and Wordsworth, you give me so many ideas. I can't aspire to be anything like him but I can try."

It wasn't the first time Samuel had found inspiration from other poets. He had written with Charles Lloyd, Charles Lamb and Robert Southey. But he had never before experienced this meeting of minds. There was no denying his style of writing was different from Wordsworth's and his method of writing especially so, but the collaboration worked perfectly when they wrote separately and brought their work together afterwards for correction and criticism by all three of them, Dorothy sitting between them at the desk while they read aloud for hours and she copied down to their dictation, writing it out again neatly afterwards.

If Sara hoped that the cold, damp November mornings and cloudy, dull days would stop Samuel going out so much, she was sadly mistaken.

"I'm off," he announced one day.

"What? Now?" Sara said. It was mid-afternoon on a dismal-looking day.

"We're walking over to Watchet."

"Wouldn't it be better to wait till morning? It'll be dark soon."

"If we go now we can watch the sun go down and the moon rise over the sea." Samuel didn't need to look at Sara's face to know she thought they were quite mad.

"How long will you be gone?" she asked.

"Oh, I don't know. Two or three days."

"I don't know why you have to go at all," Sara said. "It's such an unnecessary expense with the inns and eating houses to pay for."

"It's research," Samuel said vaguely. "For a new poem."

She didn't believe him but she let it go, leant her face towards him for his goodbye kiss. He turned swiftly away from her to lift Hartley into his arms. "Goodbye my sweet boy," he said. "Look after Mama for me."

Sara wasn't the only one to be concerned about the costs though. "All these inns are so expensive," Wordsworth complained. "We need to earn a bit of money to pay for them."

"We could write a poem together," Samuel said. "A ballad. For the *Monthly Magazine*, John Aiken's new project. It's like my *Watchman* magazine: intended to appeal to 'persons of free enquiry'. When I went to Bristol in August Mrs Barbauld, Aiken's sister, told me they would pay £5 for a ballad on a supernatural theme. They're very popular at the moment. I can't say I like them much myself. I hated reviewing them, all those castles and ghosts. But if it pays well…"

"I've been reading George Shelvocke's *A Voyage round the World, by way of the Great South Sea,*" Wordsworth said. "You like travel and adventure, don't you? We could use some ideas and descriptions from that."

"A sea voyage," Samuel mused. "A seafaring man telling a story…"

"An unnatural crime," William added excitedly. "A curse…"

"John Cruikshank told me about a dream he had," Samuel said, "about a spectral ship, crewed by dead sailors…"

"In George Shelvocke's book they often saw albatrosses. Suppose they kill an albatross," William said. "That could be your mariner's crime. And the spirits of the South Seas demand revenge…"

"Mariner," Samuel said. "The Ancient Mariner. The Rime of the Ancyent Mariner Spelled R-I-M-E, A-N-C-Y-E-N-T"

"Yes, yes!" Wordsworth laughed. "As if it's a recently discovered tale. Something that happened hundreds of years ago…"

"A ballad," Samuel went on. "We need short verses, simple words, frequent repetition…"

He was still talking about it when they arrived at the Bell Inn at Watchet and he hurried to a table, took out pen and paper and jotted down the ideas he had come up with.

From that moment on the poem was constantly on his mind. Walking out onto the harbour side later that evening, he decided it was from here that his mariner would set sail. The next day, as they continued on to Dulverton, more ideas came flooding into his mind: he could use the steep woods near Culbone for the setting of the hermit's woodland home and he thought of a way the poem could sound as if it was an old sea legend. Wordsworth suggested a couple of lines, a couplet here and there, the description of the wedding guest listening, "like a three years' child," and of the mariner looking, "long and lank and brown, as is the ribbed sea sand." But even then he could see Samuel was racing ahead of him. The way he was approaching it, the ideas he had — the very way he worked was far too different from his.

"You go on with it," he said generously. "It's yours, it suits your style. I can't contribute anything more."

Back at home the poem grew rapidly. It consumed Samuel; he thought about it while he ate and drank, ran over it in his mind when he walked over to Alfoxton, dreamed about it at night, sometimes leaping out of bed first thing in the morning to scribble down something that came to him while Hartley tugged at the hem of his nightshirt. "Hartley," Sara admonished him, "Papa is working. It's important…" *This* might be the work that made their fortune.

As Samuel wrote, the poem developed a life of its own, changing from a gothic pastiche written to appeal to the modern market to a metaphor for life, the mariner experiencing a spiritual journey on his sea voyage and incorporating Samuel's philosophical views of guilt, redemption and the origin of evil.

"I've changed the traditional ballad style," Samuel told Wordsworth excitedly. "Instead of sticking to the four line, four stress verse I'm varying the number of lines to make it more flexible and musical. And using a lot of repetition. Listen:

Down drop the sails, the sails drop down
'Twas sad as sad could be
And we did speak only to break
The silence of the sea."

"It's magnificent," Wordsworth said.

By the end of November he had written three hundred lines and it was clear it was more substantial than the original £5 project they had envisaged.

"How about making it into a book with some other poems on supernatural subjects?" Wordsworth said. "I could put some of mine in."

In the meantime, Samuel sent three short poems to the *Monthly Magazine* instead of the *Ancient Mariner* under the deliberately ridiculous pseudonym of Nehemiah Higginbottom.

"It's a joke," he told Cottle. "I've made fun of my own poems."

"And Lamb's and Lloyd's," Cottle remarked drily.

"They won't mind," Samuel said glibly. "Anyway, it's mine mostly. I've used my own lines here, look…"

But Lloyd did mind. He had an uncle called Nehemiah. He was sensitive, thin-skinned, he thought he was being made a fool of, that everyone was laughing at him.

Dorothy came rushing over from Alfoxton one morning. She was in tears. "I've had a letter from

Charles Lloyd," she managed to say. "Here…" She thrust it into Samuel's hand.

Samuel skim-read it and started laughing. "So he thinks I'm a villain does he? That I've neglected him, turned against him? Oh, forget it, Dorothy! It's childish rubbish!"

But worse was to come.

"I've had a letter from Edith," Sara said. "She says she and Southey are not coming to Alfoxton now. I was so looking forward to seeing her again."

"Why aren't they coming?" Samuel asked, dreading the answer.

"Charles Lloyd has written to him. He's told him something you said about Southey years ago. And Southey thinks one of those poems you wrote in the *Monthly Magazine* was getting at him. It was a line…" She looked at the letter. "'Now of my false friend playing plaintively.' Southey thinks you mean *him*."

"I'll write to him," Samuel said, "explain everything, make amends. Don't worry…" He kissed Sara's cheek.

"I was looking forward to seeing Edith again," Sara said. "And Southey wanted to see the Wordsworths."

"I wish I'd never written or published those sonnets!" Samuel said.

When he wasn't working on the *Ancient Mariner*, revising, re-working, reviewing, changing the odd line here and there, he was hard at work on other projects. He studied French and German and worked on a translation of Wieland's *Oberon*.

He was still waiting to hear about his tragedy *Osorio*. "I don't think it will be accepted," he told Cottle. "But Sheridan could at least have replied. *He* was the one who asked me to write it in the first place. I reckoned on a profit of £500 to £600..."

Although he had inured himself against failure it was still a big disappointment when, at the beginning of December, he heard the worst: Sheridan had rejected it.

"He says the last three acts are obscure," Samuel told Wordsworth.

"I've had better news," Wordsworth said. "Harris is keen on *The Borderers* but he'd like me to make a few alterations. Dorothy and I are going up to London to discuss it with him."

"If it's a success we're thinking of going on a walking tour through Wales and up to Yorkshire and Cumberland," Dorothy said excitedly.

Samuel thought wistfully of the things he had planned with his £500 profit. He was pleased for Wordsworth, of course he was, but the disappointment over *Osorio* still stung.

"Everyone loved it!" Dorothy said when they came back. "I never expected it but it looks like it will be accepted.

But it wasn't.

"Due to the metaphysical obscurity of one character," Wordsworth said dolefully. "It just about sums up the state of the stage at present. I can't believe that they'll accept Monk Lewis's *The Castle Spectre* and reject *our* work."

Samuel was now desperately worried about money. "I need to find a way to earn a regular income," he told Wordsworth. "I thought first of all about another lodger-pupil like Charles Lloyd but now I'm wondering about setting up a school. Basil Montagu, little Basil's father, you know, is interested in helping me. It wouldn't be a conventional school, more a programme of systematic study, where Basil and I wouldn't be teachers but sort of managing students. Eight students at £100 a year..."

But nothing came of it. Then he was approached by Daniel Stuart, the editor of the *Morning Post*, who offered him a guinea a week for regular contributions of poetry or political essays.

Samuel worked out he needed about £100 a year to support himself and his family, including the £20 a year allowance he gave Sara's mother. A guinea a week would cover about half that and the £40 annuity that had been set up by Poole a year ago would help make up the rest. It wasn't quite enough but it would have to do until he could think of something else.

Then, the week before Christmas, he received a letter that seemed to answer all his problems. The Unitarian church in Shrewsbury had a vacancy for a minister and John Prior Estlin had recommended Samuel for the position.

"£120 a year," he told Sara proudly. "And a house, worth £30 in rent."

"A house..." murmured Sara, dreamily. She could see it now. Shrewsbury was a town, with proper streets and big houses, shops and society. Oh, she would miss the few friends she had made here but they would soon make new ones and as the wife of the minister she would have some position in the town. And Samuel would be parted from the Wordsworths...

"Shame it's so far away," she said. She scarcely saw her family now but she'd see even less of them miles away in Shrewsbury. "Are you going to accept?" she went on.

"Yes…" he said slowly. "Well, I suppose I'll have to go up there, preach a few sermons, meet the congregation, see if they like me. But yes…"

Samuel was still preaching in Taunton and Bridgwater. He knew it was something he could do, something he believed in, despite some of his unorthodox views. It would be a good position, a steady income, the only thing against it being moving away from Wordsworth and Dorothy. But their lease would expire next summer anyway and maybe they would follow him wherever he went.

There was another knock at the door.

"Letter for 'ee," Milton said grumpily. "Two in one day," he complained, just loud enough to make sure Samuel heard, as he shuffled off. Milton was their only link to the outside world, driving his wagon and horses from Stowey to Bridgwater, where he dropped off and collected letters and parcels at the Angel Inn, and then on to Bristol with post collected at The Bear and, since Samuel had lived in Stowey, at Cottle's bookshop in Wine Street. He would also bring odd bits of provisions like cheeses and kegs of cider, even the occasional passenger. He wasn't keen on Samuel, who often kept him waiting while he finished writing letters and grumbled at him when correspondence and books arrived later than he expected.

Samuel turned the envelope over in his hand. "I don't recognise the handwriting," he said.

"Well, open it!" Sara said impatiently.

As he drew out the sheet of writing paper a cheque fluttered to the ground. Sara picked it up, looked at it

141

incredulously. "£100!" she whispered. Then, more loudly, "£100, Samuel, a fortune!" She squinted at the signature. "Who's sending us £100 and why?"

"Tom Wedgwood," Samuel said. "Tom and Josiah. A gift," he read out, "to enable you to defer entering into an engagement we understand you are about to form, from the most urgent of motives..."

"How did they know?"

Samuel shrugged. "I don't know. Oh, what am I going to do, Sara? If I accept this, I'll have to give up the ministry position."

"Why can't you do both?"

"It wouldn't be right; you know it wouldn't..."

"No, I suppose so..." But she was sure other people would do it.

He turned the cheque over in his hand. "One year's gift, at the end of which we'll have to start again, as opposed to a lifetime's steady income? Which do I do?"

"Well, it's obvious isn't it?" Sara said sharply.

"Oh, I don't know, Sara." He sat down, put his head in his hands. "The Wedgwoods believe in me. They think I have talent, prospects. They'd never think of giving me money otherwise. I'd be letting them down if I give it all up and go into the church... I think I'll go and talk to Poole about it."

"Take it," Poole said. "The Wedgwood cheque. Stay here and write. It's what you were born for. You'd be wasted as a minister."

"But Estlin thinks I'd be a good minister."

"I'm sure you would. But is it what you really want? You'd have no time to write. Not like you do now."

142

"But even if I accept the cheque I'm only buying time. A year. That will soon go. What happens after that?"

"I might be able to extend your £40 annuity for another year."

"I didn't think I'd get it *this* year," Samuel said wryly. "I can't go on relying on charity and hand-outs. That's what Sara says. And she's right. I have to earn a proper living. We're sure to have more children. I need to support my family."

Returning home to Hartley tottering towards him unsteadily with his hands outstretched and Sara straightening from the cooking pot with her swollen belly, Samuel knew he had made the right decision. It didn't stop him having doubts though, waking in the night, picturing his life as a mundane minister in a busy county town, compared with the freedom he had now, to write and compose and bask in the beauties of nature in the Somerset countryside.

On 5th January he picked up his pen and wrote to the Wedgwoods, returning the cheque. "I do not wish to conceal from you that I have suffered much from fluctuation of mind on this than on any former occasion and even now I have scarcely courage to decide absolutely." He set out all his reasons for deciding on the Shrewsbury post, including the fact that it would pay £120 a year and came with a house.

"I wish I could come with you," Sara said as he packed his books and notes. "Like I did when we went to Derby."

"We didn't have Hartley then," Samuel said. "And there's this one to think of too…" He patted her stomach fondly.

"I would have liked to have seen what Shrewsbury is like," she said wistfully. "And to see the house…"

In her mind she saw a house like Mrs Evans' in Derby: a comfortable town house in a street with shops. She could hardly wait.

"I'll tell you all about it," Samuel promised.

He arrived in Shrewsbury late in the evening of Saturday 13th January, ready to preach the first of two trial sermons in the Unitarian chapel. Shrewsbury was a busy county town, the streets noisy and dirty, people hustling by without a friendly smile and he was immediately homesick for Somerset. "It is chilling to be among strangers," he wrote to Estlin. "And I leave a lovely country."

The next day, Sunday morning, a cold, dark, dismal day, Samuel made his way through the unfamiliar streets to the Unitarian chapel. As the strains of the organ playing the 100th psalm faded away he stood up. The congregation looked up at him expectantly and, as usual, all his nerves faded away. He could do this; it was what he was good at.

He gave out his text, "And he went up to the mountain to pray, himself, alone," his voice rising in volume and strength. He judged his sermon well, talking about peace and war, church and state, on the spirit of the world and the spirit of Christianity. He talked about those who had, "inscribed the cross of Christ in banners dripping with human gore," and in order to show the fatal effects of war he contrasted the life of a simple shepherd tending his flock with the same boy kidnapped, brought into town and made drunk and then forced into the army. "A wretched drummer boy with his hair sticking on end with powder and pomatum, a long cue at his back, and tricked out in the loathsome finery of the profession of blood."

He could feel the congregation being swept along with him as he spoke. He knew he had done well. Afterwards people gathered around him to shake his hand.

"Sir, sir..." a voice said. He was on his way out of the church but he turned back. "Sir," the young man repeated, "William Hazlitt, sir. Honoured to make your acquaintance." He bowed. "May I walk with you?"

He was a young man, seventeen or eighteen maybe, pale, fresh-faced, dark wavy hair, wide-set dark eyes.

"My father is the minister of Wem," he said. "He would be pleased to meet you." Samuel wasn't surprised: it was usual for dissenting ministers to exchange visits with their neighbours. "He has asked me to invite you to come and stay with us," the boy went on. "It's not far."

"Unfortunately I can't stay tonight," Samuel said. "Maybe in a couple of days."

"Thank you. I'll tell my father. Thank you," the boy mumbled. He was shy, Samuel saw, shyer still when he visited two days later. He scarcely spoke at the dinner table. His father turned out to be a learned man.

"What do you think of Mary Wollstonecraft's influence over William Godwin?" he asked Samuel.

"I think it's an example of the ascendancy that people of imagination exercise over those of mere intellect," Samuel said.

The conversation moved on to which was the superior philosopher, Edmund Burke or James Mackintosh.

"Burke is a metaphysician," Samuel said confidently. "Mackintosh is a mere logician." Later they discussed Holcroft. "He barricades the road to truth," Samuel said, "setting up a turnpike gate at every step we take."

The next morning Samuel received a letter, brought on to him from his previous lodgings. This time he recognised the writing. It was from Tom Wedgwood.

"I've been offered an annuity!" he burst out excitedly.

William Hazlitt had just come into the room.

"From the Wedgwood brothers!" Samuel explained, laughing at the boy's face. "£150 a year, why, that's more than I can get here. To give up my present post and devote myself entirely to poetry and philosophy."

"But sir," Hazlitt said, "you would give up your ministry? You are so gifted…"

Samuel looked down to avoid the man's disappointed face. He saw that his shoelace was undone and bent to do it up.

"Poetry and philosophy," he said softly, almost to himself. "It's what I've always wanted to do."

# Chapter Nine

Sara was disappointed. She had no idea how much she had been looking forward to leaving until it was taken away from her. It would have been a long way away from her family, but she saw little of them now, and to be the wife of a minister, a position with kudos, in a little house, in a town with streets and shops, proper shops selling the sorts of things she used to buy in Bristol... Oh, she couldn't deny it was wonderful to have the money from the Wedgwoods: they could pay off money they owed, including her mother's £5 quarterly allowance. But now she was stuck in this miserable little cottage forever. She turned Samuel's letter over and over in her hand; his happiness radiated off the page with every word. "I can't believe it..." he wrote.

He had written to everyone: Josiah Wedgwood, first of all, thanking him for his support and belief in him; then to Poole, "I am not certain that I am not dreaming," to Estlin, who still thought he should be a minister and disapproved of the Wedgwood annuity, to Thelwall, "I am astonished and agitated," and to Wordsworth, "I accepted it on the presumption that I had talents, honesty and propensities to perseverant effort."

Samuel longed to be back in Somerset but he had undertaken to do two more sermons and it was another eleven days before he could set off for home. On his way home he felt obliged to go by way of Westbury-on-Trym to say thank you personally to the Wedgwood brothers at Cote House.

Sara had plenty of time to compose herself. She couldn't show Samuel how disappointed she was. Tears could fall now but by the time he came home she had a welcoming smile on her face.

"Isn't it the most marvellous news, Sara?" he burst out breathlessly almost before he had opened the door. "Oh, Sara, oh, my love, I'm to be a poet. A properly paid, well, supported poet. To devote myself entirely to poetry and philosophy. It's like a dream. I must go and see Wordsworth and Dorothy."

He seemed almost on the point of going out again immediately.

"Wait, wait!" Sara said. "Let me get you something to eat first…"

Hartley began to stir from his afternoon nap.

"Let me, Sara," Samuel said, going over to him. "Your papa, David Hartley, is going to be a poet," he told the red-faced, sleepy-eyed little boy, "and a philosopher, like your namesake." He laughed boisterously, picked him up and held him high in the air. The little boy's face crumpled and he began to cry.

"He's always like that when he first wakes up," Sara laughed. "Here, let me…"

She took Hartley from him and he snuggled into her shoulder, still whimpering and rubbing his eyes.

"He'll be all right in a minute or two," she said, bending with difficulty and putting him down on the floor, where he continued to grizzle.

"Here," she passed the loaf of bread towards Samuel. "And let me get you some ale."

"Yes, and then I'll go over to Alfoxton. Or maybe I should see Poole first. Yes, that's what I'll do…"

Poole was overjoyed, of course. It was what he had always wanted, to have Samuel recognised as the great man he already knew he was, properly recognised and supported financially, rather than being propped up on an ad hoc basis by himself. Cottle, Estlin and the others. And now he could stay near him in Stowey. The Wordsworths would soon be gone and Samuel would be free from their influence.

Samuel had said goodbye to Dorothy and Wordsworth once already. When he went up to Shrewsbury he wasn't sure when he would see them again. Now he was reunited with them, even if only for a short time. The lease on Alfoxton was due to expire in the summer.

"I've started writing a journal," Dorothy told Samuel when he went over, "a record of our final months here. I write down what I see and what we do together."

Conscious that these last months together were precious, the three of them met every few days. Sometimes Poole came along. One day he took them to see his cousins at Marshmills.

"Sing one of your arias for us, Penelope," he asked her. "*Come, Ever Smiling Liberty;* it's one of your favourites."

"No," said Penelope firmly. "*Your* idea of liberty is quite different from mine."

Mostly, though, they were happy on their own, just the three of them.

"I am working on my poem *The Ruined Cottage*," Wordsworth told Samuel one day. "I'm trying to develop the character of the pedlar and make it more into a moral tale."

"I'm still working on the *Mariner*," Samuel said. "It's such hard work, getting the meter right..."

February was a cold month with snow showers, sharp frosty mornings and icy cold nights.

"You're not going out in this?" Sara asked day after day as Samuel wrapped himself up in his coat, hat and scarf.

"It's lovely out there, Sara," he would reply enthusiastically, "once you get walking."

But Sara was too heavily pregnant to risk a fall on the icy streets. It was bad enough going out to the courtyard every morning to break the ice on the well and draw up the heavy bucket of water.

There was the odd milder day when she ventured out, enjoying the fresh air and Hartley's chatter as she walked up to Alfoxton with Samuel, but she was so tired all the time. "I think I'll go up to bed now," she often said as soon as Hartley was settled for the night.

"Yes, you go my sweet," Samuel would reply absently, his finger on the page in the book he was reading or his pen poised over the paper. "I'll bring Hartley up later."

One evening, as he sat by the fireside, his thoughts went back over the day he had spent with Wordsworth and Dorothy, the frosty walk over to Alfoxton, twigs and dead leaves cracking under his feet, his breath streaming out in front of him. His mind wandered from there to his childhood, his school days in London. It wasn't very late but such a cold night that the village street outside had fallen silent. All he could hear was the fire crackling gently in its last embers and Hartley's gentle breathing in his cot next to him. *"Hartley, my son,"* he thought fondly, looking down at him sleeping so peacefully. *"I will give you such a childhood, the like of which I didn't have myself. I won't send you away to school at nine years old. You will wander freely on the hills like your papa does. I will show you such things, nature will be your best friend...."* He stopped, picked up his pen, began to write feverishly. Suddenly an owl hooted loudly. So close it sounded, as though it were just outside the cottage. He crossed to the window, drew back the curtain. Frost was beginning to form tiny feathery patterns that he thought he could almost see growing as he watched. He sat down again, squinting in the feeble light as his pen scratched away on the paper.

"The frost performs its secret ministry,
Unhelped by any wind. The owlet's cry
Came loud—and hark, again! loud as before.
The inmates of my cottage, all at rest,
Have left me to that solitude, which suits
Abstruser musings: save that at my side
My cradled infant slumbers peacefully."

*Frost at Midnight* was a paean to his life in Stowey, his happiness in the little cottage in the country, his pride in his son and his wife, the future he saw for them all. He concluded it:

"Suspend thy little soul; then make thee shout
And stretch and flutter from thy mother's arms
As though wouldst fly from very eagerness."

As spring wore on, Sara began to find it too far to walk to Alfoxton and Samuel went on his own.

"Stay the night," Dorothy would urge as it grew late while they were still talking or walking. "Sara knows where you are; she won't mind."

Sometimes he stayed a few days. Sara was tired, he told himself. It would make it easier if she didn't have him to cook for and look after.

From the house they could walk in the deer park and the surrounding beech woods and down to Putsham, Holford and Crowcombe. They wandered the Quantock Hills and down to Kilve with its desolate rock and boulder strewn beach and its grey forbidding sea. One misty afternoon in late February they climbed the great Iron Age hill-fort at Dowsborough, with its wonderful view stretching for miles.

"Such a union of earth, sea and sky," Dorothy marvelled. "Look at the clouds above, the mist below us…"

They loved walking at night, seeing the countryside by the light of the moon.

"Let's go up to the castle!" Dorothy exclaimed one evening. "It's a beautiful evening. Up high on the hill we can look at the moon, the valley below…"

"It's late Dorothy," Wordsworth said, "and cold. I'm going to bed."

"I'll come with you," Samuel said, "and walk you back afterwards."

Wordsworth was right, it was a cold night, but Samuel had his big, warm coat and Dorothy was bundled up in shawls and a cloak and bonnet. The moon was bright. Dorothy took his arm, sometimes talking, sometimes silent, perfectly attuned to his mood in a way Sara never seemed to be nowadays.

152

There was nothing left of the castle above Stowey, just the bumps and mounds of grassy hillside where walls and ditches had been. It was a steep climb to the top of the hill but Dorothy was hardly out of breath when they reached the top.

"Look at it, Samuel," she breathed. "The world below us. Just you and me awake. Everyone else dead to the world."

It wasn't quite true of course. Voices drifted from the street as people returned from the alehouse, some cottages still had smoke curling from the chimneys and candlelight dimly visible behind the curtained windows.

Dorothy sat down, then lay back like she had so often done on the hillside in the Quantocks. Samuel didn't need to be told now. He lay down next to her, gazed at the sky above him. The world below him retreated, the ground barely supporting him. Lying like this, no earthly sign visible, he felt like he was floating in space, at one with the stars, moon and planets above him. He had never been so aware that he was on a planet too, so small and insignificant, a tiny part of God's creation. He didn't need to speak. He knew Dorothy was feeling the same. It was holy, reverential, the most wonderful feeling he had ever known.

"My father used to tell me about the stars," Samuel said softly. He sensed Dorothy's silent encouragement.

"That's the Pole Star," Samuel pointed up. "Sailors like your brother John, my brother Frank, they use that to navigate." Dorothy had told him about John. She was nearly as fond of him as she was of William. "There's Jupiter," he went on. "It's a thousand times larger than our world. The stars are suns with worlds rolling around them. Space is vast. We're so tiny, so unworthy..." His voice broke. He knew she understood. Theirs was a communion like no other.

They walked back in silence, feeling that they had experienced something special, a never-to-be repeated experience. Maybe Dorothy would tell Wordsworth, almost certainly she would: she told him everything. He would understand. But he could never tell Sara.

Samuel's admiration for Wordsworth grew daily. "You're a far better poet than me," he told him when Wordsworth had read out his latest lines for *The Ruined Cottage*. "Have you ever thought of writing a great philosophic poem? It was something I myself considered once. An epic poem. I thought it would take me about twenty years to do. I told Cottle about it last year. But I don't have the talent. You do."

"It's a wonderful idea," Wordsworth said. "Yes, I could do that. I know I could."

"I told Charles Lamb about it too," Samuel said. "He feels that nothing but an epic poem can satisfy the vast capacity of true poetic genius. Having one great end to direct all your poetical faculties to, and on which to lay your hopes and your ambition, will show to what you are equal."

Samuel was so pleased that Wordsworth liked his idea.

"He's going to call it *The Recluse or Views of Nature, Man and Society*," he told Poole. "He reckons it will take at least eighteen months. The Giant Wordsworth, God love him! Even when I speak in terms of admiration due to his intellect, I fear lest those terms should keep out of sight the amiableness of his manners. He has written nearly 1,200 lines of a blank verse, superior, I hesitate not to aver, to anything in our language which any way resembles it."

"I think it's an excellent idea," Poole agreed. "It is as likely to benefit mankind much more than anything Wordsworth has yet written."

"He needs to borrow more books though," Samuel said. "Can you let him have John Wedgwood's copy of Erasmus Darwin's *Zoonomia?* He has written to Tobin to ask him to send any books on travel."

"It's frustrating," Wordsworth told him later. "There's so much research to do. I don't know how I will ever finish it."

At the beginning of March Samuel began to get violent toothache.

After seeing him taking yet more laudanum, Sara sent him to the doctor.

"You've got an abscess," the doctor said.

"Can you take the tooth out?" Samuel asked.

"I can try…"

The doctor struggled. Samuel writhed in agony. "Stop! Stop!" he yelled finally. "Leave it. I'll put up with the pain."

"What? He couldn't do it?" Sara asked when he returned home, his jaw wrapped up in a cloth.

"No, and I'm not going back," Samuel said. "I'd sooner put my hands in a lion's mouth than put my mouth in his hands."

"Come and stay with us for a while," Dorothy said generously.

"I can't leave Sara with the baby so nearly due," Samuel said. "Especially in the hands of that doctor, who's inherited little skill from Aesculapius."

Dorothy laughed. "Well, bring her too, then. And Hartley. There's plenty of room. It will be fun…"

From Alfoxton he wrote to his brother George. "I don't like to be estranged from my family," he told Sara. "I rely on George's support."

He told George about the pain he had been getting from his tooth. "Laudanum gave me repose, not sleep," he wrote. "But you, I believe, know how divine that repose is — what a spot of enchantment, a green spot of fountains and flowers and trees, in the very heart of a waste of sands! God be praised ... I am now recovering apace, and enjoy that newness of sensation from the fields, the air and the sun, which makes convalescence almost repay one for disease."

"I've told him I'm no longer interested in radical politics," he told Sara as he sealed the letter. "I said I know that many people still think of me as a democrat and a seditionist but that I am now thoroughly disenchanted with the French Revolution. I have said that, with the annuity from the Wedgwoods, I will devote myself to poetry that elevates the imagination and to prose that introduces the reader to the beauty and simplicity of nature. I want other people to appreciate, like I do, the fields and woods and mountains. It is here that I have found benevolence and kindness growing within me and I wish to implant that feeling in others."

Sara was enjoying her stay at Alfoxton. She loved the house. It reminded her of the villa her parents had owned in Westbury before her father was declared bankrupt: the same spacious, gracious rooms, the wooden floors, dark panelled walls, echoing corridors. It was furnished like a grand house. There was a fireplace in their bedroom and a view across the lawns.

While she was there she had to help Dorothy in the house, of course, but it was nothing to the things she had to do at the cottage. Here, Dorothy shared the chores. True, she was a bit slapdash for Sara's liking, more than a bit really, the way she wiped the range cursorily when she had used it and left dirty cloths hanging around the place, but it wasn't Sara's house, why bother with it herself? There was a maid who came in once a week to do the heavy cleaning and sort the washing and things and Peggy Marsh all the time, the older, experienced, competent and confident sort of nanny that Sara would have liked for Hartley.

Little Basil, now six years old, was besotted with Hartley, treating him like a little brother to be shown everything as though it was brand new. "This is my bedroom," he announced solemnly, holding the toddler by the hand. "And Peggy sleeps here. You'll sleep over there." He pointed to a truckle bed, next to Peggy's, made up for Hartley. "You can put your toys here if you like…"

Sara had brought a couple of Hartley's favourite toys with him and Basil treated them with respect mixed with a degree of superiority. "I used to play with things like that," he said, looking at the hobby horse Hartley was dragging around the room, "but I'm too big now."

At eighteen months old, Hartley was now a lively little boy, rushing around the place, eager to explore the big house. More like Samuel than Sara, with his dark hair and grey eyes, he was slimmer built than either of them with skinny little arms and legs.

With Basil and Hartley playing happily together and Peggy Marsh to chase around after them, Sara reclined in the armchair by the window, looking out at the lawns beyond, the snowdrops carpeted under the tress, the fern-clad hillside beyond. The days were beginning to draw out, the weather grow milder. The baby was due in early May. Not like Hartley, born in the winter. She would be able to hang the nappies and baby clothes on the line outside to dry…

Swathed in shawls and blankets and holding his aching jaw, Samuel sat opposite her, either reading a book or dozing or sitting with his pen in his hand and his lap stuffed with sheaths of paper. He was still working on *The Ancient Mariner*. "I've asked Cottle if he will include it in the third edition of my *Poems,*" he told Wordsworth, "and cut out nearly half of the old poems to make room for it. They're so juvenile now compared to what I'm writing. And add in three of my most recent poems, including *This Lime Tree Bower* and *Frost at Midnight*."

In the evenings he would read it to Wordsworth and Dorothy, over and over again, changing the odd word or phrase to get it right. The conversation would range way above Sara's head as they discussed meter, cadence, the ballad form, line variations. And yet, living here at Alfoxton with them, even for so short a period of time, Sara began to feel included in a way she hadn't before.

Dorothy asked her every day how she felt. "My aunt always found these last few months so exhausting and dull," she said. And Sara had a glimpse of the life Dorothy had had before she almost literally ran away with Wordsworth: a life of looking after babies and children, in a household where she was treated as little more than an unpaid nursery maid.

Every day, when Sara heaved her huge stomach from the dining room to the sitting room, Wordsworth rushed to put the footstool under her aching legs and swollen ankles and Sara saw the side of him Dorothy saw: the man who looked out for every little comfort for someone he cared for. No wonder she wanted to be with him all the time.

Even Samuel seemed more solicitous. When Dorothy and Wordsworth went for their daily walk he made sure she was comfortable before he installed himself in his chair with his books and papers. True, he still often forgot she was there as he huffed and puffed and crossed out words he had written, substituting them with others that he muttered out loud, but on her own with him like this, she had a vision of how their lives might be once the Wordsworths left and she had him back to herself again.

"We do need to decide where we are going to go," Dorothy said one evening.

"There are no houses to let around here," Wordsworth said. "And, really, nothing to keep us here. Except *your* friendship." He nodded towards Coleridge and Sara. "And Poole's."

"We don't want to lose *you* either," Samuel said quickly. Sara said nothing. She'd like nothing more than to prise Samuel away from the two of them and she knew Poole felt the same. "Maybe we should think of moving too," Samuel went on, "so we can all stay together."

"There's Racedown, of course," Wordsworth mused. "I know Pinney would let us have it back. We'd probably have to pay rent this time though," he laughed.

"But do you really want to go back there?" Dorothy asked. "You felt it was too remote last time."

"I know, but we have to live somewhere. Oh, I don't know. Maybe while we decide what to do we could go on a walking tour somewhere."

"Wales, maybe," Dorothy said excitedly. "And then back up north. We could go and stay with Mary Hutchinson in Sockburn. She's always inviting us."

"But then we'd still have to find somewhere to live after that," Wordsworth said miserably.

"What about going abroad?" Samuel suddenly asked. "All of us," he said, warming to his subject. Sara looked up from her sewing, ran her hand over her swollen belly. Did Samuel mean her and the children as well?

"Germany!" he said suddenly. "I've always wanted to learn German. Oh, Wordsworth, think of it! The four of us, in a village, near a university, in a pleasant area, near the mountains maybe." He knew how Dorothy and Wordsworth loved mountains.

It wasn't the first time Samuel had talked of going to Germany. Just after Hartley was born, before they had moved to Nether Stowey, he had told Sara of a plan to go and live there and study chemistry, anatomy, theology and philosophy. "Germany is where all the most exciting developments in philosophy are taking place," he had told her.

"I should put the annuity the Wedgwoods have so generously given me to good use," he went on now, "to further my knowledge. That's what they expect of me."

"Germany!" Dorothy exclaimed, her eyes shining. She turned to William. "To travel and see other countries. Oh, William, say we will."

"It's tempting," Wordsworth said carefully. "I'd prefer Switzerland. I went there on a walking tour eight years ago. It's beautiful, Dorothy. I'd love to show it to you. And we could still learn German there."

"That's impossible though, isn't it? Dorothy said sadly. "Now that the French have invaded."

"France, Holland, Spain: all at war with us," Wordsworth agreed. "There are few countries in

Europe safe for an Englishman to travel nowadays. And Belgium overrun, Switzerland under France…"

"It would have to be Germany then," said Dorothy decisively.

"Once we're established, others can join us," said Samuel. He could see it, a Pantisocratic community living, working and studying together, just like he had always wanted.

Wordsworth agreed readily, "There's James Losh, a friend of mine. He's recently married. This is just the sort of scheme he's interested in. I'll write to him."

"What about Basil?" Dorothy said suddenly. "We can't take him."

"We're looking after him for nothing at the moment since his father has left the legal profession," Wordsworth reminded her. "We can't go on doing so."

Sara waited for one of them to say the obvious: what about Hartley and the new baby? If they were thinking of going in July she would have a two-month-old baby and a child under two to take on a long, difficult and dangerous journey. But sitting there by the fireside, with the three of them so carried away and excited by their plan, she hadn't the heart to throw cold water on it.

It was Dorothy who brought up the next stumbling block.

"How are we going to pay for it, William?"

Wordsworth looked over at Samuel. "How long do you think we would be gone?"

"Two years," Samuel said decisively, as though everything was already arranged. "That should be long enough to master the language and learn the sciences…"

"We already owe money to Poole and Cottle," Wordsworth said quietly. "It can't be done."

"William," Dorothy said. "You can *earn* money. Through your poetry."

"You know I don't want to go into print," Wordsworth said. "Not yet. Not until I'm ready."

"Write to Cottle," she urged. "*Please* William. It's the only thing to do. Poetry is your profession. You need to earn money from it."

"You could ask him to publish our two tragedies together," Samuel said. "*Osorio* and *The Borderers.*"

"Or my *Salisbury Plain* poem and the *Tale of a Woman.* And a few others I'm working on…"

Samuel could see him coming around to the idea.

"I'll write to Cottle on your behalf," he offered.

"Don't ask it as a favour though, just because I'm your friend," Wordsworth said. "Tell him to treat the matter purely in a business fashion. We'd need about thirty guineas I would say, to pay for the trip."

"Well, you could give him first refusal and tell him you'll approach other publishers if he can't come up with it."

By the time they returned to the cottage, Samuel had nearly finished *The Ancient Mariner* and had started writing another ballad-style poem, *Christabel.*

On March 23rd he walked triumphantly up to Alfoxton with the completed manuscript of *The Ancient Mariner* which he read to Wordsworth and Dorothy in the parlour.

"Maybe we should publish it *with* some of my poems," Wordsworth said. "Like we talked about before."

"It's a wonderful idea," Dorothy agreed. "Now that you've written so many more, William."

"Mine could be on supernatural or romantic subjects and yours on characters and incidents from everyday village life," Samuel suggested.

"I'll have to get to work," Wordsworth said. "I have some ideas I've been thinking about for a while. I want to keep the words plain and simple, make them accessible to everyone."

"It will be provocative," Samuel said, "writing in such a different style. I think we'll have to make it clear the poems are experimental."

"Maybe we could put a preface in to explain that," Wordsworth suggested.

"We need a title."

"That will be tricky with the different subjects we're covering. We can't just call it *Poems*."

"And some of mine are ballads," Samuel said. "Maybe Cottle will come up with something. I'll write to him."

# Chapter Ten

"I've written to Cottle and told him about our collaboration," Samuel told Wordsworth. "I've asked him to come and stay so we can talk it through when we have our work set out properly. If he comes in May we can walk to Lynton and Lynmouth. We can show him the Valley of Rocks. He can see everything at its best with the woods and waterfalls and the cliffs..."

At the beginning of April Samuel received a letter from his brother George.

"He's inviting us to Ottery to stay with them," Samuel told Sara.

"When?"

"Now. But it's impossible with the baby so near."

"You go," Sara said. "It's important to get on with your family."

"I can't leave you like this."

"I can go and stay with her while you're away," Dorothy said when Samuel told her.

164

"Would you?" Samuel said. "Are you sure?"

"Of course. I had enough practice with my aunt. I know just what to do if necessary."

Dorothy brought a book with her. "It's Godwin's *Memoirs of the Author of A Vindication of the Rights of Woman,*" she told Sara. "It arrived today. I thought we could look at it together."

"Mary Wollstonecraft? I was taught all about her at school."

"Everyone is talking about this book," Dorothy said. "It's quite shocking, the things she did, living with Gilbert Imlay, having an illegitimate baby..."

Sara was flattered. Dorothy had never involved her in conversations like this before.

But it was short-lived. When Samuel came home again, the three of them were together more than ever, Samuel spending most of his time over at Alfoxton as they worked on the book of poems together or walked and talked, often at night.

He and Wordsworth were both in a period of intense creativity. "I've written eleven poems since March," Wordsworth said. "I can't wait to read them to Cottle. What with those I've already written I reckon I'll have enough for a second volume of poems later on."

Wordsworth's poems were either autobiographical or they dealt with the lives of the country people around them. Like Samuel, he kept the language simple; the main idea, they decided, was to be natural. Samuel was still working on *Christabel,* which he hoped he could finish in time to be published with Wordsworth's poems. The supernatural theme of this and *The Ancient Mariner* would balance out the down-to-earth themes of Wordsworth's poems. They decided on four long major poems: *Christabel* and *The Ancient Mariner* from Samuel and *The Idiot Boy* and *The Thorn* from Wordsworth. Dorothy sat with them, writing and re-writing their work, correcting and advising, and writing postscripts and asides in the letters Samuel wrote to his friends. Her company was as necessary to Samuel as Wordsworth's. He loved their night-time walks, where she strode along, oblivious to the rustlings and cries of night-time animals, revelling only in the nature surrounding her, like the gypsy type lady he had in mind in *Christabel*.

As she walked along the familiar paths, Dorothy sometimes said things out loud, the odd description or phrase, repeating it over and over to get it right. "I want to write it in my journal when we get home," she would say and Samuel would find the same words and phrases coming to him when he sat down to write his poems.

"There are nightingales in the woods near Dodington Hall," Dorothy said excitedly one evening. "It's a beautiful evening. If we go late tonight we can listen to them singing."

Samuel never forgot it: the company of his two closest friends, the soft April evening, blue sky deepening into dusk, the fresh spring green of the leaves on the trees, the birds singing.

When he came home he started his poem *The Nightingale,* dedicating it to "My Friend and thou our Sister!"

The poem described their walk, their very special relationship, the "old mossy bridge" they sat on at Halford before they said goodnight to go to their separate homes.

"My friend, and thou, our sister! we have learnt
A different lore: we may not thus profane

Nature's sweet voices, always full of love
And joyance!"

As he was writing it he remembered an incident he
had recorded in his notebook. Hartley had fallen down
and hurt himself and was crying and, in order to take
his mind off it, Samuel had taken him outside to look
at the moon. "He ceased crying immediately," Samuel
had written in his notebook, "and his eyes and the trees
in them, how they glittered in the moonlight."

It was the sort of incident, like the spectre ship in
*The Ancient Mariner,* that he kept a note of ready to use
at the right time.

In *The Nightingale* he changed it slightly to fit the
theme of the poem and form an ending:
"My dear babe,
Who, capable of no articulate sound,
Mars all things with his imitative lisp,
How he would place his hand beside his ear,
His little hand, the small forefinger up,
And bid us listen! And I deem it wise
To make him nature's play-mate. He knows well
The evening-star; and once, when he awoke
In most distressful mood (some inward pain
Had made up that strange thing, an infant's dream)
I hurried with him to our orchard-plot,
And he beheld the moon, and, hushed at once,
Suspends his sobs, and laughs most silently,
While his fair eyes, that swam with undropped
tears,
Did glitter in the yellow moon-beam."

Knowing this special time with the Wordsworths
was nearly over inspired in Samuel an elegiac feeling, a
wish to capture this precious time together. In April he
wrote a poem, *Fears in Solitude,* about the possibility of

167

a French invasion, but even here he found his love for the Somerset countryside coming out. He set it in the Quantocks, in a "green and silent spot, amid the hills," and ended it:

"... And after lonely sojourning
In such a quiet and surrounded nook,
This burst of prospect, here the shadowy main,
Dim-tinted, there the mighty majesty
Of that huge amphitheatre of rich
And elmy fields, seems like society —
Conversing with the mind, and giving it
A livelier impulse and a dance of thought!
And now, beloved Stowey! I behold
Thy church-tower and, methinks, the four huge elms
Clustering, which mark the mansion of my friend;
And close behind them, hidden from my view,
Is my own lowly cottage, where my babe
And my babe's mother dwell in peace!"

It was the second week in May when Samuel received a letter from Joshua Toulmin, the minister of the Taunton Unitarian church.

"Why, Sara, this is dreadful news," he said. "Toulmin's daughter has drowned herself. In Bere in Devon. Toulmin is devastated. He has had to go down there. He asks if I will conduct his service in Taunton this Sunday."

"You must, of course you must," Sara said. "You won't be gone long, will you? Only the baby is due any day now..."

"I'll be back before you know it," Samuel said, kissing her. "And the baby will wait for Papa, won't you?" He ran his hand over her belly.

But the baby didn't wait. Soon after Samuel had left Sara felt the familiar pain. As before, she was lucky — luckier, she knew than most women. It was a quick labour and by the time Samuel returned on Sunday evening she was sitting up in bed feeding their new baby son.

"She had a remarkably good time," Samuel wrote proudly to his friend Estlin. "Better, if possible, than her last."

"We'll call him Berkeley," Samuel said to Sara later. "After George Berkeley.

Sara looked at him blankly.

"The philosopher," Samuel explained. "George Berkeley, Bishop of Cloyne, the author of works on the relation of man to nature."

She didn't mind, really, what they called him. And if it was a girl next time maybe *she* could choose the name. He was a beautiful baby. Hartley had been such a scrawny little thing, still was really, but Berkeley was a big, easy-going baby with lovely grey eyes.

Samuel was very proud of him. One day he saw a neighbour passing the cottage.

"Quick, Nanny!" he said, grabbing Berkeley from her arms. "Let me have him a moment!"

"But, sir, he's only half-dressed," the poor girl answered.

"It doesn't matter." He rushed outside. "See my second son!" he said proudly to the startled neighbour. "Berkeley. Such a handsome fellow, isn't he?"

"Well," said the neighbour, "I have to say, this is something like a child!"

A stab of pain went through Samuel. Was she saying Hartley was inferior? He whisked the baby back inside and handed him back to Nanny.

"Bercoo Baby Brodder!" Hartley said, pointing at Berkeley.

"But *you're* just as beautiful!" Samuel told him, dropping to his knees on the floor next to him.

But Baby Berkeley wasn't enough to keep Samuel at home.

"We're going up to Cheddar," Dorothy told him, two days after the baby was born.

"I'll come with you," Samuel said impulsively.

"Are you sure?" she asked uncertainly.

"Oh, Sara doesn't need *me* around," he said confidently. "I just get in the way. Anyway, we won't be gone long…"

They stayed overnight in Bridgwater and a second night at Cross, just outside Cheddar.

"I think I might go on to Bristol," Wordsworth said when they had done enough sightseeing. "Can you escort Dorothy back home for me?"

"Yes, of course. You're thinking of seeing Cottle, are you, to discuss the poetry book?"

"Yes…" said Wordsworth slowly. "And I thought maybe I'd see what I can do to patch up the quarrel between you and Charles Lloyd. I believe he's in Bristol at the moment."

Lloyd had just published his novel *Edmund Oliver,* in which the hero, a drunk and a lecher, left his university in Oxford and enlisted in the dragoons. It was clearly meant to be Samuel and he was deeply hurt that Lloyd should parade his secrets in public in order to humiliate him. He was even more hurt when Southey and then Lamb took Lloyd's side against him. "How am I meant to concentrate on my writing with all this going on around me?" he had said to

Wordsworth and now Wordsworth was good enough to try to help.

Samuel had only been back a couple of days when a visitor arrived. Just for a moment he didn't recognise the awkward-looking young man standing at the door. "Hazlitt, sir," the boy mumbled. "William Hazlitt. You invited me in January…"

"Yes, yes, of course!" Samuel exclaimed. "Come in, come in! You're very welcome. I've been looking forward to seeing you again."

He remembered now, pressing his address into the boy's hand that frosty morning in January when they had walked back from Wem to Shrewsbury together. "Come any time," he had said generously.

"Who is it, Samuel?" he heard Sara calling out. "I'm feeding Berkeley."

"Oh, please sir, I have no wish to disturb you and Mrs Coleridge. I had no idea…" The sound of a baby wailing, coupled with a small boy yelling peevishly pierced the air.

"No, no, please," Samuel said, as the boy edged away nervously, "wait there a moment. Let me just…"

He darted back inside in time to catch sight of Sara's skirt trailing up the stairs, while Nanny stood by the fire with Hartley in her arms.

"Come in, come in!" he called out.

"He *can't* stay here," Sara hissed at Samuel in the bedroom while she held Berkeley to her breast. "It's not… Well, it's not seemly. A young man, here, in such a small place, with me like this every few minutes…" She gestured to her breast.

"I'll take him to Alfoxton," Samuel said. "Dorothy won't mind."

"But she doesn't even *know* him," Sara said. "And Wordsworth isn't back yet."

"He's a minister's son, Sara," Samuel reminded her. "Perfectly trustworthy. Anyway, you haven't even met him yet. He wouldn't say boo to a goose."

Hazlitt was still hovering nervously in the parlour downstairs. "I can stay at the inn," he said.

"Nonsense!" Samuel said. "Come on. I'll walk you over to Alfoxton."

If Dorothy was surprised to see him arriving with a guest for her, while her brother was still away in Bristol, she didn't show it. "Of course you must stay," she said. "*Both* of you."

Samuel was hoping she would say this. A night away from two babies was just what he needed.

"I'll put you in the St Albyn room," she told Hazlitt.

"It's full of old family portraits!" Samuel laughed. "I hope they don't give you nightmares!"

"I don't have much food to offer you," Dorothy went on. "I don't usually bother much when William's away. I was going to have porridge myself. My teeth are troubling me so. I think there might be some bread and cheese…"

Samuel woke early the next morning, after the best night's sleep he had had in a week, to hear a stag bellowing in the woods. After the same sort of frugal meal they had had the night before, Dorothy brought out a sheaf of papers.

"William's manuscripts," she said, "for the joint poetry book. I thought you would like to take a look at them, Samuel."

"Yes, it's a lovely morning," Samuel said. "Let's take a walk in the park first, then we can read these under the trees."

172

After a tour of the deer park, they sat down on the trunk of an old ash tree that stretched along the ground and Samuel read some of Wordsworth's poems out loud to Hazlitt and Dorothy.

"It is only a shame that Wordsworth does not agree with me about traditional superstitions associated with places," he said as they walked back to Nether Stowey in the moonlight that evening. "His poetry is more matter-of-fact," he went on. "His genius is not a spirit descending to him from the air. It springs from the ground like a flower or unfolds itself from a green spray on which a goldfinch sings. I'm only referring to his descriptive poetry of course, the poems he's written for our book. Now, his philosophical poetry, that's quite different. It has a grand and comprehensive spirit in it, so that his soul seems to inhabit the universe like a palace, and to discover truth by intuition, rather than by deduction."

They were back at the cottage when Wordsworth arrived the next day. Hazlitt stood around nervously while he and Samuel greeted each other. "I had a wasted journey," Wordsworth was saying. "Lloyd had already gone back to Birmingham."

"It doesn't matter," Samuel said. "It was good of you to try. This is my friend Hazlitt." The two men bowed to each other.

Sara saw how Hazlitt hung around nervously while Samuel and Wordsworth talked, taking in their every word, but not uttering a word himself.

"How beautifully the sun sets on that yellow bank!" Wordsworth said suddenly, glancing past Samuel's shoulder and out of the low lattice-paned window. It was the sort of thing they said all the time and Sara scarcely noticed it but she saw Hazlitt gazing adoringly at him.

"We will show you the Somerset countryside!" Samuel burst out next. "Lynton and Lynmouth, the Valley of Rocks. I'll walk back with you to Alfoxton."

"You're going again?" Sara asked.

"Well, I should help entertain Hazlitt," Samuel said. "And Wordsworth and I have a lot to discuss…"

In some ways Sara didn't mind. When Samuel was home he was always bringing people back, people she had to find refreshment for, people who arrived just as Hartley had settled for his afternoon nap, or when she was feeding Berkeley, as had happened with Hazlitt. She only wished Samuel wouldn't sound quite so eager to get away from her and the children all the time.

As they walked back together Hazlitt said, "You'll be having the new baby baptised soon I suppose."

"Oh no," Samuel said quickly. "I thoroughly disapprove of infant baptism. They can decide to do it later if they want. But to decide for them while they are still babies? No, it just doesn't seem right."

The following evening, as they sat outside under the trees, Samuel was surprised to hear Hazlitt's voice raised in argument.

"No, sir, no, I disagree," he was saying.

Samuel stopped mid-way through telling Dorothy about the different notes of the nightingale. Hazlitt was arguing with Wordsworth. He would never have believed that shy, nervous boy would have the spirit to stand up to the mighty Wordsworth. "You have a point…" Wordsworth was saying.

Samuel's heart swelled with pride. This was the sort of conversation he had envisaged when he first thought of Pantisocracy: people feeling free to express their opinions without censure. Here, at Alfoxton, he had achieved something like his dream. If only he could make it happen permanently.

He was keen to show Hazlitt the Valley of Rocks while he was staying in the area. "I've asked John Chester to come with us," he told him.

Chester was a few years older than Samuel and Wordsworth. He was from a well-off farming family: his father had rented Dodington Hall from the Marquis of Buckingham and farmed a vast area of land around it. When his father died the family moved into another house in Stowey, also rented from the marquis. On the face of it, Chester had little in common with Samuel and Wordsworth, but they had known him a little while now — he had been one of the guests at the housewarming party at Alfoxton that had caused so much trouble — and he was good company, although he scarcely spoke a word but was content to sit back and listen. He agreed to join Samuel and Hazlitt on their walk to the coast and arrived looking like a typical country farmer, in corduroy breeches and sturdy boots and, as always, carrying a hazel stick. He was stout and bow-legged but kept up easily with the pace set by Samuel, despite his slightly dragging sort of gait.

They walked to Minehead first, past Dunster with its castle on the hillside. "What a lovely village," Hazlitt said. "It looks like a landscape painting by Poussin."

When they stopped at Broomstreet Farm for a rest, Hazlitt pointed to the bare masts of a ship standing out starkly against the setting sun. "Look!" he cried, "the spectre ship from *The Ancient Mariner*."

It was nearly midnight when they arrived at Lynton and they had some difficulty waking up their hosts, who had given up on their arrival and gone to bed. The next morning they walked on to the Valley of Rocks in sweltering heat that soon turned into a thunderstorm. Everyone rushed for shelter, except Samuel, who ran out bareheaded to enjoy the storm. It was short-lived however: just a few claps of thunder and a quick shower.

At the end of May, Cottle arrived at Alfoxton to discuss the book of poetry.

"I'm not sure about the wisdom of a collaborative venture like this," he said. "I still think Wordsworth's poems will stand up well alone."

"But they lack variety," Wordsworth said. "I suppose *Peter Bell* or *Salisbury Plain* might work alone, but the others would be better with Samuel's."

"I'm just a bit worried about the archaisms in *The Ancient Mariner*," Cottle said.

"But that's the whole *point* of it," Samuel said. "To make it sound like it's a work I discovered! Wordsworth and I definitely think it should be a joint volume," he went on decisively, "and that we should publish anonymously. Wordsworth's name is unknown to anyone; to a large number of people mine *stinks*."

"And we still need a title," Wordsworth added.

It wasn't all work. They were keen to show Cottle the places they loved, the places that had inspired them. Aware that these were the Wordsworths' final weeks at Alfoxton, nostalgia tinged their favourite walks to Kilve beach, Holford Combe, Hodder's Combe and up on the Quantocks. For the second time that summer they walked to the Valley of Rocks. Unused to walking such distances, Cottle struggled while the others strode ahead, revelling in the places they loved, the dizzying views from the zig-zagging coastal path, the green wooded hills, the beautiful sweep of the beach and sea below them.

By the end of the week, when Cottle had to return to Bristol, Samuel and Wordsworth had managed to get a deal.

"Thirty guineas," he said, stretching out his hand first to Wordsworth, then to Samuel, "for the joint volume: *Lyrical Ballads.*"

"Thirty guineas," Wordsworth said when he had gone. "Exactly half of what I was hoping for."

"But enough to cover the journey to Hamburg," Samuel pointed out.

"Yes, but we need money to live on once we are there. I was hoping the final payment on the legacy I'm getting from Raisley would have come through by now. I'll write to my brother Richard and see what I can sort out." Raisley Calvert, a friend of Wordsworth's, had died three years earlier when he was only twenty-two. He had always supported and believed in Wordsworth and had generously left him £900 in his will.

Sara was still hoping that the whole idea of going to Germany would be dropped. The thought of the dangerous boat journey with two small children, one just a few months old, then the lack of hygiene in a foreign country, the conditions they would have to live in, the illnesses they would be subjected to, was almost unbearable. She couldn't help thinking that, on his own, Samuel might have given up on the idea, just as he had given up on others in the past, but the Wordsworths remained set on it and now she had heard John Chester was going too.

"Chester?" she had repeated incredulously when Samuel told her. "It will never happen."

Hard to imagine the rustic Somerset farmer, dressed in his brown corduroy, travelling to Germany. He scarcely uttered a word of his own language; how would he cope with a foreign one?

"He's financing himself," Samuel said quickly. "It's all arranged."

She shouldn't have been surprised really. Samuel had always had the power to attract people, people who would do anything, go anywhere, just to be with him.

Whether Sara liked it or not, plans were taking shape. It was all they talked about nowadays.

"I've made enquiries," Wordsworth told Samuel. "Lodgings are so expensive in university towns. I think we will have to find accommodation in some small town or village until we can speak German fluently enough to go to university. People tell me Saxony is very beautiful and a cheap place to live. Dorothy and I could board with some respectable family."

"We'll need a house though," Samuel said. "Sara and I and the children. And a servant. Once we've mastered the language we can earn some money by translating."

"Do you think we might travel to Switzerland while we're over there," Dorothy asked, "if the political situation improves? William is so keen to show me all the places he has been to."

"It all depends on what we can afford," Wordsworth said.

"Well, we can travel as far as our meagre income will allow us."

Poole tried to dissuade Samuel.

"You have everything you need here," he said. "I will lend you my books, I can get you any you need, you can use my book room…"

"Southey agrees with him," Sara said, gesturing to the letter in her hand. "Edith says he doesn't understand why you have to go to Germany to learn a language you could learn home here. Why can't you listen to your friends, Samuel?"

"The Wedgwoods expect me to *do* something with the money they've given me…" Samuel began.

"But you can write poetry *here*." She thought back to that week in March at Alfoxton, Samuel working contentedly in the chair opposite her, the Wordsworths gone away somewhere, anywhere…

"I want to study philosophy," Samuel said.

"You can do that here too. Poole said he'll get you the books. Or you can get them from the Bristol library. We could move back to Bristol…" Back to civilisation, near her family, away from this miserable cottage.

"But I want to learn German," he went on quickly before she could come up with another argument. "I need to hear it spoken, to live amongst German people. Then Wordsworth and I can go to a German university. It's so exciting!"

"Is Dorothy taking little Basil?" Sara asked.

"No. She thinks it's too dangerous," Samuel said. Basil was six years old. Sara waited for him to say it would be dangerous to take Hartley and Berkeley but he didn't.

After three weeks, Hazlitt left Stowey on a Sunday morning.

"I have to preach in Taunton this morning," Samuel told him. "Then I'm walking up to Bristol to see Estlin and going on afterwards to the Wedgwoods in Surrey to discuss the Germany trip. I'll meet you in

Bridgwater after the service; we can stay the night there and walk up to Bristol together."

After leaving Hazlitt to make his way back to Shropshire, Samuel spent the day in Bristol with Estlin.

"Don't go," Estlin told him when he explained about the Germany scheme. "It's a silly idea. You have everything you need here. Your reputation is growing. Look at the way you are being asked to write poetry and articles. If you go away now people will forget about you."

Daniel Stuart of the *Morning Post* thought highly of Samuel's work. He had already published *Lewti, The Dark Ladie* and *The Old Man of the Alps* and would be happy to accept more.

"But the Wordsworths are going," Samuel persisted. "It's such an opportunity for us."

At least he knew he had the support of the Wedgwood brothers, especially Tom Wedgwood, who had the same sort of restless enquiring mind as Samuel. They had just moved into their new house and were proud to show it off and to talk to Samuel about his plans.

"This place is a noble large house, in a rich pleasant country," Samuel wrote to Tom Poole. "But the little toe of Quantock is better than the head and shoulders of Surrey and Middlesex."

The Wordsworths' lease on Alfoxton Park ran out on 24th June. Exciting though the new project was, they were sad to leave Alfoxton, the seat of so much of their happiness. On Saturday 23rd June they walked for the last time down the driveway, past the Dog Pound and the waterfall. "Oh, William!" Dorothy said sadly, "I can't bear to think we will never hear the sound of this waterfall again."

Since they weren't sailing to Germany until September they were temporarily homeless. It made sense to be in Bristol to supervise the publication of *Lyrical Ballads* and Cottle had offered to have them to stay in his rooms in Wine Street but he couldn't put them up until 1st July. Sara had no choice but to have them to stay in the cottage.

"Samuel's still in Surrey," she said apologetically.

"That doesn't matter," Wordsworth said. "Can we leave some of our things here when we go up to Bristol? There won't be room at Cottle's place and we don't know where we will live after that. We hope to go and see James Losh while we're there. He and his wife are still thinking of coming to Germany with us."

"And William needs to take his new poems to Cottle," Dorothy said proudly. "He has written two more: *Expostulation and Reply* and *The Tables Turned*. He wrote them while Hazlitt was here and they had a philosophical argument."

"I can't imagine Hazlitt arguing with anyone," Sara said.

"No, we were surprised too," Dorothy laughed.

When Samuel returned from the Wedgwoods' house a few weeks later, he went to see Wordsworth and Dorothy, who had moved into lodgings near the Losh's house in Shirehampton.

"It was so noisy in Bristol after Alfoxton," Dorothy said. "We're close enough to Bristol here but it's quieter."

"And I've written another poem!" Wordsworth burst out. "Dorothy and I have been on the most wonderful walking tour to Wales, to the Wye Valley, and I've composed a poem. For Dorothy." He turned proudly to his sister. "Lines, Written a Few Miles

Above Tintern Abbey, On Revisiting the Banks of the Wye During a Tour, July 13, 1798."

"It's a beautiful poem, Samuel," she said. "It *must* be included in *Lyrical Ballads.*"

"It's not a ballad," Wordsworth said quickly.

"We may have to change the title," Samuel said. "We can talk to Cottle about it. And about your new poem. Tell me about your trip."

Samuel listened, entranced, as Wordsworth and Dorothy described the beautiful countryside, the flowing river, the crumbling ruins of Tintern Abbey.

"But you must show them to me," he said. "Can't we all go together? Thelwall lives not far away from there. A place called Llyswen, just above Hay. We can go and visit him at the same time."

"We need to see Cottle first. To finalise the poems."

"Yes, of course, but that won't take long. Then we can go."

The original idea had been to have four long poems: *The Ancient Mariner* and *Christabel* from Samuel, and *The Idiot Boy* and *The Thorn* from Wordsworth. Only one of these was, in fact, a ballad, but together they did make a good balance of styles.

"It's such a shame I haven't been able to complete *Christabel*," Samuel told Cottle. "I was so upset about the Charles Lloyd business that I just couldn't do it."

Wordsworth, meanwhile, had composed many new poems, none of which were ballads, but all of which Cottle thought should be included. The resultant volume was strangely unbalanced: there was only one ballad and Wordsworth's *Tintern Abbey,* too good to be omitted, was quite different from his original idea of humble poems of rural life. With *Christabel* still not finished, Coleridge's other poems consisted of two extracts from *Osorio* and *The Nightingale,* a last-minute substitution for *Lewti,* which had already been published in the *Morning Post.*

Finally, however, with the finished manuscript of the newly entitled L*yrical Ballads with a Few Other Poems* safely delivered to Cottle, they were free to go on their tour of Wales.

The night before they left, Samuel sat down to write a letter to Poole. He needed his advice. More than that, he needed his support. For some time he had been wondering whether it was a good idea to take Sara and the two boys to Germany. It would be so expensive and so much inconvenience for them. If he went alone he could send for them in say, three or four months, once he had mastered the language. He would be relying on Poole, of course, to look after Sara and the children while he was away. He knew Poole would say yes.

Sara was surprised when she heard the tentative knock at the front door of the cottage. It was rare to have a visitor when Samuel was away. "Tom!" she said delightedly. "How lovely to see you. Can I offer you tea?"

"I've had a letter from Samuel," he began awkwardly.

She laughed a bitter sort of laugh that sounded strange even to her.

"So have I," she said in a strangled sort of voice. "Oh don't worry, Tom, you don't need to tell me anything. Although that's not what Samuel says." She waved her hand to a letter lying open on the table. "'Poole will explain everything', is what Samuel says.

But I know. I didn't want to go anyway. Not with the babies. It's far too dangerous."

"It's only the expense," Poole said quickly. "It's a trip of 'intellectual utility' he says." He had memorised the exact term Samuel used. "And economy. And he's promised he'll write. Twice weekly to you and me alternately. Just three months, that's all. Then he'll send for you. Why, he's been gone nearly that long already."

"And not thought to come back and see us before he sails," Sara said, so quietly that Poole scarcely caught it.

"Oh, he will, I'm sure he will. He's so busy supervising the poems for the book…"

Samuel set off for Wales with a lightness of heart and a clear conscience. He had done his duty by Sara. Poole and his mother would look after her, he would send money for her. Sara was happy there with her babies. She didn't need him around the place getting in the way. And he was furthering his education, providing a future for her and the children. He was sure she understood that. And now, with Wordsworth and Dorothy by his side, the two people who contributed to his well-being and development, he was free to go anywhere, do anything, achieve everything, away from the stifling domesticity of the cottage.

The three of them walked up the Wye, through the beautiful countryside that the Wordsworths had described, and then on to the Brecon Beacons between Builth Wells and Hay on Wye, ending up in Llyswen, where John Thelwall lived. Thelwall and his wife Stella made them so welcome that they stayed several days before heading back to Bristol.

A few days later, at the end of August, they set off again, this time to go up to London in preparation for their voyage to Germany. They travelled at a leisurely pace, walking some of the way, taking the coach or going by waggon or post chaise and stopping off at Blenheim and at Oxford University.

"It's a shame the Loshes couldn't come with us in the end isn't it?" Samuel said.

"I think he was keen, I really do," said Wordsworth. "But he's just too ill now. That same nervous complaint he had before."

"It was lucky we went to see him in Bath," Dorothy said. "While we were there we dined with his friend Reverend Richard Warner and he told us about his book *A Walk Through Wales*. That was why we went to Wales. And then William wrote *Tintern Abbey*."

"Well, we have one more fellow passenger," Samuel said, determined to change the subject back to the forthcoming trip.

"John Chester." Wordsworth smiled. "I never thought to see him leave Somerset."

"He'll use the trip to study German agriculture," Samuel said. "And he has the money to do it."

"So many of those Somerset farming families have money," Wordsworth said. "Look at Poole's father."

When they arrived in London they found that Wordsworth had forgotten to bring a letter from Cottle to Thomas Longman, a London publisher.

"Does it matter that much?" Dorothy asked, seeing him going through all his papers and pockets again.

"Yes. The thing is, the book is printed but Cottle doesn't have the necessary finances to publish it. He needs someone else, preferably a London publisher, to take it on with him. Worse than that, he's already printed up some title pages giving his own name as printer and Longman's as publisher."

"Can't you just go and see Mr Longman and explain what's happened? Maybe he'll just do it anyway…"

But Longman refused. "I'm sorry. It's just too risky," he said.

"I've put too much into this for it to fall at the final hurdle," Wordsworth said.

"But you've got your thirty guineas, William," Dorothy said. "It's not *your* fault Cottle is in financial difficulties."

"He did it as a favour though didn't he?" Wordsworth said. "It's only fair we should help him now." He thought for a while. "What about Johnson?" he said suddenly. "He published *An Evening Walk* and *Descriptive Sketches* for me five years ago. I'll go and see him. Come with me, Samuel. Together, I'm sure we can persuade him!"

The moment Samuel saw Mr Johnson he doubted they would get anywhere. He was an elderly gentleman, not the type to be swayed by two young radical poets, but they had to try. He listened to them carefully, then, to Samuel's surprise, he agreed to go ahead with *Lyrical Ballads*.

"And you have some more poems of your own, sir?" he asked Samuel.

"Yes. *Fears in Solitude* is a particularly good one of mine, but there are others."

"Well, I think I could consider a volume of yours as well…"

It was only a few days before they were due to sail. Time was running out. But Wordsworth dashed off a letter to Cottle telling him what he had done and asking him to transfer his interest in *Lyrical Ballads* to Johnson.

"It's all I can do now," he said to Samuel. "I've left our brother Richard in charge of my finances while we're away."

Now it was time to forget England, to look forward to the new exciting chapter in their lives. They left London on 14th September and two days later they sailed from Yarmouth.

# Chapter Eleven

*"I do languish to be at home" September 1798 to March 1799*

Strangely, Samuel suddenly missed his babies as they set sail and land receded from view.

"I saw their faces so distinctly," he told Wordsworth. "I miss them already."

Wordsworth scarcely seemed to hear him. Clutching his stomach, he rushed to his cabin. Dorothy stayed maybe only a moment more before she, too, disappeared below with Chester following soon after.

Samuel, however, found the motion of the ship exhilarating and loved to watch the grey waves and the frothy foam crashing up against the side of the ship.

With the others prostrate with sea sickness, Samuel quickly made new friends on board: a heavy drinking Danish man, an elderly Prussian gentleman and a Swedish nobleman, who enjoyed arguing politics with him. Samuel loved it when he overheard people talking about him as a great philosopher.

Before they sailed he had bought himself a huge, heavy overcoat for the journey, with big enough pockets to carry books and a collar that would come up right over his head. In the evenings he wrapped himself up in it and sat on the deck of the ship, watching the sea and the stars and writing everything down in his notebook.

The crossing to Cuxhaven took forty-eight hours. Wordsworth, Dorothy and Chester were ill the whole time, Dorothy the worst, vomiting and groaning and crying for the entire voyage.

As the ship left the open sea and sailed into the calmer waters of the Elbe estuary, they finally emerged onto the deck.

"I thought we'd be able to see the shore by now," Dorothy said, looking around in dismay at the vast still water.

"Hamburg is another sixty-two miles inland," Samuel told her. "The captain has agreed to take us there for half a guinea each."

Not being able to speak German or French, Chester stayed firmly with their little group. Dorothy knew enough of both but she was still feeling too ill and too uncertain of herself to speak to anyone so instead she began writing a new journal to record their experiences to look back on with Wordsworth in the future.

Wordsworth gravitated naturally to a fifty-year-old French emigré, Monsieur de Leutre. "It's so good to speak French again after nearly six years," he told Dorothy.

With the ship anchored overnight in Cuxhaven, Samuel began a letter to Sara.

"Over what place does the moon hang to your eye my dearest Sara? To me it hangs over the left bank of the Elbe; and a long trembling road of moonlight reaches from thence up to the stern of our vessel, and there it ends … Goodnight my dear, dear Sara! Every night when I go to bed and every morning when I rise I will think of you with a yearning love, and of my blessed babies."

It was 19th September when they finally set foot on German soil, arriving at Altona, the port of Hamburg. Here, Wordsworth and his new friend de Leutre went to find accommodation and Samuel rushed into town to the booksellers and merchants with his letters of introduction from the Wedgwoods.

"What a dreadful place!" Samuel said when he returned to Dorothy, Chester and de Leutre's servant who were guarding their luggage. "All huddle and ugliness, stink and stagnation!"

"William has found us a hotel," Dorothy told him. "Der Wilder Man. It's not the usual sort of place we would stay but there's nothing else available. The only problem is that there is not enough room for William. But he's looked up an old friend here, John Baldwin, who has said he can share his bed while we look for somewhere else."

The Swedish nobleman Samuel had been friendly with on board ship had recommended the Hotel de Hamburg but Samuel knew Wordsworth could not afford it and had obviously gone to a lot of trouble to find him somewhere so he said nothing.

It was market day the next day and they were woken early by the sound of the stalls being erected in the street below their window. Dorothy and Chester set off to explore the town while Samuel and

Wordsworth went to introduce themselves to Mr Chatterly, an English merchant, one of the people on the list given to him by the Wedgwoods. As they had hoped, Mr Chatterly turned out to be a useful contact; he took them to meet his German partner Victor Klopstock who was the proprietor of one of the Hamburg newspapers. Samuel recognised the surname immediately: Victor's older brother was a famous poet and dramatist. Victor spoke no English so he spoke in German to Samuel and in French to Wordsworth. He took them around the town in a fruitless search for a cheap coach to buy, so that they could travel around more easily, and introduced them to his friends.

That evening they dined with de Leutre at the French hotel, le Saxe, which they thought would be cheap but wasn't, and then went to the French theatre, which was dreadful.

The next day, after another unsuccessful search for a carriage, Victor Klopstock took Samuel and Wordsworth to meet his brother. It was a disappointing visit. The famous poet lived on the outskirts of the city in a long row of identical houses on dull flat land and Friedrich Klopstock, now seventy-four and wearing a huge frizzled wig, could hardly stand to greet them on his grossly swollen legs and had scarcely any teeth in his sunken mouth.

He became animated once they began talking though, switching easily to French, because Samuel and Wordsworth didn't know enough German, and discussing politics and literature with them.

"Such a shame to see a great man reduced to that," Samuel said on the way home.

"His mind is still as lively though," Wordsworth said.

"I can forgive him anything except that dreadful wig," said Samuel. "I can't imagine why he wears it. He should just go bare headed."

Later on Wordsworth came to Samuel. "I'm really worried about money," he told him. "We can't afford to stay here."

"We'll start looking for somewhere outside the city," Samuel said.

The next day he and Chester rode out to investigate the possibility of living in Ratzeburg, thirty-five miles out of Hamburg.

Samuel asked around for lodgings and was advised to try the local pastor, whose rectory was right on the shores of the lake.

"You'll love it there!" Samuel enthused to Wordsworth and Dorothy when they got back to Hamburg. "It's so beautiful, with a lake and woods all around we can walk in. I've found us lodgings for thirty-six marks a week."

"We can't possibly afford that!" Wordsworth gasped. "I don't know what we're going to do."

They talked late into the night. Finally, they decided the only thing to do was to split up.

"We're thinking of Lower Saxony," Wordsworth said. "Right in the countryside. It will be much cheaper to live there than so close to the city."

They stayed in Hamburg for the Feast of St Michael and then Samuel and Chester moved into their house in Ratzeburg, leaving Wordsworth and Dorothy to make their way to Lower Saxony.

Samuel and Chester soon settled into their lodgings with the pastor. Samuel fell into a rhythm of working in the mornings, going for a walk in the afternoons and going out every evening to dinners and the weekly balls and concerts that were held in the town. Ratzeburg was a wealthy town where rich merchants mixed with retired noblemen. Everyone was pro-English, *Rule Britannia* was played at concerts and at one hotel, when they found out Samuel and Chester were English, they gave them a special meal, "in honour of Nelson's victory."

Samuel soon had a wide circle of friends but he was particularly close to the pastor, who helped him learn German by letting him follow him around the house and gardens, telling him the German name for everything they saw. The pastor's children liked him too and he found that playing games with them was also a quick and easy way to learn conversational German as they patiently repeated words with him and laughed when he pronounced them wrongly.

It was nearly six weeks before Samuel heard from the Wordsworths. "I don't know what to think," he told Chester day after day. "It's not like Wordsworth not to write. It's ominous."

It was Dorothy who finally wrote, giving him their address in Goslar, a small town on the edge of the Harz mountains.

"She says Wordsworth is working hard, but not at German," Samuel told Chester. "How strange. I speak nothing else. Except to you, of course."

Without Wordsworth and Dorothy he felt so alone.

"You have all in each other," he wrote to them. "But I am lonely and want you!"

He had Chester of course but, although he was loyal and supportive and a good friend, it was nothing like the relationship he had with Wordsworth and Dorothy. But it was someone to talk to, someone to share the strangeness of the customs of a new country.

"Look at these feather beds!" Chester laughed on their first night in Germany. "One above and one below, instead of sheets and blankets!"

But despite Chester's company he felt lonely and missed Sara and the children dreadfully. "O my love! I wish you were with me!" he wrote. "O God, I do languish to be at home! Kiss my Hartley and Bercoo Baby Brodder. Kiss them for their dear father, whose heart will never be absent from them many hours together!"

As promised, Samuel wrote alternately to Poole and Sara twice a week. He also wrote a journal, cataloguing everything he did, the new places he saw, all his new experiences. He sent this off at regular intervals, intending it to be published when he returned to England.

In October, reviews of *Lyrical Ballads* began to come out. The critics were mostly impressed, if a bit bewildered by the new style, but Samuel was disappointed to find that Wordsworth's poems were praised more than his. An unsigned critic writing in the *Critical Review,* however, was particularly scathing, singling out *The Ancient Mariner.*

"Many of the stanzas are laboriously beautiful," he wrote. "But in connection they are absurd or unintelligible."

"Southey writes for the *Critical Review,*" Samuel told Chester miserably. "I can't believe he can be so hurtful to me."

On 20th October Samuel at last had a letter from home. It was from Poole.

Samuel laughed when he read it.

"He sounds just like my brother George!" he told Chester. "He used to write letters like this to me when

I was at university. Listen to this. 'What you have to do is to attend wholly to those things that are better attained in Germany than elsewhere ... Begin no poetry — no original composition — unless translation from German may be so called ... Beware of spending too much time with Chester. Live with Germans. Read in German. Think in German. Make a strict arrangement of your time and chain yourself down to it ... It would counteract a disease of your mind — which is an active subtlety of imagination ... this many of your friends falsely call irresolution. No one has more resolution and decision than you.'

"He's pleased we've separated from the Wordsworths," Samuel went on. "He thought we might start on another joint project and forget what we had come here for. But that was never my intention."

"We are going on at Stowey just as when you left us," Poole went on. "Mrs C and the children are perfectly well. Mrs C keeps up her spirits ... She will write you a long letter next."

Samuel rushed off a letter to Sara, begging for, "A very, very long letter —write me all that can cheer me — all that will make my eyes swim and my heart melt with tenderness!"

He began to get worried when by the end of November he still had not heard from her.

"I don't understand it," Samuel told Chester. "It's not like Sara not to write. Doesn't she understand how much I miss her? How much I need to hear about her and the babies?"

Chester said nothing. He hadn't had any letter from his family yet.

Samuel tried again, "How is this, my love? Why do you not write to me? Do you think to shorten my absence by making it insupportable to me? Or perhaps you anticipate that if I received a letter I should idly turn away from my German to dream of you — of you and my beloved babies! Oh, yes! I should indeed dream of you for hours and hours … and of the infant that sucks at your breast, and of my dear, dear Hartley — and with what leaping and exhilarated faculties should I return to the objects and realities of my mission. But now — nay, I cannot describe to you the gloominess of thought, the burthen and sickness of heart, which I experience every post day."

His longing for Sara inspired him to write the poem *The Day Dream, From an immigrant to his absent wife.*

"Across my chest there liv'd a weight so warm
As if some bird had taken shelter there
And lo! upon the couch a Woman's Form!
Thine, Sara! thine! O Joy, if thine it were!"

It was early December when he finally heard from her.

"Oh, no! Berkeley is ill!" Samuel burst out when he opened the letter. "Oh, my poor baby! You have no idea what it's like to be a father and to suffer like this, Chester!"

"What's the matter with him?" Chester asked.

"A smallpox vaccination that seems to have gone wrong," Samuel said, scanning the letter for details. "This letter is so damaged I can hardly make it out."

"About three weeks after you left Stowey, Mrs R Poole proposed to inoculate her child and sent round to the inhabitants," Sara wrote. Samuel read on to get to the important part. "My dear baby on the eighth day began to droop, on the ninth he was very ill and on the tenth the pustules. He lay upon my lap like a dead child, burning like fire and all over he was as red as scarlet. I was almost distracted! I had no husband to comfort me and share my grief — perhaps the boy would die and he far away!"

"But I don't understand," Samuel said. "This letter is dated 1st November. Why has it taken so long to get to me? And why did Poole say in his last letter that they were all well?" He quickly read on. "Ah, I see; he didn't want to worry me."

"The letter's in a dreadful state," Chester remarked, looking at the torn pages. "Maybe it was lost in the post."

"My poor Sara. How she has suffered. On top of everything else she says she has an eye infection."

"Will you go back to England?" Chester asked.

"I couldn't possibly think of it in the winter," Samuel said. "In any case, Sara says the babe is out of danger now. And she is almost recovered. See, there's a postscript here telling me she's reading Maria Edgeworth's book on the practical education of infants and giving me news about her sister. Everything is fine now. There's no point in my going home. I will write to her immediately."

"When I read of the danger and the agony..." he wrote. "My dear Sara! My love! My wife! God bless you and preserve us. My wife, believe and know that I pant to be home and with you."

It was a cold winter, the coldest in living memory. The frozen rivers and snow blocked roads meant that no more letters from home could get through. Homesickness and worry forced Samuel into activity. He went on several outings, including a river trip to the medieval town of Lubeck on the Baltic, with its beautiful churches, old buildings and narrow streets, and he continued to record everything he saw religiously in his journal.

"In the evening I wish myself a painter," he wrote. "Just to draw a German party at cards. One man's long pipe rested on the table, smoking half a yard from his mouth by the fish-dish; another who was shuffling, and of course had both hands employed, held his pipe in his teeth, and it hung down between his thighs, even to his ankles, and the distortions which the attitude and effort occasioned him made him most ludicrous phiz."

He loved visiting the churches: "Every picture, every legend cut out in gilded wood-work, was a history of the manners and feelings of the ages."

In December the lake froze over completely and Samuel went skating, a first-time experience for him. He was so taken by it that he wrote a letter to Wordsworth as well as to Sara, describing the tiny particles of ice that were thrown up by the skates, the shadow of the skater seen in the water where the ice was thin enough, and the melancholy keening sound of the skates on the ice.

Dorothy wrote back.

"You speak in rapture of the pleasure of skating. In the north of England amongst the mountains whither we wish to decoy you, you might enjoy it with every possible advantage. A race with William upon his native lakes would leave to the heart and imagination something more dear and valuable than the gay sight of ladies and countesses whirling along the Lake of Ratzeburg."

Samuel missed Wordsworth and Dorothy even more as Christmas approached and everyone else gathered friends and family around them. One night, unable to sleep, he sent them a few lines of poetry.

"William, my head and my heart! Dear Poet that feeblest and thickest

Dorothy, eager of soul, my most affectionate sister!

Many a mile, O! many a wearisome mile are you distant,

Long, long, comfortless roads, with no one eye that doth know us."

There was, he added, a great deal more, but he had forgotten it because he didn't write it down.

Christmas in Germany taught them such a different tradition from the English Christmas. Samuel and Chester were invited into the pastor's parlour to see the Christmas Eve tradition of bringing in the yew bough and decorating it and the children putting out the presents they had bought for their parents. Samuel was moved to tears when he saw how the pastor clasped his children tightly to him.

The next day it was the children who had presents, brought by 'The Servant Rupert', a mysterious man in a white robe and a mask who said that Jesus Christ, his maker, sent him there.

"The parents and older children receive him with great pomp of reverence," Samuel wrote, "while the little ones are most terribly frightened."

One of the things that fascinated Samuel was how the older children, even when they found out that The Servant Rupert was only a man dressed up, kept the secret from their younger brothers and sisters.

With the River Elbe still frozen, no letters had been able to get through from England but in early January Samuel at last had a letter from Poole.

"Mrs Col and the little ones are perfectly well," he wrote. "Berkeley was, as you have heard, well peppered with the smallpox, but never in any danger."

Samuel sat down to write a reply. "I've told him what I've decided to do," he told Chester. "Now that I am fluent and can read in German as easily as in English we can move down to Göttingen to go to the university there. While I am studying there I plan to work on two pieces of literary work: the first a series of letters addressed to Josiah Wedgwood, to be made up later into a book perhaps, on bauers, or peasants, in Germany. The second to be a biography of Lessing, dealing also with the true state of German literature today."

He knew Chester would go with him of course. He paid his own way and even lent Samuel money if he needed it. It was an unlikely sort of friendship, one Samuel wouldn't have sought, but there was no doubt they got on. Samuel wasn't entirely convinced that Chester was acquiring much knowledge of German agriculture — he had only learned enough German to get by — but he made sure he was included in all the social events he was invited to.

"Do you know what Wordsworth's plans are?" Chester asked.

"He told me in his last letter that he and Dorothy are touring the Harz mountains to visit Nordhausen," Samuel said. "He's still thinking about where to live when they go back to England. He wants to go back to the north but I have told him that I can't leave Stowey and he wants to be near me."

"What does Dorothy want?"

"She only ever wants what Wordsworth wants. He should never have brought her here to Germany though. No one believes she is his sister. Over here they assume she is his mistress so no one wants to socialise with her. And Wordsworth won't go out without her. Shut up together, speaking only English, they may as well be back in England as in Goslar."

On 14th January Samuel had another letter from Sara. He stood for a long time turning it over in his hand.

"It's bad news, I know it is," he said to Chester.

"Just open it, why don't you?" Chester snapped.

Dated a month earlier, it had obviously been delayed by the bad weather. Sara was still distraught. Her previous letter had been delayed, she explained, because she was in such a state over Berkeley that she hadn't put the right postage on and it had been returned to her. In the meantime, she had been having a dreadful time.

"Our dear children were charmingly recovered from the smallpox," she wrote. Samuel heaved a sigh of relief. "Berkeley had the day before taken his last powder and, in spite of his red spots and little pustules, began to look a little like himself when, on the night of 20th November, he was taken very ill, a violent suffocation and fever."

It seemed Berkeley now had a violent cough.

"His complaint is an inflammation of the lungs," Sara wrote. "I suppose his complaint will end in the whooping-cough, for half of the children in the town are dreadfully afflicted with the most grievous malady; our little ones will both have it, I fear, unless I can get them to Bristol in time to avoid it.

"I am aware that this account of the dear child will very much wound you my dear love but the instant I have a glimpse of comfort I will sit down to impart it to you. Poole has been here," she went on. "He insists on my not telling you about the child until he is quite well — I am sorry I let my feelings escape me so. I

201

should be much hurt if you were to return before you had attained the end of your going."

This was the bit Samuel wanted to hear. Yes, the baby was ill, and he was worried about him and about poor dear Sara but he didn't need to come home; she had Dr Lewis there and Mrs Poole and the ladies from Stowey to support and help her. Even John Chester's mother had rushed in to help, looking after Hartley for Sara so she could concentrate on Berkeley.

Samuel replied immediately. "Ah, little Berkeley — I have misgivings — but my duty is rather to comfort you, my dear, dear Sara! Take care of yourself — You do right in writing me the truth — Poole is kind — but you do right, my dear."

"And we're still going to Göttingen?" Chester asked when Samuel told him the latest news.

"Of course. I've told Sara in my letter. She said she wants me to do what I came here for."

Ten days later he had a letter from Poole with better news. Sara had gone up to Bristol with the children to stay with her mother. "Poole says Berkeley merely has a bad cough that has been going around the village," Samuel told Chester. "And that the change of air is doing him good. Sara is very well. He thinks she was wrong to cause me distress me about the children. He says I must let nothing trouble me and keep my mind on what I have come here to achieve. When Berkeley had the smallpox, he says, everyone rejoiced that I was not at home. You see, it will all be alright!"

On 6th February Samuel and Chester started off on their 200-mile journey from Ratzeburg to Göttingen, six days on treacherous roads, travelling in stagecoaches which jolted, lurched and creaked over the icy roads. Huddled in coats and rugs, there was little protection from the freezing wind that blew through the split panelling of the coach and they often had to stop because of snow drifts blocking the road.

Sipping from his brandy flask, Samuel made notes of everything he saw: the cosiness of the lighted lamps in the windows of the houses; the twists of sweet white bread they could buy from the stall at a village fair because it was so rare, like the gingerbread that was sold at fairs in Stowey; the poor people he saw sharing a bed of straw at an inn.

It was another bitterly cold day, 12th February, when they arrived at last in Göttingen but the weather couldn't detract from the beauty of the place, a typically German medieval walled city with ramparts and turrets, steeply roofed half-timbered houses and a fine large marketplace in the centre.

The only lodgings they could find at first were poky, dark, dirty rooms in a narrow side street.

"They'll do for now," Samuel told Chester. "Once I'm at university I can ask around for somewhere better."

The university was in a fine neo-classical building with arched windows. Samuel went in with his letters of introduction and asked for Professor Heyne. A diminutive man burst into the room, bowing several times, jumping up and down and brimming over with enthusiasm. He spoke so quickly, with a little nervous cough between each phrase, that Samuel had difficulty understanding him.

"An English man!" he enthused. "And these letters of introduction … and a life of Lessing, you say? We have plenty of books that will help you in our library here. You must borrow whatever you need. I will make a special arrangement for you."

"Something they usually only afford to the professors here," Samuel told Chester proudly later on.

Samuel signed up for lectures in theology, physiology, anatomy and natural history.

One evening he had a visit from a group of English students, some of whom had also been to Cambridge.

"Come out with us," they urged and he was soon in the full swing of university life again, like the student he had been back at Cambridge. There was a difference though. The odd party and even heavy drinking session was acceptable but he took his responsibilities seriously; he had come here to work, he had left his wife and family in order to better himself. Not only Sara and Poole, but people like the Wedgwood brothers were relying on him to prove himself. He worked hard, harder than he had ever worked before, attending all his lectures and reading as much of the German poets as he could. He spent £30, nearly a quarter of his annual allowance, on books which he planned to use to write a major work on metaphysics later in life. He longed to buy more but he just couldn't afford it.

Here at Göttingen he really felt himself to be at the heart of the intellectual life of Europe, honoured to be in the company of so many distinguished professors, renowned not only in Germany but throughout Europe. This is what he wanted: not to be just a provincial Englishman but to be part of a group of world-renowned European scholars.

He went out in the evenings with the German professors he admired so much, thrilled to be included in their company, and made friends with both the German and English students.

As he had hoped, he found better accommodation in rooms owned by one of the professors in the centre of the student quarter and close to the university library.

His only worry was that, while the weather was so bad, he had still received no letters from England. He was worried about Sara and the children. In March he wrote to Sara, "Why need I say how anxious this long interval of silence has made me? I have thought and thought of you and pictured you and the little ones so often and so often, that my imagination is tired, down, flat and powerless; and I languish after home for hours together in vacancy; my feelings almost wholly unqualified by thoughts…"

He sealed the letter and posted it, even though he knew it would wait many more weeks yet until the River Elbe thawed and letters could get through.

# Chapter Twelve

At first nothing changed for Sara when Samuel sailed to Germany. He had been away for months already; the fact that he was now in another country made little difference. Life was hard in the cottage. There were only her and Nanny to do all the chores and Nanny had such a dreadful cough she wasn't as much help as she could be. It was an unusually mild autumn but it wouldn't be long before those golden days would turn to frosty mornings and dark, damp evenings. There were apples to be picked, winter vegetables to dig out of the cold, hard ground. Soon the road outside the cottage would be muddy and the open gutter choked with autumn leaves and rain. Before long they would wake to find the water in the well frozen.

The steady mundane routine of looking after a small boy and a baby kept her going from morning to night. Poole kept to his word and came to see her regularly, bringing produce from his own garden with him. People in the village learned she was on her own. She made new friends; John Chester's mother and sisters began visiting her, the bond of having their menfolk living together miles from home bringing them closer. She still saw the Cruikshanks and the Roskillys regularly and through them she had met the Misses Brice, whose father was a vicar.

It was hard to imagine Samuel living so far away. She had seen so little of him before he went that sometimes she imagined he was only living in Bristol or Surrey or London, somewhere he could come home from at any time.

She cried when she read Samuel's letters. They were so tender and loving, a reminder of the man she had known when they first married. And he missed her so much and missed the children. A small voice inside her still asked why he didn't spend more time with her when he *was* at home but she reminded herself that this was his work, the separation no worse than if he was in the army or the navy and away for months at a time. She felt a smug little glow of satisfaction when she heard he had separated from the Wordsworths. Maybe the separation would be permanent. Maybe they had lost their hold on him and he would be come back to her and her alone.

She was proud of Samuel for pursuing his dreams; he was thinking of the future for her and the children. She knew he was brilliant; she had always known it from that very first moment she had met him. One day he would be a great man. This present separation would mean nothing then. So although she was pleased when people asked how she was coping on her own, the last thing she wanted was to be thought of as the poor little wife left alone. She wanted everyone to know she was behind Samuel in everything he did.

When she had read Samuel's letters she had to pass them on to Poole's apprentice, Tommy Ward, to be copied out with strict instructions from Samuel to leave out the more intimate parts. He had told them that both the letters to her and to Poole would contain descriptions of his life over there, which, in addition to the journal he was keeping, would be made into a book when he returned. Ward was thrilled to be entrusted with such a responsible task. He had always been willing to do anything for Samuel. When he was away in London or Bristol Samuel was always writing to Poole to ask Ward to look for a certain book and put it on the Exeter coach for him or send off a parcel.

Knowing the letters were intended to be read by other people made it easier to bear the lively descriptions of what a good time he was having: the twenty different kinds of soups he had tried, the beer and wine-drinking sessions, the styles of carriages in the streets, the unusual brass doorbells, the churches and museums, the long hours he spent in the company of people she would never know. As she read all this she comforted herself with the heartfelt protestations of tender love he wrote intended just for her. She and Samuel had a sacred bond, one she knew he held dear. Whatever happened they were bound together by love and by their children.

"Smallpox is going around in the village," Mrs Poole told her one day. "My daughter-in-law is advising all the mothers in the village to have their children vaccinated. You should ask Dr Lewis to do Hartley and Berkeley as soon as possible."

"But it's so warm," Sara said. "I've read that it can be dangerous to vaccinate in the warm weather."

Everyone was having it done though and, after a few weeks, Sara felt she had no choice.

Hartley was ill first.

"He doesn't seem to have taken the vaccination," Dr Lewis said. "I'll have to try again."

He injected him again and again until Hartley's arm swelled up in a great head. Then, miraculously, he was well again.

Eight days after the vaccination, however, Berkeley began to look poorly. On the ninth day he was pale and listless and she couldn't get him to feed.

The next morning when she went to him she found him covered in huge pustules. She knew Nanny was up: she could hear her coughing downstairs. "Nanny, Nanny!" she cried. "Send for Dr Lewis!"

Nanny took one look at the baby, turned and flew out of the door.

Sara could feel the heat from Berkeley's body as she lifted him up. He made no sound, he didn't move, just lay in her arms as though he were dead.

She saw the fear in Dr Lewis's face when he saw him. The pustules were clogging his nose; the baby could hardly breathe. He gave him laudanum.

"Keep him cool," he advised. "Try to get him to feed. I'll come back soon."

Sara's life turned into a living nightmare. It was heart-rending to see her child like this. His eyelids were so covered in pustules that he couldn't open them, his mouth full of them so he couldn't cry, only make the most dreadful noise in his throat, a sound that broke through the odd few minutes of sleep that Sara managed to snatch.

Dr Lewis came every couple of hours. Poole and his mother rushed around to see her the moment they heard.

"I will write to Samuel as soon as I can," Sara said.

"No," Poole said quickly.

"What?"

"You know how any upset stops him working. He will only worry. There's nothing he can do so far away. Leave it for the time being. You have too much to do. I'll write to him and say everything's fine. By the time he gets the letter, the baby will be better."

"Are you sure?" Sara asked. She was so tired, so distraught, she couldn't think straight. Poole was right: the slightest upset caused Samuel such strain and brought on his neuralgia. And what could he do? Even if he set off for home it would take weeks to get here and Berkeley could be better in a few days and all the effort and money to go to Germany would be wasted.

People in the village soon heard that Berkeley was ill. They knew Samuel was away so they rallied around. Anna Cruikshank came over, Mrs Roskilly and Mrs Chester, other women that she had hardly spoken to before, all offering help, bringing food, taking Hartley away for a few hours to play with their children. They cried when they saw the baby, comforted Sara when she cried. But it was Samuel that Sara needed, the father of her child, the one person who would understand and share her suffering. She couldn't help thinking how awful it would be if the baby died while Samuel was away. All the responsibility for the baby's life rested on her.

One night they reached a crisis point: the itching from the pustules was so bad that she and Nanny had to sit either side of the cradle holding Berkeley's hands to stop him thrashing about and banging his head.

"I can only give him more laudanum," Dr Lewis said.

The next morning Berkeley seemed a little better but he was fretful and only at peace when suckling at

Sara's breast. Soon, however, she found pustules on her nipples, which swelled so large that she couldn't bear anything to touch them, let alone have Berkeley suck at them.

"We can try getting him to drink cow's milk through a tube," Dr Lewis said. "And I'll ask around the village. There may be someone who would suckle him for you."

James Coles' wife arrived soon after. "I'll do it for you during the day," she offered.

Sara was so grateful. Not many women would want to suckle a child as ill, as horribly disfigured, as fretful as Berkeley was.

At night she tried to get him to take the cow's milk but he turned his head away from the cold hard tube. Sara's own milk had to be expressed, an excruciating process with her tender breasts and swollen nipples.

She had never felt so bad. Everything was disorder and chaos. She couldn't ask Nanny to help at night because her coughing disturbed Berkeley just as he fell asleep. He whimpered when she put him down in his cradle so she ended up sitting for hours with him in her arms or on her lap, getting cold and stiff and numb. The chimney in the parlour smoked so badly that she often nursed Berkeley upstairs in the bedroom, swathed in shawls and blankets because there was no fire in there. Sometimes she was so tired during the day that she lay down on the hard parlour floor by the fire with Berkeley in her arms.

One day, just when she felt at her lowest ebb, Sara felt a sudden stabbing pain in her eye. Within a few hours it had closed up completely, her face and neck swelled up and her head was swimming.

"You've caught a violent cold in the head," Dr Lewis said as he bandaged up her eye. "You must try and get more rest."

How could she rest? She was in a constant state of torment. And yet, gradually, gradually, Berkeley began to improve. The pustules healed everywhere except on his head where they were clogged with his hair. "We may need to cut it all off ," Dr Lewis warned. "But otherwise I think we can say he is out of danger."

Sara heaved a huge sigh of relief. Her little baby, who had been so beautiful, was left horribly scarred and disfigured, but he was alive and that was all that mattered.

At last, with the danger past, she could sit down and write to Samuel. What a relief it was to pour out her catalogue of woe.

"Don't make him think he has to come home," Poole had warned her. He was right of course, there certainly wasn't anything Samuel could do if he came home now, but knowing his child had been in such danger, hearing how much she needed him, she still hoped he might.

Things gradually improved. Sara's eye was still bad but the pustules on her nipples healed, her milk came back and she could feed Berkeley again. He was easier, more comfortable and more like his old self. Something like a normal routine returned and for the first time in ages she could sleep at night.

One night she had a dream. She thought she heard Samuel calling her. He sounded in distress, shouting like he did when he had nightmares. She groped the empty bed next to her. "Samuel, Samuel, I'm here," she said. The bunched-up bedclothes in her hand turned into a great grey seabird that croaked distressingly and flew around the room with great flapping wings. She woke up in a hot sweat. She could still hear the bird. Then she realised the sound came from the cradle at the foot of the bed. It was Berkeley. He was ill. She fumbled to light a taper, leant over the cot. He was red hot, that great rasping sound she could hear was him struggling for breath. As soon as it was light Nanny went for Dr Lewis again.

"I'll need to give him an emetic to clear the poisons," he told Sara.

She watched helplessly as her poor baby vomited, choked and coughed; he seemed on the point of suffocation. She sat up with him all that night and the next, unable to do anything to ease his wheezing.

"Half the children in the village have whooping cough," Mrs Poole said.

"Dr Lewis says it's just an inflammation of the lungs. But if we stay here he and Hartley might catch the whooping cough. It might be better if I took the children up to Bristol."

But Berkeley was far too ill for her to think of travelling.

"I'll have to give him a blister," Dr Lewis said the next time he came, "to bring down the fever."

"No, no!" Sara protested. "He's suffering enough already."

Dr Lewis left but five minutes later he was back. "I've been to see Mrs Poole," he said. "She advises you to do what I suggest. She says she will pray for you all."

What could she do? She watched helplessly as he spread the irritating paste onto Berkeley's chest.

"This will need to stay on for a few hours," he said. "It will irritate him but when the blister has formed I will be able to drain the poisons out and his fever will come down."

Half an hour later Berkeley was writhing in agony from the itching and instead of getting better he became worse and worse, the hacking cough distressing as he struggled to breathe. For the second time Sara was convinced he would die. A few days later, however, despite the cough, he seemed a bit brighter. He opened his eyes and looked around and seemed to breathe more easily. Small signs, but enough to give her some hope.

Hartley was touchingly solicitous about his little brother, peering worriedly into his cradle when he coughed, doing his best to stay quiet when he slept. It was hard though: he was only two and he would forget. Sara and Nanny told him, "Shh!" so often that when he heard other children playing in the road outside he would crane his neck and call out, "Boys, you must not make such a noise to wake my little brother Bercoo — I horse-whip ye, naughty boys!"

As soon as she had a moment Sara sat down to write to Samuel.

"Don't tell him anything," Poole said again. "Not until Berkeley is better. There really is no point. It will only worry him and take his mind off his work."

But this time she took no notice. Her first letter to Samuel hadn't arrived. He had written to her berating her for not writing. It was only fair he should know the reason.

Once she started writing she couldn't stop. Every detail, her own suffering and Berkeley's, flew from her pen to the paper. She cried as she wrote, wiping her wet face and sniffing. It was cathartic to pour out her feelings to the one person who would truly understand. As she neared the end of the letter she had a sudden vision of Samuel's reaction to it. This second crisis would make him realise he must come home, that he must spend every moment of his life with his family who meant everything to him, more than his work, more than his friends, old and new. Yes, it would take weeks to get here, yes, God willing, Berkeley would be better, but she would have him back, that's all that mattered. Then she pictured Poole's reaction, Wordsworth's, Dorothy's, the Wedgwood brothers'. They would despise her, say she forced him to come home. Samuel himself would resent her for standing in the way of his ambitions. She picked up the pen again.

"I am sorry I let my feeling escape me so," she wrote. "Be assured, my darling, I am as comfortable as my situation (with respect to my child) will admit and that I am truly glad that you are not here to witness his sufferings as you could not possibly do more for the boy than has been already done for him. I should be much hurt if you were to return before you had attained the end of your going."

Another thought occurred to her and she went on, "I am very proud to hear that you are so forward in the language — and that you are so gay among the ladies: you may give my respects to them and say that I am not at all jealous, for I know my dear Samuel in her affliction will not forget entirely his most affectionate wife."

She had her pride. No one, not even Samuel, could ever say she had made him feel guilty about having a good time while he was away.

The letter safely posted and Berkeley slightly better, Sara decided to go up to Bristol. Her mother and Edith both thought it was a good idea; a change of air was what he needed, they both said, away from the cold, damp cottage and the whooping cough germs going around Stowey. And she needed to be with her family. She felt so alone, worn out and wretched after these long weeks of illness and worry. It was the end of December, not the best time to travel, but if she left it any later the roads would be worse.

They went up in a chaise. Sara wrapped Berkeley up in flannel and kept him tight against her breast the whole time. His cough seemed to have subsided and he travelled quite well, given the state of the rutted bumpy roads. Nanny's cough, on the contrary, was no better and she wheezed and hacked the whole time.

"My mother shares rooms with Mrs Lovell, the mother-in-law of my sister Mary," Sara told her.

Nanny looked around excitedly as they entered the city with its busy crowded streets lined with shops.

The baby stirred in Sara's arms and opened his eyes. "See, Berkeley, we're nearly there," Sara said. The familiar city streets opened out around her. Lamps were being lit and Berkeley gazed at them in awe, struggling to get out of her arms to get a better look.

"Nearly there," Hartley repeated sleepily. "Grandmama…"

The chaise drew up outside one of the houses in Newfoundland Street. The door opened and Mrs Lovell hurried out.

"Let me take the babe," she said to Sara, "while you bring Hartley."

As they entered the lighted house Mrs Lovell looked down at Berkeley. "Why, he's scarcely marked at all," she said. "What a beautiful child. I can hardly believe he's been so ill."

Sara's spirits rose. Mrs Lovell was an experienced mother; Berkeley obviously wasn't as ill as she thought. He would soon get better here in the city, away from the germs and squalor of the village. She looked around her approvingly; this was the sort of house she was used to, the sort of house she had lived in all her life until she met Samuel. The rooms were large with high ceilings. Outside the window she could hear the noises of the city streets. She felt like she had come home. That night she slept better than she had for a long time and the next day she woke to find Berkeley no worse for his long journey in the cold.

Sara missed Poole and Mrs Poole, who had come in every day to see her, but here she was never alone. Her sisters Mary and Eliza, her mother and Mrs Lovell all took it in turns to sit with her and Berkeley and to begin with she was sure he was getting better.

A week later, however, she woke to hear him coughing again and struggling for breath. When she picked him up and held him to her breast she could feel he was red hot again and he wouldn't feed. Frightened, she sent for her mother's physician, Dr Morris.

"He doesn't seem too bad," he said when he looked at Berkeley. "There's no need to be alarmed. As soon as the warmer weather comes his throat and chest will improve. I will send over some syrup for him."

He came every other day but Berkeley's condition went on deteriorating. He was feverish again, drenched in sweat when she went to him at night. She couldn't get him to feed and she could see he was losing weight. He showed no interest in anything around him and scarcely moved his arms and legs.

"I think it's his throat rather than his chest," Dr Morris said. "I will need to apply a blister to it."

"Oh, I don't know," Sara said. "It was so bad last time he had a blister."

"It's the only thing I can suggest," Dr Morris said.

For the second time she watched Berkeley endure the agony of the irritant paste. A blister formed and was drained but by then he was so ill it was clear it wasn't going to work.

At the end of January Dr Morris told her, gravely, "You must prepare yourself for the worst."

Sara had been writing regularly to Poole, who had very clear views about what she should do.

"He says if Berkeley dies I must not tell Samuel until he comes home," she told her mother. "It doesn't seem right."

"He isn't a parent," her mother said. "Of course you must tell Samuel. It's your duty. And his right to know, however bad it is."

"But I don't want to be the one who stops his work. That's important too. And he may blame me."

In the end she did what Poole wanted. "He says Samuel should have finished his work by the middle of March. Until then he should be shielded from anything that might upset him so that he can concentrate. Then Poole will write first to prepare him for bad news."

The baby lingered on for two more long dreadful weeks. Sara never left him. Someone always sat with her: her youngest sister Eliza, her mother, Mrs Lovell. Usually not Nanny because her cough disturbed him.

Sunday 10th February: a date she knew she would never forget. It was the early hours of the morning. Sara and Eliza were sitting by the cot. Suddenly she saw the cot shudder as baby began to shake convulsively. Sara leapt up. "Mrs Lovell! Nanny!" Sara yelled. "Come quickly!"

The fit was violent and quick, soon over, and Berkeley was dead. Sara let out a huge wail of agony. "My baby! My son! My Berkeley! No! No! I can't bear it!"

Her mother held her while she wept, huge great sobs that wracked her body. "Samuel, Samuel!" she cried inwardly. "Samuel, I need you. Why aren't you here with me to help me?"

Hartley was too young to understand what had happened. He knew his baby brother was ill, he knew he was no longer there and everyone was upset, but he didn't realise the baby would never come back. Sara could see how upset he was at seeing her so unhappy.

Southey came as soon as he could. "Leave everything to me," he said. "I will deal with the interment. Then you must come to Westbury with me and Edith. You can't stay here."

"Thank you," said Sara, grateful for a man at last to take over. "I can't bear to be in this house without him here."

"Of course, of course," Southey said quickly.

"I can't bring Nanny," Sara said. "The doctor says her cough is consumption. He wants her to go back home."

"It's no problem. Edith and I will take care of everything."

Edith and Southey were renting a house in Westbury that they nicknamed Martin Hall after the house martins that nested in the eaves. They couldn't have been kinder to her, leaving her alone when she wanted, sitting with her if she needed someone to talk to, holding her when she wanted to cry.

"The doctors say he died of consumption," Southey told her gently.

It made no difference to Sara what he died from. He was gone, that was all that mattered. She veered wildly between trying to put a brave face on things for everyone else's sake and violent outbursts of grief. When she combed her hair at night great long strands fell out in her hands and after a few weeks she was left with only a few long straggly bits. "I shall have to cut it short," she told Edith sadly, "and wear a wig. I hope it grows back by the time Samuel comes home." She had always been proud of her thick brown hair and knew how much he loved it.

After a few weeks she felt well enough to go back to Bristol. Her mother had knocked a barrel over on her foot and couldn't move from her chair. With her to look after and no one to help look after Hartley, Sara was rushed off her feet. In some ways she welcomed the constant work; it took her mind off the pain in her heart.

Poole had hoped to come up and see her in Bristol but in the end he couldn't get away. He wrote to her regularly though and was the only person outside her family that she felt she could confide in. "I am almost ashamed always to write to you in strains of complaint," she wrote. "But I expect you to pity and forgive me."

It was the middle of March when a parcel of letters arrived from Poole; Samuel's letters from Germany had arrived. Sara's heart sank when she read he was going to Göttingen. She had hoped he might be coming home soon. But this letter was dated 14th January. He would be there by now, enrolled in the university. He would never be home before May. Of course he knew nothing about the tragedy but it was hard to read his long accounts of heavy drinking sessions.

"I am weary of this long absence," Sara wrote to Poole, "and shocked at the description of jovial parties. Their manner and their mirth must be excessively disgusting. I wonder how Chester likes them?"

She found some comfort in his words of love and broke down in sobs when she read, "Ah, little Berkeley — I have misgivings … You do right in writing me the truth." Now he needed to know what had happened. She longed to write herself but she had promised Poole that he would write first. He sent the letter by messenger to her to read and send on to Germany. Her eyes scanned over the first few lines. She read them, read them again. By the time she had finished it she was shaking with rage and indignation, tears of anger and frustration pouring down her face.

"Mrs C is very well…" she repeated under her breath. "She was much fatigued during the child's illness but her health was very good and she very wisely kept up her spirits ... She felt as a mother but she never forgot herself. She is now perfectly well and does not make herself miserable by recalling the engaging, though remember, mere instinctive, attractions of an infant a few months old ... I have myself within the last month experienced disappointments more mighty than the death of ten infants..."

She sat with the letter in her hand a long time. She admired Poole, he was her confidant and support. But how could anyone speak of the loss of a child in such a callous way? "When the infant becomes a reasonable being, then let the affection be a thing of reason, not before. Brutes can only have an instinctive affection." To call her beloved beautiful Berkeley a mere brute, an animal not a person. And to give Samuel the idea she was perfectly well, that she hadn't grieved, wouldn't go on grieving for the rest of her life. "Don't conjure up any scenes of distress that never happened," Poole wrote. All this to save Samuel's feelings, to protect him from knowing the truth. It wasn't fair. It wasn't right. She *had* to post the letter on. She had made a promise. But she would write herself, she would put the record straight for the sake of herself and Berkeley.

"My dearest love," she wrote. "I hope you will not attribute my long silence to want of affection; if you have received Mr Poole's letter you will know the reason and acquit me. My darling infant left his wretched mother on the tenth of February and tho' the leisure that followed was intolerable to me, yet I could not employ myself in reading or writing or in any way that prevented my thoughts from resting on him — this parting was the severest trial that I have ever yet undergone and I pray to God that I may never live to behold the death of another child for O my dear Samuel! It is a suffering beyond your conception! You will feel, and lament, the death of your child but you will only recollect him a baby of fourteen weeks, but I am his mother and have carried him in my arms, and have fed him at my bosom, and have watched over him by day and by night for nine months; I have seen him twice at the brink of the grave but he has returned, and recovered and smiled upon me like an angel — and now I am lamenting that he is gone!"

On and on she wrote, every tiny detail, from when she left Stowey, to Berkeley's gradual decline, to the last moments of his life. Samuel must have the truth, however unpalatable.

"I cannot express how ardently I long for your return, or how much I shall be disappointed if I do not see you in May. I am much pleased that you 'languish to be at home'. I hope you never more will quit it."

# Chapter Thirteen

---

*"My poor Muse is quite gone — perhaps, she may return and meet me at Stowey"* *April 1799 to July 1799*

---

Samuel read Poole's letter through again. He looked at the date. Poole had written on 15th March and even then Berkeley had been dead a month. It was now 4th April. Nearly two months and he hadn't known. *"Berkeley dead."* Even thinking the words made no sense. How was he going to say them out loud? To Chester? To his friends? *"Berkeley dead."* His little baby. He had dreaded it yet somehow he knew it would happen. It was his fault for going away and leaving them. If he had stayed they would have come to no harm.

He wished he could cry but no tears came. He felt numb.

"I'm going for a walk," he told Chester, who was hanging around him concernedly, at a loss as to how to react to the news.

In England the snowdrops would have come and gone, yellow and purple crocuses would have pushed through the cold earth, daffodils would be coming into bloom. Here, a cold spring had followed on from the glacial winter, a blanket of snow still lay on the ground and the air he breathed in was like ice cutting into his lungs. He walked for miles under the iron grey sky, across the flat dreary fields, down to the river where he stopped on the bridge and threw stones into the river like he did when he was a boy. He thought about life, about death, about the metaphysics of it all.

"My baby has not lived in vain," he wrote to Poole when he got back. "Nothing is hopeless. What if the vital force which I sent from my arm into the stone as I flung it into the air and skimmed it upon the water — what if even that did not perish! It was life! It was a particle of being — it was power — and how could it perish." He included one of Wordsworth's Lucy poems:

"A slumber did my spirit steal
I had no human fears
She seemed a thing that could not feel
The touch of earthly years
No motion has she now, no force;
She neither hears nor sees;
Rolled around in earth's diurnal course,
With rocks, and stones, and trees."

Chester came in while he was writing. "We'll be going home soon now, won't we?" he asked.

"Oh, no, no," Samuel said. "Not for at least six weeks, maybe eight. I have far too much to do. My professors are expecting me at lectures. I still have to find material for my book on Lessing. I'm at a critical stage in it."

In the evenings he went for long walks on the medieval ramparts of Göttingen, listening to the nightingales in the oak trees that lined the walk. It was still bitingly cold, the new buds on the trees covered in a frosting of snow like icing on a cake. The poor birds forced to sing in the snow reminded Samuel of the spring of last year when he walked with Wordsworth and Dorothy in the new spring green of the Quantocks. The poem he had written then, *The Nightingale,* brought Hartley so sharply to his mind that he suddenly thought how awful it would be if he too were to die before he returned home. "It's my fault, *my fault,*" he muttered to himself as he walked along. "If I had been there, Berkeley wouldn't have died."

"My dear Poole," he wrote when he got back. "Don't let Hartley die before I come home. That's silly — true — and I burst into tears as I wrote it."

Poole was the only one who really understood him. "Of many friends, whom I love and esteem," he wrote to him. "My head and my heart have chosen you as the friend — as the one being, in whom is involved the full and whole meaning of that sacred title."

Writing to Sara seemed far more difficult. "It is one of the discomforts of my absence, my dearest love!" he wrote. "That we feel the same calamities at different times." He wondered if the baby's death might bring them closer. "To have shared —nay, I should say — to have divided with any human being any one deep sensation of joy or of sorrow, sinks deep into the foundations of a lasting love." He knew he was partly to blame for their past arguments. "When in moments

226

of fretfulness and imbecility I am disposed to anger or reproach," he went on. "It will, I trust, be always a restoring thought — We have wept over the same little one — and with whom am I angry? With her who so patiently and unweariedly sustained my poor and sickly infant through his long pains."

He added that he still had so much work to do that he couldn't possibly be back for at least another ten or eleven weeks.

Sara was devastated when she read his letter. "Another ten or eleven weeks!" She sighed to herself, "Poole said six or eight. And before that the middle of March…"

There was no one she could talk to about it. She couldn't tell someone like Anna Cruikshank, it was disloyal to Samuel and to her marriage and Anna might tell someone else; gossip was rife in a small village like Stowey. Poole, her usual confidant, always took Samuel's side, unless it was something to do with the Wordsworths when he was firmly on hers. Her mother would say, "I told you so." She had liked Samuel at first. She had fallen under his spell like everyone else did, but she would still have preferred Sara to marry someone with money. And now, although Samuel continued to help her financially, she was growing more and more disillusioned with him.

Southey was someone Sara could have confided in. She had known him a long time and he had been so good to her when Berkeley died. She didn't know what she would have done without him. He had looked after her with so much care, seen her when she was at such a low ebb. And those two weeks living with them in Westbury she had seen the way he was with Edith, always making sure she had everything she wanted, caring about her happiness. He had married Edith in secret against his family's wishes. Oh, she knew they weren't always the perfect couple. They, too, had their problems. Both of them suffered from their nerves, Southey controlled his through his strict self-control and by hard work but Edith had always struggled: she had difficulty sleeping at night, she wouldn't, or couldn't eat, she worried about the least thing.

But Southey took his responsibilities as a husband seriously, facing up to difficulties and dealing with them on Edith's behalf, whereas everyone, especially Poole, seemed to think that Samuel should be shielded from the harsh realities of life like a child, leaving Sara to deal with them on her own. She was losing respect for Samuel; she could feel it happening. If only she had a husband like Southey. At one time she thought they might have made a match: he had been interested enough in her to write to her when he was at Oxford. But it would never have worked out: the shy modest Edith was much more Southey's type. He was a reserved sort of man, slightly prim. Sara was too outspoken, too quick-tempered and passionate for him. She needed a passionate man like Samuel, although sometimes she wondered if they were suited after all. The very qualities that had attracted Samuel to her — her independence, her forthrightness, her spirit — now seemed to repel him. Maybe he, too, would have been better with someone like Edith who didn't stand up for herself and did what she was told without question. Or, more likely, someone like Dorothy who spent hours transcribing his poetry and would have slavishly followed Wordsworth to the ends of the earth.

Edith was the only other person Sara could have talked to. They had always been close. But Edith would only tell Southey and it would be one more weapon in his campaign against Samuel.

Although they had tried to patch up their original quarrel over Pantisocracy, their disagreements had resurfaced over Charles Lloyd's *Edmund Oliver* book and Samuel's satirising of Lloyd's and Lamb's poems.

Quite apart from wanting Samuel home anyway, Sara was worried about money. She had already had to borrow two lots of money from Poole as the money Samuel had left her had run out.

She didn't know how she would stand it. The cottage, where Berkeley had suffered so dreadfully, was hateful to her now, every room a reminder of an empty cradle, a life cut short so cruelly and painfully. She would prefer to stay somewhere near Edith and Southey, who had been so supportive to her, but frankly she didn't care where they went as long as they could move from this horrible cottage. It seemed so unfair that she was so unhappy while Samuel was having such a good time. He was lucky to have his work to channel his energies into and his friends to help him take his mind off things. Oh, she had people who were kind to her, good friends like Poole and his mother, the Cruikshanks, the Chesters and the Roskillys but her social life couldn't compare with Samuel's and she found herself resenting each lengthy description of his evening drinking sessions and parties.

It was Samuel's solace: his work and the company of his friends. It was the only way he could deal with things, blocking them out by immersing himself in activity. He was four or five years older than his fellow students and enjoyed the way they looked up to him. Now he had been at the university a while he had gathered a small group of English students around him — Clement Carlyon, George Greenough and Charles Parry — and after they had been out for the evening they would sit and talk late into the night on subjects as diverse as geology, religion, linguistics, witchcraft, metaphysics and agriculture. Samuel didn't know how he would have coped without them to take his mind off things at home.

It was the middle of April, two weeks after he had received Poole's letter, that Samuel received a letter from Sara dated Easter Sunday, 24th March. By then Berkeley had been dead five weeks. He still found it hard to believe. But, as he read on, it began to sink in. Sara's words, torn from her heart, the vivid descriptions of Berkeley's suffering. Suddenly it was all too real and the tears, dammed up for so long, began to flow. His chest ached, the pain so bad, so overwhelming, he didn't know how he could bear it. After he had finished reading it, he sat for a long time wiping his eyes, sniffing, dabbing at his face, the letter still in his hand.

When he finally got up to move he was stiff. He felt a twinge of pain in his left knee. A dose of laudanum, that would help, a generous dose to ease the pain in his knee and the pain in his heart and mind...

He slept better that night than he had done for a long time and although he woke up with the same feeling of dread that something awful had happened, he nonetheless felt ready to throw himself into his work again. When he came home from university that day he was told he had visitors: a man and a woman, the servant said. Samuel hurried to the door, half-hoping, not daring to believe and there they were.

"Wordsworth! Dorothy!" He held out his hand but they both rushed to envelop him in the German hug that everyone here used but Samuel had always thought effeminate.

There was so much to talk about but Samuel knew that first he must tell them about Berkeley. He expected Dorothy to cry but he was touched when Wordsworth too broke down in tears.

"You will come back with us of course," Dorothy said. "Now. We're going now."

"It hasn't been a success for us, this trip," Wordsworth said sadly. "We just haven't had the money. We can't afford to socialise like you do but in any case the weather has been so bad, so bitterly cold you can't imagine, that we haven't been able to get out at all. I've learned nothing of the language. So we decided to make the best of it and at least see some of the countryside before we return. We've been walking in the Harz mountains."

"I hear they're very beautiful," Samuel said. "I was hoping to see them before I go back. But I'm not sure that I'll get the chance."

"Surely you'll come back now?" Dorothy said again.

"Please don't try to persuade me," Samuel said. "It's hard enough for me as it is. I long to go home. It's all I think about. But if I go now it will be a waste of time and money having come at all. I'm working as fast as I can, reading and transcribing from eight to ten hours a day. But it is impossible for me to collect the material I need in less than six weeks from today. I've written to Sara and explained."

"You enjoyed the poems I sent you?" William asked.

"They're wonderful," Samuel said. "You've written so much. It's not been a complete waste of time for you."

"And I've been writing a journal of everywhere we go, everything we do."

"Me too," said Samuel. "But I've written no poetry. I've tried. I start a poem but I can't finish it. My muse has left me. Maybe she will meet me when I get back to Stowey."

Dorothy and Wordsworth exchanged a glance. "We were hoping you'd like to come up to the north with us. We've decided to move back to Cumbria."

Samuel shook his head. "No, no. Sara would hate it. I can't possibly take her somewhere she wouldn't know anyone. Especially now."

"She'd know us," said Dorothy. "And she'd make friends. Oh, *please* Samuel. We *need* you."

"There's the expense," Samuel said. "It's a long way to go. And there's Poole. I couldn't bear to be parted from Poole. He's the man who first gave me an anchor."

When he thought of Poole he saw himself flying into his arms and hugging him like Wordsworth had hugged him earlier.

To Samuel's amazement, Wordsworth's eyes filled with tears again. "*I* can't bear not to be near *you*. You'd love it in the north, I know you would. We could go skating on the lake in the winter like you did in Ratzeburg. I would race you! And there's a library nearby, Sir Frederic Vane's, for all your research."

"No, that's no good to me. It's old books I need chiefly and they're not the sort I'd find in a gentleman's modern collection."

"Oh, please, at least think about it," Wordsworth begged.

"My mind is made up," Samuel said determinedly. "I've asked Poole to find us a house in Stowey. We can't stay in that cottage after what has happened. Why don't we find out if we can get Alfoxton again for you?"

Wordsworth shook his head. "Dorothy and I are decided on Cumbria. It's our home. It's where we belong."

"But you'll be so isolated from everything, From London, from society and politics."

"I will have nature all around me, the library that I need nearby, I can write undisturbed…"

And so they argued on, all the next day, until it was time for the Wordsworths to move on to catch the coach to Hamburg. Samuel walked five miles along the road with them and then they parted.

After they had gone Samuel thought back to their descriptions of the Harz mountains. Wordsworth and Dorothy had gone in the winter, when snow and ice were on the roads, but now it was May, the weather warm and balmy. Springtime was supposed to be one of the best times to visit. He had heard the legends about witches and devils and the Brocken spectre on the mountain, a strange phenomenon caused by one's own shadow on the misty mountainside.

It wasn't hard to find friends willing to come with him: Chester, of course, Carlyon, Parry, Greenough and the son of one of his German professors, Professor Blumenbach.

"My dear Sara," he wrote in haste on the back of a letter to Poole, "on Saturday next I go to the famous Harz mountains, about twenty English miles from Göttingen, to see the mines and other curiosities. On my return I will write you all that is writable. God bless you, my dear, dear, dear love! With regard to money, my love! Poole can write to Mr Wedgwood, if it is not convenient for him to let you have it."

Sara broke down in tears when she read the letter: what had she done to be treated like this? She felt neglected, deserted, uncared-for. All those protestations of love, the beautiful poems he wrote her, they were just empty words. He didn't love her, he couldn't possibly love her, he would never treat her like this if he did.

And she was so worried about money. She had already had to borrow ten guineas from Poole, she hated having to ask for more, from him or from the Wedgwoods, especially when Samuel seemed to have limitless funds to spend on drinking, parties and holidays in the Harz mountains. It was now the middle of May. "I hope you will soon be here," she wrote. "For oh! I am so tired of this cruel absence. My dear, dear Samuel do not lose a moment of time in finishing your work — for I feel like a poor deserted thing — interesting to no one. You must not stay a minute by the way, but fly from Yarmouth and be with me at

quarter-day! Pray write a few lines from Yarmouth...
My dear husband, God almighty bless you and see you
safe home to your affectionate — Sara Coleridge."

Samuel's trip to the mountains had been and gone
by the time Sara's letter arrived. He was away for a
week, a real holiday that made him forget all about his
troubles at home. As they walked he recited *Christabel*
to his companions.

"Oh, you must finish it!" they told him
enthusiastically.

"Yes, you're right. But it's not as easy as that..."
Samuel said.

It was a tough walk. Samuel's feet ached dreadfully,
especially his toes. Climbing the Brocken they often
had to stop to rest and get their breath. It was a clear
day, so no chance of seeing the Brocken spectre. When
they reached the top, breathless and exhausted, they
stood looking at the scene below them.

"How would you describe sublime?" Carlyon
asked.

Of course everyone had a different idea of it but no
one could come up with a satisfactory answer.

"What do you think, Samuel?" someone asked
finally, noticing he had said nothing.

"It is a suspension of the powers of comparison,"
Samuel said.

They had a map and a compass but much of the
time they followed the well-worn paths made by
animals and drovers, stopping off to visit any pretty
village they came to: Rübeland, Blankenburg,
Wernigerode and Goslar, where Wordsworth had
stayed with Dorothy. Here the mountains were no
higher than the mountains in Wales or the Lakes, as

Dorothy had told him, "The cataracts nothing more than kittenracts!"

At night they slept in country inns on beds of straw after basic suppers of bacon, coffee and schnapps.

Samuel made notes all the time to write up into a report in his next letter to Sara and to publish when he got home. He also started a poem, beginning with the view from the Brocken. The very German-ness of the countryside made him homesick for England.

"O 'dear, dear' England, how my longing eye
Turn'd westward, shaping in the steady clouds
Thy sands and high white cliffs! Sweet native isle,
This heart was proud, yea, mine eyes swam with tears
To think of thee; and all the goodly view
From sovran Brocken, woods and woody hills,
Floated away, like a departing dream
Feeble and dim."

Having started it though, he couldn't continue. It was true, what he had said to Wordsworth, his muse had left him. And yet he had written some poetry: the poems he had sent to Sara about how much he missed her.

How he longed for home, longed for England and everything English. And yet now the time came, now he had nearly finished everything he needed to finish, he was reluctant to go. Here, he was a student, free from any responsibilities, he could do what he liked, go where he wanted, everyone liked him, admired him even. When he went back he would have to make a lot of decisions: where they would live and what he would do. The Wedgwoods' annuity was generous but he had overspent on everything, especially books, while he was in Germany. Hopefully, the publication of his German work would make up the shortfall but he had harsh critics in England. *Lyrical Ballads* had had poor reviews. In Sara's last letter she had said that everyone she knew had laughed at it.

There was another reason he half-dreaded going home: he was just beginning to come to terms with Berkeley's death. When he went home it would all come back to him. Worse than that, he would have to take on Sara's grief as well as his own. His mind darted away from it.

Deep down, he knew he would have to face up to all these things. But he found himself easily distracted.

"I've been wondering if there's anything else I should be doing while I'm over here," he told Chester one evening. "I don't want to get home and wish I had done more. Scandinavia perhaps, a walking tour, in the footsteps of Mary Wollstonecraft."

Two of his English student friends, the Parry brothers, were keen on the idea when he told them. "We'd need to write and ask our father's permission first," they said.

Samuel spent the next few weeks feverishly making sure he had all the material he needed before he had to leave Göttingen. He still had work to do on the biography of Lessing and he wanted to go to the library at Wolfenbüttel, where Lessing had worked from 1770 to 1781.

Back in Nether Stowey, Sara ploughed her way through the long letter describing Samuel's walking tour. How carefree he sounded, like the student he, of course, was. He seemed to have forgotten he had her and Hartley. And they were struggling financially while he was off on a week's holiday. Oh, he might have been sleeping on beds of straw, but the inns had to be paid for, food, however meagre, had to be bought. And all this while Sara owed money to tradesmen and had the ignominy of having to borrow from Poole all the time. She had gone past making excuses for Samuel to herself; he should be home by now, with her and Hartley, facing up to his responsibilities, supporting his family, not gallivanting around Germany without a care in the world.

In May Edith came to stay. Southey was in London where he was studying law. Edith and Southey were going through a difficult patch. "Maybe the time apart will be good for us," Edith said.

Part of the problem, Sara suspected, was that Edith hadn't been able to have children. "But you're so thin," Sara told her. "If only you'd eat more."

"I can't," Edith said. "My stomach hurts too much."

Sara noticed she didn't write to Southey even though letter after letter arrived from him. "It's not fair to him, Edith," she told her. "He needs to know that you're all right."

The mysteries of marriage... Sara realised everyone had their problems.

When Edith went back the cottage felt lonelier than ever. Samuel had said he would be home by late June but the weeks went by and she had given up trying to pin him down.

It was 24th June when Samuel packed his books into a chest to be sent to Cuxhaven.

"Let's go up to the Brocken again before we start our journey home," Samuel said to Chester. "We didn't see the spectre last time and I'd like to try again."

Carlyon and Greenough, who had gone with them before, were only too eager to go again. But the weather conditions still weren't right for the unusual phenomenon of the Brocken spectre, even though they went back at dawn the next morning for a final attempt.

After that they took a leisurely route to Brunswick, where they met the Parry brothers.

"Good news!" they said. "Our father says we can go to Scandinavia!"

Faced with the reality, Samuel suddenly realised he didn't want to go. The strangeness of another country, being away from England, seemed just too much. "I'm sorry," he said. "I'm just so homesick. But I still want to do it. Spring next year. I promise."

There were still some pieces of material Samuel wanted for his book on Lessing, so he and Chester moved on to Wolfenbüttel, where he spent every day at the library but unfortunately he still couldn't find everything he needed.

After that they walked from Brunswick to Helmstedt. It was hot, their feet were sore and their legs ached. In order to travel light they had brought as little as possible with them and Samuel was down to his last clean shirt. They both stank. "I shall be glad to get to Cuxhaven and find some clean clothes," Samuel said.

When they arrived, however, they found the boxes of clothes and Samuel's all-important books were not there waiting for them. The ship was due to sail. They had no choice but to go as they were: dirty and smelly.

As Samuel watched Germany retreating from view the last ten months seemed almost like a dream. What had he achieved? He was fluent in German, both written and spoken, though he had been told that his accent was abysmal. He had gone to lectures in physiology, anatomy and natural history and he had read and researched Lessing for his book. He had also gathered material in German on Thomas Malthus' essay on population, giving him new insight into Godwin's and Condorcet's philosophical arguments. There were his journal and his letters and notes to be written up for publication on his return. And finally he had written six long letters to the Wedgwoods on the German peasantry, one of which he had already sent, and there were another five he would take with him when he went home. He could be proud of his work.

Now, as the ship left the calmer waters of the harbour and headed out to sea, Samuel knew it was time to move on, to leave behind him the heady carefree student days and put to good use everything he had learned these last ten months.

But first there were Sara, Hartley, Poole and beloved Stowey.

# Chapter Fourteen

*"Beloved Stowey" July 1799 to December 1799*

When he pictured going home Samuel had always seen himself landing at Shurton Bars and walking the four miles to Stowey and into Sara's arms. But of course it was only a fanciful image dreamed up by a poetic mind. Homecomings were never as expected and, as the ship edged into the port of London on a typically grey gloomy English day with a touch of damp mizzle in the air, Samuel longed not for Stowey and Sara's arms, but clean clothes and a comfortable bed.

Their luggage and Samuel's box of books still hadn't caught up with them so, while they were waiting, Samuel called in on Wordsworth's brother Richard, who lent him some clean clothes. Then he went to see Daniel Stuart to arrange for the first of his translations to be published in the *Morning Post* in August.

Samuel had been away from home for almost a year. His journey through the heart of England in high summer was more beautiful than he remembered. To his eyes every tree, every field, every hedgerow looked new and exciting. As he finally trudged the hot dry dusty lanes into Stowey nostalgia overwhelmed him.

He hadn't known exactly when he would arrive and he knew Sara wouldn't be expecting him.

The windows to the cottage were open but there was no sound from indoors. Maybe she had gone over to one of her friends, Anna Cruikshank perhaps. He pushed the front door open. Now he could hear voices in the garden: Sara's and Hartley's. Tears rushed to his eyes and his throat tightened.

"No," Sara was saying, "it's a 'd' not a 'p'. Try again."

They were sitting on a bench in the garden, their heads bent over a children's reading book. Hartley, not the small toddler he remembered but a dark haired elfin-looking little boy, was kicking the leg of the bench impatiently with his foot. He looked up. "Man," he said, pointing at Samuel.

Sara looked up, gave a small strangled cry, the book fell to the ground and suddenly, he scarcely knew how, they were in each other's arms, clinging together.

She felt thinner; he could feel her ribs. He stepped back, held her at arm's length. She looked different. Then he realised she was wearing a wig, a strange-looking flat, dark affair that looked like it was clamped to her forehead. She saw him looking and her hand flew to her head.

"You'll find me changed, Samuel," she said.

"No, no…" he said quickly. But she was. Her face was thinner too, pale, the pain showed in her eyes, the merry, round-faced woman he had left a year ago had gone. Here was a woman who had suffered; it was etched in the mouth that tried to smile, the eyes that no longer sparkled.

"Hartley!" she said, turning away from his scrutiny. "Here's Papa come home."

"Man," Hartley said again.

"My sweet, sweet boy!" Samuel said, reaching for him. But Hartley shrank back, hiding behind Sara's skirts. "He's going through a shy stage," Sara said quickly. "He's like it with everyone. Oh, Samuel! It's so good to have you home. I have so much to tell you. I was hoping you'd be back sooner." She stopped herself. She hadn't wanted to start nagging him the moment he arrived. "Come on, come inside. You must be hungry and thirsty."

They were awkward with each other, neither wanting to say what they knew they should say, neither of them daring to mention Berkeley's name. Where they were four, now they were three, Samuel acutely aware, once they were inside the cottage, of the missing cradle by the fireside.

Hartley still hung back silently while Sara prepared food for him. "We have a new maid," she said. "Fanny. She's a bit older than Nanny." She lowered her voice. "Not very good," she went on, "but it's early days yet."

Samuel ate silently. The guilt he had been feeling for so long washed over him. He should have been here. He would never see Berkeley again. Hartley didn't know him. How was he going to pick up the threads of his life again?

"You'll want to go and see Poole," Sara said when he had finished.

"Yes." Samuel jumped up quickly. At the doorway he turned. "You can come too," he said. "You and Hartley."

"No, no," Sara said. "You'll want to see him alone. We can talk later."

Her eyes filled with tears as she saw how eager he was to escape already when he had only just got back.

Samuel hurried down the street to Poole's house, waited impatiently for someone to answer the door.

Poole's face when he saw him was a picture: disbelief, wonder, love, the expressions all flitting across it one after the other. He wrung Samuel's hand as though if he were to let it go he would disappear again.

They talked and talked. It grew late, later than Samuel realised. The cottage was in darkness when he walked back. Sara had gone to bed. He slid in next to her. Was she still awake? For a moment he considered reaching out, pulling her towards him, but he was dead tired and before he knew it sleep had overcome him.

He woke the next morning with that strange disconnected feeling of not knowing where he was. He had slept in so many different beds recently, in so many different places. He could hear a child's voice talking quietly to itself, the sound of a maid moving around downstairs. He turned to look at the head next to him on the pillow: a round head with fine short strands of hair flattened against it. A shiver of revulsion ran through him. Then Sara opened her eyes. "Samuel…" she murmured sleepily. He had no choice. He put his arm around her, laid the strange-feeling head on his shoulder, tried not to think of the lustrous dark hair that used to spread across the pillow, fall across his face and get into his mouth. Luckily she didn't seem to expect more.

"You'll be hungry," she said quickly, slipping out of bed. "And Hartley will want his breakfast."

Hartley regarded him with suspicion over his breakfast of bread and milk.

"Papa will play with you later," Sara told him.

It wasn't at all what Samuel had expected. He had envisaged jubilation, enthusiasm, not this heavy weight of sadness. He could sense Sara's disappointment in him, he knew she thought he had let her down and that even now he wasn't coming up to her standard. The Sara he had missed, always happy, always positive, someone he knew would always be there for him, bore no resemblance to this new Sara, the sad Sara, the bitter Sara, the Sara who had had to cope on her own, who would never forgive him for being away when she needed him.

Sara knew she should try harder. She had hoped they might recover some vestige of their former happiness but the hope had quickly faded. She knew she must make an effort at their marriage. They had made their vows. For better, for worse, in sickness and in health. She knew Samuel took them as seriously as she did. And they mustn't go on arguing, for Hartley's sake. He was old enough now to understand the friction between them. But she just couldn't get past the disappointment she felt in him. She had never been very good at hiding her feelings. They bubbled close to the surface: anger, sadness, joy. But there was no joy anymore. For the first few days they were on their best behaviour, polite to each other, careful what they said, but after a week or so the effort was just too much and they began to get on each other's nerves, snapping at each other over the stupidest things. Occasionally one or other of them would apologise, they would try again, but they were caught in a cycle that was hard to break.

How Samuel had longed to be home at Stowey but now he was here he felt like he had great hooks attaching him to Sara, to Hartley, to the cottage, to domesticity, and he found himself thinking longingly of his student room and the freedom to come and go without anyone asking him where he was going or what he was doing.

At least Hartley had begun to accept Samuel, chattering to him in a mixture of ordinary speech and a strange sort of baby-talk that Sara had to interpret for him.

"No, Papa," he said to Samuel one day, taking one of his wooden soldiers away from him. "Not like that. That's not how Uncle Southey does it."

"He talks about Southey all the time," Samuel said moodily.

"We've seen so much of them recently," Sara said. "They came in only a few days ago on their way to Minehead on holiday. Edith isn't at all well."

Samuel didn't seem to be interested but she pressed on regardless. "They were so good to me, Samuel, when Berkeley died." Her voice broke slightly on the baby's name but she forced herself to continue. "I do wish you would make it up with Southey. You owe it to him for everything he has done for me. And it's hard for me and Edith that you and he don't get on."

The time she had spent with Southey had made her see his side of the argument and she believed Southey would make peace with Samuel if only one of them would make the first move.

Samuel hoped she would let the subject drop but she returned to it again and again. He had forgotten how persistent she could be. But in the end he realised he would have to give way if he wanted a quiet life. He sat down and wrote a letter.

"I am perplex'd what to write, or how to state the object of my writing," he began. "We have similar talents, sentiments nearly similar, and kindred pursuits ... we have likewise in more than one instance common objects of our esteem and love ... I pray and intreat you, if we should meet at any time, let us not withhold from each other the outward expression of daily kindliness, and if it not be any longer in your power to soften your opinions, make your feelings at least more tolerant towards me."

He had only just sent the letter when Sara heard from Southey.

"He says that Edith is much worse," she told Samuel. "He wants to go on a walking tour to Lynmouth and the Valley of Rocks but he doesn't want to leave her alone."

"I thought your other sister was there with her."

"Yes, but Eliza's so young. And it's *me* Edith wants."

"But I've only just come home," he said peevishly. "Your family's more important to you than I am."

"Don't be silly. I'll only be gone a few days. I'll bring her back here where we can look after her."

"I don't see why *we* should look after her. Southey should be doing that."

"*She* looked after me when I needed help," Sara said. "It's only fair."

Southey's reply to Samuel's letter arrived while Sara was away. The letter was full of righteous indignation; of course, Southey thought everything was Samuel's fault.

Samuel rushed around to Poole's house. "I don't know what to do," he said. "I've made things worse, not better."

"This is all Charles Lloyd's fault," Poole said. "It isn't just the book he wrote. He went around spreading malicious rumours. Even Lamb began to believe them. Let me write to Southey. I'll give him both sides of the story and he can make up his mind."

A few days later Sara, Edith and Eliza arrived in Stowey in a chaise, Edith still looking desperately fragile, but with a warm smile on her face for Samuel. "Southey is following on foot," she told him.

Samuel waited with a mixture of fear and hope but as soon as he saw Southey coming down the street he knew it would be all right. Without thinking, he opened his arms in that continental way he had always scorned. Southey ran towards him and there in the middle of the street they held each other close.

They stayed two weeks. It was a crush in the cottage but the warm summer meant they could eat all their meals outside and, although Edith was far too weak to do anything, there was still Eliza to help Sara with the chores. With so many people around and so much going on all the time, Samuel and Sara had no time to bicker. And Sara could sense Southey's support, his willingness to help her out and to make her marriage work.

Hartley was in his element with Uncle Southey to play with and if Samuel was jealous he didn't show it. He and Southey, reunited after such a long time, were like a newly-wed couple, scarcely able to let each other of their sight, talking, talking, talking all the time.

They went everywhere as a crowd, Sara included in a way she had never been with the Wordsworths. They spent most of their time looking for a house for her and Samuel to rent. "By the sea maybe," Samuel said. "Kilve or Watchet…"

Sara still saw herself in a town or a city, somewhere near Bristol preferably where she could see her family, but she would go anywhere as long as she could leave the cottage, with its associations with Berkeley and all her unhappiness.

A week later Samuel suddenly announced they should visit his family at Ottery.

"They've never met you, Sara," he said in his new generous way and she could see he was trying hard to make things up to her. "Now is the perfect time."

"We'll come with you," Southey said. "I'd like to take Edith to Sidmouth. The sea air would do her good."

So they all packed up, taking the new maid Fanny to help with Hartley, and set off for Ottery.

Sara was nervous: what would Samuel's family make of her? She was no longer a pretty young bride but a married woman of several years with a three-year-old son. And she still wasn't looking her best; she had lost a lot of confidence since she had to wear a wig and her figure hadn't regained the curves that she knew suited her. But Samuel's family seemed to like her.

"You must stay as well," George Coleridge told the Southeys and Eliza.

"Thank you, that's very generous of you," Southey said. "We are hoping to find accommodation in Sidmouth. For my wife's health."

But it was high summer, there was nowhere to stay in Sidmouth, so they ended up in Exeter, in rooms big enough for Sara and Samuel with Hartley and Fanny to join them.

Sara liked Exeter with its shops and busy streets and she kept Edith and Eliza company while Samuel took Southey on a walking tour to Totnes and Dartmouth.

The three sisters were in the parlour one morning when they heard a strange sound from the stairwell: a thumpety, bumpety, bump followed by a thud. There was a moment's silence, then a loud shriek. Sara rushed out. Hartley was lying at the bottom of the stairs yelling and sobbing and clutching his arm.

"It hurts, Mama! It hurts!" he cried.

Sara scooped him up. "Silly, silly boy!" she said. "How many times have I told you not to run down the stairs?"

"My arm!" he sobbed, pulling away from her. "Don't touch it!"

The arm was already swelling up. "I'll fetch a doctor," Eliza said.

"The bone isn't broken," the doctor said, "just badly bruised. I'll bandage it up and let you have an ointment to help bring down the bruising."

When they returned from their walking tour, Samuel and Sara took Hartley back to Ottery.

"Stay as long as you like," George Coleridge said.

"Two or three weeks maybe?" Samuel said to Sara. Her heart lifted. Here she was accepted as family. Samuel had to be kind to her in front of his family. She could tell they liked her. And she was away from that hateful cottage with its awful associations. They had only been there a week, however, when Fanny came to her one morning.

"I think I've got the Itch," she said, her face burning with embarrassment.

"What? Let me see," Sara said urgently.

Fanny lowered her bodice; an angry-looking bright red mottled rash ran across her front.

"Oh no," Sara said. Scabies was a disease of the lower classes. It was highly contagious. How dreadful to have brought it to Ottery, to pass it on, maybe, to George's children, possibly already to have infected Edith and Eliza.

"We'll have to go," she told Samuel.

It was a dreadful journey back: Fanny squirmed and scratched and cried all the way.

Back in Stowey the apothecary examined them all.

"Well, none of you show any signs of it," he said. "But you must get rid of the maid. Then you'll have to clean everything, burn Hartley's clothes, wash all the bedding and fumigate the house. I'd advise you and your husband to wear mercury girdles as a preventative. As for young Master Hartley, you must paint him with brimstone. That will stop it." He produced a bottle of bright yellow ointment.

Hartley thought it was hilarious. "I be a funny fellow, and my name is Brimstonello," he laughed.

Frustrated at being shut inside, he was up to all sorts of mischief, getting in Sara's way everywhere she went. One morning he darted through the door just as she was closing it and she trapped his arm in it. "Ow! Ow!" he yelled.

Sara cried as she cuddled him; he had only just got over one injury and here she was inflicting another one on him.

Fanny had gone back to her father's house immediately. Worried about how she was getting on, Sara wrote to her. A few days later she heard back. Fanny's father wouldn't let her use the brimstone ointment but allowed her to wear the mercury girdle. She had been up to Bristol where she was offered a position and asked if Sara would write a reference for her.

For Sara the carefree days of the summer were suddenly over. The weather had turned. It was dull and dreary with constant rain. Without a servant to help with the heavy work, without Edith and Eliza to share the cooking and cheer her up with their chattering, without Uncle Southey to play with Hartley, everything was suddenly overwhelming. She stripped beds, flung open windows, boiled water for washing and pounded the sheets in the tub. The whole house stank of sulphur.

The constant heavy rain filled the open gutter that ran outside the cottage until finally it overflowed, bringing mud and silt and foul-smelling water into the cottage. Now Sara had mopping to do on top of everything else. The damp brought on Samuel's rheumatism. He woke every morning with his knees so stiff he could scarcely get out of bed. The laudanum helped with the pain but did nothing for the stiffness.

He retreated to the fireside with a book. It was frustrating for Sara to see him sitting there.

"I wish you would help me," she said as she struggled downstairs with yet another pile of laundry.

"I'm not well, Sara. You have no idea how bad it is. And I'm working," he gestured to the book in his lap.

As she pushed the back door open and dumped the sheets on the floor of the scullery Sara couldn't help remembering how it was when they were first married, how Samuel used to get up at six o'clock to clean the kitchen for her and light the fires before she got up, then help her with the dinner and wash the dishes afterwards. Now, when she needed him, he wouldn't even stir from his chair. How things had changed. She went back in, reached above his head to pull down the washing hanging on the rack. Samuel had just come to an important part in his book on Spinoza. "Do you *have* to do that now?" he asked.

"Yes, I do. There's another lot to go up."

"I can't stand this!" Samuel burst out, heaving himself painfully up from his chair. "I'm going over to Poole's where I won't be disturbed."

But Poole seemed to be on Sara's side. "You should be more understanding with her," he told Samuel.

"But *she* doesn't understand *me*," Samuel said. "I am a man of genius. I have different habits and feelings from other men. Wordsworth and Dorothy, *they* understand. If only I could get Alfoxton back for them. I know they'd come back if they could live there again."

Poole shook his head. "Mrs St Albyn won't change her mind, Samuel. She thinks we're all revolutionaries."

"But I've changed my mind about the revolution."

"The damage was done long ago," Poole said, "when Thelwall was here."

Poole's house was Samuel's only escape and he stayed late intentionally, knowing Sara would be worn out and asleep in bed by the time he got home.

When he had first reached for her in bed she had responded to him hungrily and in the dark of the bedroom he had been able to forget that almost-bald head with the thin wispy hair and remember only the warm soft giving body. But as the weeks wore on and the arguments increased, she had complained of tiredness and he had used excuses to stay up or go out.

Sara wondered if she would have another baby. Not to replace Berkeley, of course, but to seal their marriage, heal the wounds, teach them to love again. If only Samuel would say it too; if he would talk about Berkeley, help her with the heavy burden of her grief. But he didn't and the unspoken words hung heavily between them.

The scales had fallen from her eyes. She had looked up to Samuel, hero-worshipped him as a great man, someone who would provide for her and her family. Now she saw him as a wastrel, a weak man who couldn't face his responsibilities and thought only of himself. Why had he married her? He didn't need a wife or children. He was happier on his own, doing everything his way. Did she still love him? Her mind darted away from the question like a sore place she didn't want to touch. But it made no difference anyway. She was bound to him. She had no choice. She had to go everywhere he wanted, do whatever he decided to do. If only he could show that he loved her, that he wanted to be with her, then there might just be a way forward. But he didn't.

Samuel felt trapped. He had started reading JG Stedman's *Narrative of a Five Years' Expedition ... in Guiana, on the Wild Coast of South America.* How he longed to travel again. Or at the very least escape from the confines of this cottage and the forever-cleaning, sharp-tongued Sara.

"I think I'll go and see the Wedgwoods," he told her. "They need to know how I'm getting on." The Wedgwood brothers were staying at Upton in Wiltshire. He could discuss his book on Lessing and his other plans for the future with them.

"Wordsworth is writing a verse poem called *The Recluse,*" he told them. "He's going to dedicate it to me. I would love to go up to the north to visit him."

The Wedgwoods' house didn't bring him the relief he wanted though. The long journey made his rheumatism worse and once he arrived he felt fidgety and restless.

After a few days he headed back to Stowey, where the cottage still stank of sulphur and floodwater, and sat by the fire, dreaming of a poem set in Arabia. This would be the perfect time to finish writing *Christabel* and he asked Tom Poole's apprentice, Tommy Ward, to cut him some pens so that he could settle down and write it. When he received them, beautifully done, Samuel wrote one of his special punning letters to thank him, folding it up into a pentagonal shape and addressing it on the front: "To Mr Ward, this pentagonal letter comes pencil'd as well as penn'd." And on the reverse: "Your messenger never came nor went penniless."

"Most exquisite Pennefactor," he wrote, "I will speak dirt and daggers of the wretch who shall deny thee to be the most heaven-inspired, munificent penmaker that these latter times, these superficial, weak and evirtuate ages, have produced to redeem themselves from ignominy! And may he, great Calamist, who shall vilipend or derogate from thy pen making merits, do penance, and suffer penitential penalty, penn'd up in some penurious peninsula of penal and penetrant fire, pensive and pendulous, pending a huge slice of eternity. Were I to write 'til Pentecost, filling whole Pentateuchs, my grateful expressions would still remain a mere penumbra of my debt and gratitude."

Before he started work, however, Samuel decided he needed his book-box, which still hadn't arrived.

"It must be in Bristol waiting for me," he told Sara. "I'll go tomorrow. And if it's not there I'll go on up to London to look for it."

Sara sighed inwardly and thought, *"Any excuse to get away."* But in all honesty she could manage better without him there. They were arguing constantly; a break might do them good. How ironic that she had wanted him back so much and now she couldn't wait to see the back of him. And as she watched him walk down the street with a spring in his step and a cheery wave she knew he felt the same way. He didn't need her. She wasn't even sure she needed him, except to provide for her and Hartley. Edith and Southey were more important to her. They cared for her in a way Samuel didn't. They were pleased to see her, they enjoyed her company, they missed her when she wasn't with them. She would be happy if she could live near them and see them every day. But she would have to go where Samuel wanted. She had no choice.

She didn't know whether to laugh or cry when two days after Samuel had set off jauntily down the road there was a knock at the door and Milton the carrier was there with Samuel's travelling chests, including the all-important book box, at his feet.

Sara sent messages via Milton to all the places she thought Samuel might be but she heard nothing back. She didn't know what to do. She hadn't been able to get another maid and it didn't seem worth trying too hard when they both wanted to move from the cottage. She just wished Samuel would make up his mind where they were going. When she was invited by friends to stay at Old Cleeve, near Watchet, she jumped at the chance. Here she had company all the time, the company of ladies like herself with the same tastes and interests.

She shut up the cottage while she was away. If Samuel returned he could always stay with Poole. But there was still no sign of him when she got back to the cold, cheerless cottage and no letter. There was a letter from Southey, however. Her heart lifted; she had been hoping that he and Edith would invite her up to Bristol. She didn't see how she could stay here without a servant. Her hopes were quickly dashed though: Southey wrote to tell her that Samuel had gone up to Cumbria and he and the Wordsworths had gone on a walking tour. He had given no indication of when he would be back. A strange resignation fell on Sara: Samuel was never going to settle down to family life, she realised. The best she could hope for was that he would provide for her and Hartley. She had no choice but to sit and wait for him to tell her his next grand plan.

Samuel had gone to Cottle's bookshop first of all to see if his book-box had been delivered there. While in Bristol he went to the Pneumatic Institute to see Dr Beddoes.

"You must meet my new assistant, Humphrey Davy," Dr Beddoes said. "He's fascinated by the creative process and the poetic mind. He has discovered a new gas: nitrous oxide. It makes us happy, euphoric, fills us with vivid ideas. You must try it. Davy thinks it could help relieve pain during surgery."

Davy was a slim, dark-haired, earnest-looking young man. Like Samuel he was open to all new ideas, keen to try out anything in life that would add to his experience and improve himself and his fellow man.

They were part-way through their first meeting when Samuel received an urgent message to say that Wordsworth was ill. "I must go to him immediately," he told Davy. "But I will come back soon to try out your new gas."

Cottle provided a post-chaise and they both hurried up to Sockburn, where Wordsworth was staying with Dorothy's friend Mary Hutchinson and her family.

It was a blissful reunion. Five months' absence had done nothing to blunt their friendship. Wordsworth turned out to be happy, relaxed, very well.

"Oh, I *was* depressed," he said. "Really quite ill. But I am fully recovered now."

Mary's family, her brother Tom and younger sisters Sarah and Joanna, all made Samuel and Cottle very welcome. Samuel regaled them with his descriptions of his travels in Germany, the Brocken spectre that he never saw, the strange, quaint customs of Germany and the beautiful scenery of the Harz mountains.

Samuel was particularly taken with Sarah Hutchinson. How odd she should have the same name as his wife. "But it's spelt with an 'h'," she insisted.

She looked something like Sara too. True, her hair was auburn, not dark brown, but she had the same generous full-bosomed figure that he found so attractive, the same strong personality too, with a stubborn edge. She was twenty-four, much the same age as Sara had been when he first met her.

Basking in the admiration of the whole family, Samuel would have stayed at the farmhouse longer but Wordsworth was keen to show him his native country, the scenery he had boasted about for so long.

The next day they set off on foot at a huge pace that Cottle couldn't keep up with.

"You two go on," he said, exhausted. "I'll go back to Sockburn and wait for you there."

"My brother John may join us later on," Wordsworth told Samuel. "He's on shore leave at present. I've sent word for him to meet us at Temple Sowerby."

Samuel had heard a lot about John from Wordsworth and Dorothy. The three of them were very close but because he was a sailor they saw little of him. He turned out to be a very quiet man, tall and slim, happy to tag along and fit in with any of William's plans.

With only bread and cheese to sustain them they walked on to Lake Windermere and caught the ferry across to Hawkshead.

"This is where we went to school," Wordsworth told Samuel.

Then they walked back through Rydal to Grasmere. From here they explored the whole area: Ullswater, Borrowdale, Ennerdale, Wasdale Head and Buttermere.

Samuel was overwhelmed by the scenery which eclipsed anything he had seen in the Quantocks or the Harz mountains.

The pages of his notebook became filled with descriptions, from the mountains that surrounded him to the clear glassy surfaces of the lakes, with the clouds reflected in them. Waterfalls and streams, lakes and mountains, the constantly changing weather: Samuel recorded it all.

"River Greta near its fall into the trees," he wrote. "Shootings of water threads down the slope of the huge green stone — The white eddy-rose that blossom'd up against the stream in the scollop, by fits and starts, obstinate in resurrection — It is the life that we live. Black round ink-spots from 5 to 18 in the decaying leaf of the sycamore."

"I knew you would love it," Wordsworth said smugly. "You *must* come and settle here Samuel. You really must. In Grasmere. By the lake. I have a dream: we would build a house. John would lend me £40." John nodded his assent. "And you will bring Sara and Hartley and we will all live near each other. A community. Just like you always wanted."

The idea was appealing. To live here in this beautiful countryside, with Wordsworth and Dorothy nearby. Not too far away from Sarah Hutchinson. She would probably come to visit... But he wasn't sure about Pantisocracy anymore. The rural retreat that Thelwall had in Wales didn't seem to have achieved anything. He saw himself instead producing a great philosophical work. But he could do that up here just as well as anywhere else. And with the benefit of having friends nearby.

There was, however, Sara to consider. She would hate to be transported up here, miles away from her family in the south. She had made it clear often enough that she wanted to live in a town or a city where she could have neighbours and make friends. He knew she wanted to go to Bristol but it was the last thing he wanted. There, she would be back with the Fricker family, who, with the possible exception of Edith, all made clear their disapproval of him. He wanted to be somewhere he belonged.

The biggest problem at present, however, was money. He had vastly overspent the annuity he had from the Wedgwoods in Germany and he owed them £100 on top of all the loans Sara had had from Poole while he was away and there were still outstanding bills to pay.

While he thought it all over, the three men took a last final walk, an ascent of Helvellyn, seeing it as a sort of pledge to the future that they hoped to share together. Samuel longed to be one of their family group, to be included in a way he never felt he was with the Fricker family, even with Southey who had come back to him after their long separation. Here was where he wanted to be, with the Wordsworths and the Hutchinsons.

The answer to his immediate problem of money came almost immediately, as though it was fated. When he arrived in Keswick he found a letter from Daniel Stuart of the *Morning Post,* offering him a contract as a staff writer on the newspaper.

"I will take it," he told Wordsworth decisively. "I need the money. Sara wants to live in a city. We can live in London for four or five months, pay off all my debts, and then, well, we shall see..."

He suddenly realised that he had no idea exactly where Sara was now. Maybe she was in Bristol with Southey. So he wrote to him, telling him about the position and asking him to let Sara know.

In the meantime there was no rush to get back. The autumn weather was mild, if occasionally wet, but he didn't mind that. He liked to see the landscape in all conditions, particularly enjoying the mist that rolled down so suddenly from the mountainsides and shrouded everything from view. He spent another week exploring the area and then visited Thomas Clarkson, the famous campaigner against the slave trade.

Right up to the last moment he found it hard to tear himself away. "Monday morning — sitting on a tree stump on the brink of the lake by Mr Clarkson's," he wrote in his notebook. "Perfect serenity; that round fat backside of a hill with its image in the water."

On his way back he couldn't resist calling into Sockburn to see Dorothy and the Hutchinsons. Dorothy greeted him with delight but he was already looking past her to see if Sarah was around. It was her he really wanted to see. All the way there his heart had hammered and his body fizzled with excitement. He had never felt like this before. He knew she felt the same: he saw how her face flushed when she saw him, how she dropped her eyes from his knowing gaze. The others didn't seem to notice; they crowded around him, making him feel like a king. He would have to be careful about Sarah. It would have to be a secret passion.

Living on a farm they were all busy during the day with their various chores but in the evenings they gathered together round the fire for talking, games and fun. Samuel was in his element, telling them stories, using the silly puns he had used in Germany, describing his various adventures again with greater embellishments.

One evening they stood in a group around the fire. In a moment of courage Samuel reached out and took Sarah's hand. She didn't resist. He pulled it behind his back, held it gently. He was in love. He knew it. Nothing he had ever felt compared to this. It didn't matter that it had to be secret. It was special, pure, there was nothing like it.

He stayed a week, not even writing to Poole, growing ever closer to the three women, Dorothy, Mary and Sarah, dreading the day he would have to leave.

One rainy afternoon he sat on the sofa with Mary and Sarah, Mary laid her head in his lap, Sarah sat so near to him he could feel her eyelashes fluttering on his cheek.

Sarah and Mary had always been close but the death of their sister Margaret, in between them in age, had brought them closer still. They had a special bond. Mary talked of Sarah as her 'second self' yet they were quite different personalities. Mary, who had been Dorothy's friend from childhood and was

Wordsworth's undoubted favourite, was tall, thin, quiet, very calm. Sarah was small and plump, vivacious and energetic. Like his own Sara, she was neat and well-organised around the house. And they shared the same strong-minded, independent attitude that he admired. There was one important difference between them however: Sarah Hutchinson loved the outdoors and the country walks that Samuel himself enjoyed so much. They seemed on the same wavelength in so many ways. She was pretty rather than beautiful, with her strong square jaw, but she was absolutely enchanting. He began a poem, *Love*, a medieval ballad. As the words rushed from his mind onto the paper he realised his muse had returned. Not in Stowey but here in glorious Cumbria, in the company of people he loved and who loved him. When he first started the poem he thought it might form part of a longer ballad but it was so good that he decided to submit it to the *Morning Post* when he got to London.

As the month drew to a close he could put it off no longer and on 26th November he caught the all-night coach for London to start his new job.

He slept fitfully in the cold, cramped, jolting coach and woke to a grey dawn, a flock of starlings soaring and wheeling in a murmuration over the barren winter landscape. His heart ached, the separation from Sarah, the woman he knew he would love till his dying day, was like an open wound. And what lay ahead of him? His own Sara, his little boy, his responsibilities, his future stretching out uncertainly ahead of him, taking him further and further away from what his heart told him would make him happy.

The starlings seemed to represent his uncertainty. He took out his notebook. "Starlings in vast flights drove along like smoke, mist or anything misty without volition," he wrote. "Now a circular area inclined in an arc — now a globe — now from complete orb into an ellipse and oblong — now a balloon with the car suspended, now a concave semicircle — and still it expands and condenses, some moments glimmering and shivering, dim and shadowy, now deepening, thickening, blackening."

He found lodgings at 21 Buckingham Street and sat down to write to Sara. With a rush of guilt he realised how long it had been since he had been in touch with her. In fact, he still didn't know where she would be. Was she still at the cottage in Lime Street or in Bristol with Southey and Edith? In the end he addressed the letter to Lime Street and sent another to Cottle asking him to find out where she was and to pass on the address to her if his other letter didn't reach her.

It had been six weeks since Sara had heard from Samuel. Left alone in the cottage she had grown more and more dispirited. She was worn out. She lived one day at a time with no idea what the future held. She had had the letter from Southey telling her about the position in London. "He says he will send for you when he has found somewhere to live," Southey wrote. *"Yes, I've heard that before,"* Sara thought bitterly, reading it. Samuel hadn't written to *her*. She didn't dare to hope she might be included in any of his plans. They might change at any moment; she had seen him sighing over his travel books.

But now there was this letter, just delivered. She sat with it in her hand. Maybe he had decided to go abroad again. Maybe he had written now, finally, to say he wouldn't be coming back at all and she would be stuck in this miserable cottage forever.

She opened it with shaking fingers. She had to read it several times before she could allow herself to believe it.

"Hartley, my love," she said excitedly. "Papa wants us to go and live with him in London."

She bent down to hug him but he twisted away from her to play with his wooden soldiers.

"It's a big city," she told him anyway. "With shops and lots of houses, and lots of people. Uncle Southey goes up there sometimes to work. And Aunt Southey might come too if she knows we will be there. And Papa has a job, a proper job. I can have new clothes, new furniture maybe. We will live in a big house. In a street with other houses. Oh, Hartley it will be wonderful. Such an adventure."

There was a lot to do. She packed their boxes and bags, cleaned and cleared the cottage and made her round of goodbyes to the friends she had made in the last three years. She would miss them — Poole and his mother, the Cruikshanks, the Roskillys, the Chesters — but there were too many sad memories here in the cottage itself, too many arguments and misunderstandings.

She sat by the fire on her last evening, mentally checking she had done everything. The cottage was as cold and drear as ever, worse now with most of the furniture and all the pots and pans packed up to go. She wiped a space in the misted-up window and looked out onto the dark road. There was no one around. She could hear the open gutter burbling noisily. The path below the window was its usual quagmire of mud and filth. The gutter had overflowed again recently, bringing evil smelling sludge into the cottage. How lovely it would be to see a row of houses opposite, lamps in the streets, candlelight in the windows, people walking to and from their businesses, shops and houses.

It would be a fresh start, a new beginning, back in a city where she would feel at home instead of this dead-end village where she had never felt accepted. With proper employment Samuel would settle down, there would be no more travelling, he would be kind to her again, they would have another baby, a brother or sister for Hartley. She would be a better wife to Samuel. There was a chance of happiness again.

For Samuel, already working hard on his newspaper articles, it was a new beginning too but he had no intention of staying in London. City life wasn't for him. It was a means to an end. As soon as he had cleared his debts he would be off. He had no idea what he would do next but his heart was in Cumbria with Wordsworth and Dorothy.

The three years he had spent in Stowey would turn out to be not only some of the happiest in his life but the most creative, the poetry he wrote there some of the best in the English language. He had moved there with grand plans for Pantisocracy, literacy, philosophy but he had no idea, when he wrote these words, how prophetic they would turn out to be:

"Yet the light shall stream to a far distance from the taper in my cottage window."

Samuel Taylor Coleridge, December 1796

# Epilogue

Sara did like it in London; she and Samuel socialised a lot and they made many friends. They did a fair amount of entertaining before Sara became pregnant again.

In July 1800, shortly before their son Derwent was born, they moved to Greta Hall in Keswick to be near the Wordsworths in Cumbria. Two years later they had another baby, a girl, also called Sara, but their marriage remained stormy and Coleridge spent more and more time away, complaining to his friends that his wife made his home life intolerable.

Sara, on the other hand, remained outwardly loyal to Coleridge. Always a positive and optimistic person, she put on a show of cheerfulness for the sake of the children. As part of this she had a special language, which became known as her Lingo Grande. She called herself 'Snouterumpter', spoke of 'red-raggifying' in full 'confabulumpatus', and said she would, "... play the very dunder."

When she died she left behind the uncompleted *Mrs Codian's Remembrances*, which she had dictated to her daughter, a record of her and her sisters' courtships and marriages.

Coleridge's relationships were always tempestuous. At one time or another he fell out with Wordsworth, Dorothy, Lamb and Southey. Poole was the only one he never had a serious argument with. It is hard to say how many of these disagreements were caused by his opium addiction and how many by his own character.

He was a restless man, full of great ideas and schemes, many of which he never completed, but undoubtedly one of his greatest achievements was the poetry he wrote in the three years he lived here in Somerset.

# Bibliography

Juliet Barker: Wordsworth, A Life
Hunter Davies: William Wordsworth
Stephen Gill: William Wordsworth, A Life
Richard Holmes: Coleridge, Early Visions
Kathleen Jones: A Passionate Sisterhood
Berta Lawrence: Coleridge and Wordsworth in Somerset
Molly Lefebure: The Bondage of Love
Molly Lefebure: Samuel Taylor Coleridge: A Bondage of Opium
Tom Mayberry: Coleridge and Wordsworth in the West Country
Elizabeth Sandford: Thomas Poole and his Friends
Adam Sisman: The Friendship, Wordsworth and Coleridge

# About the Author

Bethany Askew is the author of seven other novels: *The Time Before, The World Within, Out of Step, Counting the Days, Poppy's Seed, I Know You, Don't I?* and *The Two Saras: Coleridge in Cumbria.*

She has also written a short story, *The Night of the Storm,* and she writes poetry.

Her new women's fiction novel *The Next Step* is due for publication in 2021 and she is currently writing another one.

Bethany is married and lives in Somerset.

www.bethanyaskew.co.uk

# Acknowledgements

I am grateful to Kate Chandler of National Trust Coleridge Cottage for the title "Three Extraordinary Years" which is a phrase she coined while she was working here. Also, to Tina Mitchell for giving me the original idea to write a novel about the Coleridges' life in the cottage.

And my thanks to the Chester family for allowing me to use material they compiled about their ancestor, John Chester.

# Blue Poppy Publishing

Founded in 2016 in Ilfracombe, North Devon, Blue Poppy Publishing is a small but rapidly growing publisher. We always like to take this opportunity to ask you, please, to take a few moments to write a review of this book, either on Goodreads or on our own website, or even better if you host a book blog; and do let us know so we can point readers to it.

If you enjoyed this book, you might like Bethany's other books including *The Two Saras: Coleridge in Cumbria*, companion to this novel. You may also enjoy *Barefoot on the Cobbles* or *Sins as Red as Scarlet* by Janet Few and *A Breath of Moonscent* by Allan Boxall, both published by Blue Poppy.

We are keen for customers to shop at their local bricks and mortar book retailers, where all our titles can be ordered, but should anyone be unable to get to a bookshop you can also order direct from us at

www.bluepoppypublishing.co.uk